BEST SERVED
COLD

RICHARD GARNER

UMBRIA PRESS

Umbria Press
London SW15 5DP
www.umbriapress.co.uk

Printed in Poland by Totem
www.totem.com.pl

Paperback ISBN: 978 1 910074 13 8
E book ISBN: 978 1 910074 14 5

CHAPTER ONE

Roy Faulkner slowly came to that Saturday morning. He was aware of the sunlight beaming through the curtains in his hotel bedroom. His memory of the previous evening was pretty hazy – but his first instinct was to feel behind his back with his hand. He touched nothing. Good. It didn't seem there was anyone else in the bed with him. He breathed a sigh of relief and plucked up the courage to turn over and see for himself. His instincts were right. He was alone in his bed.

It wasn't a common occurrence for him to sleep with someone when at a conference but his hazy memory told him he had been with Kate Williams, the stunningly beautiful reporter from the right-wing tabloid newspaper, the *Globe*. He could remember she had been pretty drunk when he last spoke to her and that the night had stretched quite substantially into the morning.

It would not have been a meeting of minds with Kate. Politically, they would have been poles apart. Actually, he thought, she might not have had a political bone in her body. A lot of people working at the *Globe* did not necessarily share its political bent. They took the pay cheque at the end of the month and just happened to be working for a paper whose political instincts were at a different end of the spectrum to his own. Rabid right, he would describe it as.

Roy was in his late forties. Actually forty-nine, but he did not tell everybody that. There was a bit of a youth culture on his newspaper and it would not have done him any good to dwell on his age. The editor, for instance, was a good twenty years younger than him. Not that he was insecure in his job. He had built up quite a reputation for writing analytical pieces about

1

the subject that he specialised in – education. That was why he was where he was that day – at the opening day of a major conference of Britain's head teachers.

He had better get up, he thought. Otherwise, he would miss the start of the conference. As he dragged himself wearily into the bathroom, he began to ask himself why he had run the risk of something happening between him and Kate. Why had he ended up at a night club at two o'clock in the morning with a dizzy blonde like Kate – someone who was also probably twenty years his junior?

Angela, his partner of five years, would not have approved. Angela was the jealous type. She was vivacious, fun, shared a lot of interests with him – but she just did not believe in her heart of hearts that men could just have friendships with members of the opposite sex and not get into bed with them at some stage.

Angela was away at the moment – visiting friends and family in the Caribbean. If she had been in the UK, he might have invited her down to the conference with him. A weekend in a top hotel in a town with a number of restaurants to die for – Brighton. Shopping? She would have been able to have a good time even if he hadn't been around all the time to accompany her. And she liked his reporter friend Mark – or, to be more accurate, Mark's wife, Prunella. Mark Elliott was the kind of "hail fellow, well met" personality who was brought up in the days when – to be a reporter – meant to be seriously capable of downing a few pints with your mates in the evening or even at lunchtime. It was a skill that had never deserted Mark. It was a skill that Roy had possessed, too, in years gone by but he had moderated his drinking habits. Indeed, Roy had lost count of the number of occasions that he had turned down an invitation to join Mark for a snifter at lunchtime to ease the passage of the day. It was all right for Mark. Most days he only had to write a couple of hundred words for his tabloid newspaper. Everyday Roy's bosses expected something weightier from him.

His mind stopped wandering and he concentrated upon getting under the shower in the bathroom without slipping. The water cascading on to his head seemed to awaken his memory more about the previous evening. The abiding image was of looking at his watch and noting it was 2.30am. Kate had been a bit garrulous for the past hour or so and seemed to be slurring her words a bit. He had gone over to her to apologise for pulling out as he had to work the next day, a Saturday. Her paper did not publish again until the Monday. He remembered he had volunteered to walk her back to the hotel – a distance of merely a hundred yards. "No thanks," she had said. "I'm having too much fun." That was his last memory. Somehow, it seemed, he had found his way back to the hotel and into bed – on his own. Good, then. His improved memory now told him he had not even tried to proposition her. He couldn't help wondering, though. What would have happened if he had? Don't go down that road, he thought – a chill suddenly forming on his spine, as he returned to the bedroom to get dressed.

• • • • •

Philip Rivers was still lying in bed that Saturday morning. It was almost midday. He had thought about getting up but there seemed no point. He had nothing to do. Except if you counted clearing up the debris from his dinner the previous evening. It wouldn't have taken long. It was just a plate from which he had eaten his ready-to-cook meal from Waitrose. He still had some class about him even in his dishevelled state. It was always Waitrose. There was an empty bottle of wine, too. Oh, and a half full one. He must have drunk the lot. He had spent the previous evening on his own – as was often the case these days. Trying to muster a bit of resolve, he realised it would take him five minutes to clear it up. No, he just did not have the energy yet to do so. Not just yet

He had gradually got into this state during the last six months – the six months since his partner, Joanna Luckhurst, had died. Joanna had been his girlfriend. She had been diagnosed with bowel cancer. It was at quite an advanced stage and mercifully for her the pain had not been long lasting. It was, though, it seemed, for him.

Joanna had been a friend for years – and then suddenly things had just clicked. It was those sorts of relationships that were the long lasting ones, he thought to himself. You weighed up the pros and cons more carefully before entering into them because you didn't want to lose a friend.

He had thought there was something wrong with her on that holiday cruising in the Middle East just six months before she died. Their relationship had got to the point where they were the best of friends and – for much of the time – sex didn't come into it. On that holiday, though, they had shared a particularly romantic evening as the cruise ship had stopped off at Bodrun in Turkey. They had made love and he had felt quite mellow, relaxed and at ease with himself as they had sipped a glass of wine afterwards. Joanna had been troubled, though. It was as if she was in pain. She was short with him – which was not a frequent occurrence. He had wondered whether to ask her what was troubling her but decided against it. He got the feeling that she would have dismissed his concern. He smiled as he remembered the evening – not a smile denoting pleasure but a rueful one as he ruminated on what could have been a lost opportunity as a result of which he might have persuaded her to go and see her doctor sooner.

When the diagnosis came, it was a shock. She confessed to him she had been in pain for a while but had put that down to the stress of leading a busy working life. She was hired by companies to arrange conferences, prepare receptions and organise the catering for them. It involved travel and that was why Rivers had thought it quite a coup to persuade her to come

4

away on holiday with him. A holiday for her was staying at home. Apart from the incident of the pain, though, it had been a success and it had confirmed to him that their future was bright and they would be together for the duration.

There was another reason why he hadn't questioned her that night. He was a private detective. Much of his work involved asking people leading – often embarrassing – questions. To him a holiday was all about not asking questions. Letting events take care of themselves. He even disliked the idea of asking a receptionist about the quickest way to get into town.

Up until Joanna's death, he would have prided himself on his resilience. When he had thought about the future without her, he imagined that he would probably bury himself in his work and – within a few months – start socialising with somebody else even if it did not necessarily lead to a relationship. That was the trend of a lifetime. He had always found it difficult to commit to spending every evening with the same person. Joanna, too, was quite a gregarious personality. She had to have been because of her job. It was quite possible she would have fitted into a similar lifestyle.

It hadn't worked out like that. Soon after Joanna's death, Jo, his right hand man at the detective agency, had also left. His mother had been taken ill and he felt duty bound to go back to the Bahamas – where he had been born – to look after her. Jo and duty were good friends with each other and he could not be persuaded to stay and help Rivers revive the fortunes of the agency. Jo had been his rock. They had first met in the Bahamas nigh on twenty years ago when Rivers had become involved in investigating a murder after initially just going out to spend a holiday with his sister. Jo had later followed him to the UK and had ended up working as his deputy. During Joanna's illness, he had volunteered to run the agency single handed but Jo's strengths were in efficiently carrying out work that had been assigned to him rather than convincing new clients that they should hire him or Rivers to investigate their suspicions. The upshot of this was that – when Rivers resurfaced from mourning Joanna's loss – Jo had gone and there was no work in train for him to follow up on.

He was still ruminating on these facts when the doorbell rang. "Who is it?" he shouted.

"It's Nikki," came the reply. "I just wanted to find out how you were."

• • ● • •

"Where's my breakfast?" Nick Barton demanded angrily.

"It's Saturday," said his wife Charlotte wearily.

"That's not an answer," he snapped. "We still eat on Saturdays, don't we?"

She was tempted to make a glib response but thought the best of it. Such an approach never silenced him- and she always came off worst in the resulting exchanges,

"I might as well go into the station and get something in the canteen," he said as if this were a threat.

She looked at him. He was dressed in a stiff white shirt and collar. He had the trousers of his suit on and his tie was neatly tied. He did not look as if he had been contemplating a relaxing day at home even before he realised his breakfast was not prepared and waiting for him.

She, by contrast, was wearing just a pair of knickers and a casual shirt which came half-way down to her knees. Another man might have found her alluring, she thought. Nick, though, seemed past stirring up those emotions.

"How long will you be?" She wasn't really interested in receiving an answer to her question but it just seemed to trip off the tongue before she could stop it.

"If you could have dinner ready by six o'clock, I'll try and get back by then," he said curtly.

Yes, sir, she thought to herself – conjuring up the image of a Nazi salute in her mind's eye. Instead, she just nodded. His comments had not been said in a way that either of them could look forward to the evening meal – but she had become resigned to the kind of curt responses that they seemed to trade with each other these days.

She often hoped he would be horrendously busy at work and be unable to return until after a time when it would not be considered rude by him for her to have gone to bed. She would always leave him a dinner that he could easily warm up. Cooking – like civility – was not Nick's strong point, she reasoned. On these occasions, she would take a sleeping pill before his return so she had gone out like a light by the time he came back.

She had no doubt that Nick's work was important. He was after all a Detective Chief Inspector. Any murder in Brighton or serious crime would be investigated by him. He had an exceptional clear-up rate and the Chief Constable was always singing his praises on occasions when they met socially, Nick always insisted she accompany him to formal receptions. "It looks good if you have a wife on your arm," he had said to her on more than one occasion. "Makes them think there's a touch of normality in your life."

Think being the operative word, thought Charlotte. If her life with Nick was normal, then she had nothing but pity for most of the human race.

Meanwhile, Nick was busy getting the jacket to his suit out of the wardrobe in the bedroom. A quick look in the mirror to see if his tie was neatly tied and he was off to the police station – where he started his working day by tucking in to a breakfast of bacon and eggs in the canteen.

• • • • •

"Morning, old boy, how the devil are you?"

It was a typical type of greeting from Mark Elliott. Roy ambled over to join him at his breakfast table. He smiled and sat down next to him.

"Good night, then?" asked Mark. "Only you look as if you've been dragged through a hedge backwards."

"Not exactly," said Roy.

"Hmmm! Not very forthcoming, are you?"

Roy ignored the comment and poured himself a cup of tea from the pot on Mark's table. The waitress came over to tell him about the self-service arrangements. "I'm off to get some scrambled eggs and salmon," he said.

"Oh, so not too bad, then?"

"No," said Roy. "I didn't know you made it down last night. We had a booking for you at the restaurant only you never turned up."

"Who's we?" asked Mark

"In the end, it was only me and Kate Williams."

"Ah! Three would have been a crowd."

Roy gave his friend a scowl and then moved over to the self-service counter. Mark watched him go wistfully, a smile creasing over his face. It was when Roy came back that Mark realised he may have overstepped the mark with his banter.

"Look," said Roy. "Those days are behind me. Besides, Kate's not my type. We would have very little in common. Then there's Angela."

"You wouldn't have to talk all night long," ventured Mark. Then he stopped. He could see his comments had ceased to amuse Roy – indeed if they ever had done. "So how is the lovely Kate Williams?" he asked.

"I must confess when I realised it was only the two of us that had turned up for the meal I was within a whisker of cancelling," said Roy. "The restaurant weren't too pleased with us, either. We'd booked for six of us. I thought there might be a frosty atmosphere if we stayed to take up the booking."

"But?"

"Well, it was either go back to the hotel for room service on my own or a night out with Kate and an expenses paid meal. I figured I could get through that."

"And?"

"She's not quite the dizzy bimbo that you think she is. We had quite a nice evening, actually, and went on to a night club."

"Hence the panda rings around your eyes?" asked Mark.

"I remember looking at my watch and seeing it was 2.30am and thinking 'Oh, God, I've got to get up in the morning and write a story'. Kate was a little bit tipsy by that stage."

"So you made your excuses and left?"

"Something like that," said Roy. He was looking away from Mark and concentrating upon his scrambled eggs. For some unknown reason Mark got the feeling there was something Roy was not telling him. He let the thought pass, though, and the two carried on eating their respective breakfasts in silence.

• • ● • •

Nikki, thought Rivers. Good, old dependable Nikki. In his twenties, he had been in love with her. Or so he had thought. Her rotund face always had a beaming smile at the ready and they had lived with each other for nearly five years before he had developed this sudden early middle age crisis and decided to get on with his life without her. It had come as a shock to her but somehow she had weathered it, they had remained friends and she had carved out a new life for herself – ironically by marrying one of his colleagues at Hendon police station. Rivers had worked in CID before giving it all up to become a private detective. Sadly, though, Nikki's marriage had not worked out. Marrying a policeman had turned out not to be easy and the two had separated a few years ago with no children.

9

"I'm still in bed," shouted Rivers. She had come round a couple of times since Joanna's death, ostensibly to see if he was coping all right. Rivers wondered whether maybe she still held something of a candle for him.

"It's all right, I've seen it all before. You can let me in," she said.

Rivers sighed. It was obvious she was not going to take 'no' for an answer. He quickly ran his hands through his hair – as if it made a difference to his general tidiness. He eased himself to the door and opened it.

"I see you still don't wear pyjamas," she said as she eyed his rather crumpled dark blue dressing gown which had been slung on over a pair of underpants. She was in smart casual mode: an immaculately ironed pair of jeans with a nearly see-through white nylon shirt. The face still just bore its rotund bearing. There were one or two lines, though, that she had tried to cover with make-up.

"Did you have a friend round last night?" she asked as she spotted the empty and half-empty bottles of wine in the living room.

His first instinct was to tell her that it was nothing to do with her – but he stopped himself. Even in his low state, he could recognise that Nikki was good hearted and it made no sense to seriously annoy the only person in his life left who would come round to see him to find out if he was OK.

"No," he said.

"Oh, Philip," she said reproachfully. Then she thought the better of the remark. "I'm sorry," she said.

"No need. I've drunk one and a half bottles of wine. There's no point in hiding it from you. It's not a fantastic amount."

"No," she said. But it would be if you were doing it every night, she thought to herself. Then she approached the table. "Let me clear these things up," she said. She picked up the half empty bottle of wine and walked over to the kitchen where she was about to put it in the fridge.

"Leave it out," said Rivers.

"Philip, I don't think it's a good idea to start again now. It's far too early."

"No, I didn't mean that. I just thought if you left it out we could have a glass together a little later on," he said. It was his way of saying he appreciated the fact she had come round without actually saying those words himself. He had never been as good as he should have been in complimenting the women in his life.

"Oh." She smiled and picked up the plate that had been host to his ready-cooked meal and walked over to the dishwasher. He was about to call out to her to stop but then thought the better of it. If she didn't make the first move towards clearing up, it was unlikely that anyone else would and you never looked a gift horse in the mouth, he thought.

After she had tidied up, he invited her to sit down in the living-room and began to pour a glass of wine for each of them. It was still early but he felt less guilty about it as he had company. Initially, Nikki seemed to flinch at the idea of having the drink but then decided not to make an issue of it and forced a smile on to her face. He could see the good old beaming Nikki that he remembered from his twenties again.

"Are you going to get dressed?" she asked him. For a moment the comment seemed as if it had spoilt the relaxed atmosphere that seemed to have been building up between the two of them.

"All in good time," he said.

"What are you doing for the rest of the day?" asked Nikki.

Rivers thought for a moment. He didn't want to say 'nothing' but in the end couldn't think of anything else to say.

"Nor am I," said Nikki. "How do you fancy going to a film? They've got a season of old movies at the Playhouse. We could see what's on?"

"What? You and I going out on a date again? After all these years?"

"Not dating, no," said Nikki. "I know you've had it hard what with Joanna's death and then with Jo leaving – I just thought you could do with a little company. That's all. No pressure."

He smiled. Nikki would be the only person to realise that Jo's decision to go back home had had an enormous impact on him. Most people who would have seen the slovenly life-style he had adopted would have assumed it was all down to Joanna's death. Jo, though, had meant a lot to him, too. Meant a lot to a man who found it difficult to commit to just one relationship in life. A lot to a man who needed friends as well as a partner to get him through day to day.

"Also, you're not the only person in the world who's lonely, you know," she added.

"No," he said. "I know." He had finished his drink quicker than Nikki and instinctively reached out towards the bottle to pour the rest of the wine into his glass Half-way to it, he managed to stop. He didn't offer it to Nikki, though, He knew what the response would be. He picked up the local paper which was on the coffee table in front of the settee and thumbed through it until he came to the listings page. He looked up The Playhouse. It was showing 'To Kill a Mocking Bird'. Even Rivers could feel a touch of enthusiasm at seeing the performance of Gregory Peck as Atticus Finch, the southern lawyer defending a black man on a charge of rape, again.

"Okay, let's do it," he said.

"Before we do" she started.

"You want me to get dressed."

She smiled. "Yes, it would be a good idea but I wasn't thinking of that. I was thinking of work."

Rivers grimaced. "What about it?" he asked.

"Well, isn't it time you got back in the saddle? I mean it would give you something to do – a purpose in your life."

He sighed. "I still can't summon up any enthusiasm for it," he said. "Besides, there's nothing around."

"How do you know?" asked Nikki. "Have you even answered the phone to any callers?" He had to admit he had not. "Well, just try, Philip," she said. "You've got to do something. You can't just mope around all day drinking a bottle and a half of wine."

"I'm not," he said – a smile forming on his lips for the first time in many a day. "I'm going to the pictures." With that, he got up from the settee and headed back to the bedroom. He turned at the door. "Make yourself scarce," he said. "I'm also going to get dressed."

She remained sitting on the settee. However, she kept her back to the bedroom as he pottered between it and the bathroom.

● ● ● ● ●

Nick Barton wolfed down his bacon and eggs and then went to his office. His deputy, Detective Sergeant Francesca Manners, was sitting in her office next door. "What brings you in today?" he asked, surprised to see her.

"I wish I could say dedication to duty – or following up leads or something like that to impress you," she said. "Sadly, though, it's just expenses – I'm way behind on them and I know I'll never have time to catch up on them in the week."

Francesca was twenty-seven, a graduate from Oxford and she had got to her current position through a fast-track scheme set up by the force to bring on its brightest recruits. It didn't endear her to some of her colleagues in the force. Nick, though, was ambivalent about the scheme. If it brought on the best officers, so be it. It was worth rewarding them to retain them. Francesca might say she wished she could impress him by her hard work. The fact was, though, she already had and he knew that – if an emergency cropped up that day – she would be in with an offer of help quick as a flash.

"Anything in the overnight file?" asked Nick.

"I did have a peep," confessed Francesca, "and no, not really. A stabbing on the sea front but they've apprehended the perpetrator. All done and dusted. There are a few drunks in custody – but that doesn't concern us. Usual Friday night customers."

"No headteachers, then?" said Nick wryly. He knew the headteachers' conference was in town but it wasn't like the arrival of a visiting football team. No-one needed to notify the police about it. Leave did not have to be cancelled.

"Sadly, no,"said Francesca, a smile forming on her face."That would have been a nice one to give to the *Gazette* this morning if there had been."

Nick nodded and went back into his office. He started reading through some of the material in his in-tray but soon became bored with it. An afternoon with Charlotte beckoned if he couldn't find something else to do. Still, maybe she would go out shopping and leave him alone at home.

He reflected for a moment. He seemed to have a much easier banter with people like Francesca than he did with his own wife, Charlotte. Francesca was single and very personable. She was wearing a smart suit even though she had just popped in to do her expenses and her brunette hair was tied up in a bun. She had obviously dressed in the belief that it was possible she might be called out on a job – where she would have to represent the force. He continued to focus his thoughts on Francesca. Once or twice in recent months he had thought if only he were twenty years younger. She was the kind of free spirit that, yes, that Charlotte had been when he first started dating her almost thirty years ago.

The kind of free spirit that Gillian Bird had been. He winced at recalling her name. He had lost her in circumstances that he had never completely come to terms with – all because of that bastard. Suddenly, he disciplined his mind again. No point in thinking that way now. That had been over thirty years ago and he was forty-nine now. Respectably married. A daughter at university.

Francesca smiled at Nick as she put her coat on. "I'm going home now," she said. "Call me if anything happens." She had never had any romantic feelings towards Nick. He was her boss. A bit of a stuffed shirt. Unbending. A stickler for protocol, or so she had thought until she had witnessed him questioning some suspects in a burglary case he was anxious to wrap up. He had, as they say, been a little bit economical with the truth when telling them how much rather than how little evidence they had to charge them with the crime.

· · ● · ·

It was one of the rituals of the conference season. The headteachers' organisation would always spend one night of their conference entertaining the media with a reception followed by a meal. As a journalist, you never liked to miss it – it was a good opportunity to network with people who might be useful to you during the rest of the year. Mark and Roy, unsurprisingly in the eyes of many of the headteachers present, were the first representatives of the media to turn up. The old school. In search of a free 'snifter'.

Both their papers had some respect for the views of the headteachers. It had a bit more gravitas if they passed a vote of no confidence in the government than if it had happened at one of the classroom teachers' unions' conference. Then it would have been treated more or less like an everyday event. The headteachers weren't so political. Some of them had probably even voted for this government, reflected Roy. Therefore their sense of disappointment at its record was more acute.

Headteachers Roy talked to that evening noted the fact that Kate Williams had not turned up at the conference that day. During conversation, he let slip he had spent the previous evening with her in a night club. Smiles all round. Kate's looks had made an impression on the headteachers, too.

The drinks came round again and Roy and Mark filled up their glasses. The room was also beginning to fill up as their fellow journalists arrived. Soon there were about thirty in the room and it was time for them to go into the restaurant to eat. There was still no sign of Kate Williams, though. Mark thought he detected a look approaching anxiety on Roy's face. "What's the matter, old boy?" he asked.

"Kate," he said. "She's still not here. I think I'd better ring her," He pulled his mobile out of his pocket and went to his speed dial which, Mark surmised, must have included her number. That surprised him. He hadn't thought the two of them were close enough to be on each other's speed dials. Perhaps they had got closer than Roy was prepared to admit the previous evening, Mark pondered. Meanwhile, Roy was obviously leaving a message on Kate's ansafone – having not managed to get hold of her.

"You do look worried a bit, old boy," said Mark gently. He was beginning to be concerned about his fellow journalist.

"Well, yes," Roy replied hesitantly. He remained silent for a moment and then said what had been on his mind. "I know I'm not responsible for her – we're just two professional reporters on an assignment – but I left her on her own in a night club at 2.30am. She was tipsy if not to say drunk. Anything could have happened to her."

"So you were the last person to see Kate Williams alive, Mr Faulkner?" said Mark adopting the tone of an inquisitor.

"Christ, Mark, that's not remotely funny," said Roy emphatically. Before he could get the words out of his mouth, Mark had got his mobile out of his pocket and was leaving his own message on Kate's ansafone. "For goodness sake, Kate, ring either me – Mark Elliott – or Roy as soon as possible," he said. "The poor lad thinks he may have killed you."

"That's even less funny," said Roy, quietly this time.

"Oh come off it, Roy, nobody thinks that," said Mark. "I'm just trying to shake her out of her sloth so she rings back and puts your mind at rest. You're a prize-winning journalist. Well respected for your incisive analysis of the education scene. Nobody thinks you've gone and killed off the opposition."

Roy managed a weak smile at this but – as the night wore on and there was still no word from Kate – that weak smile was replaced by looks of growing concern. He was normally one of the last to leave at this annual social function but this year he decided that – rather than pretend to have fun – he would be better off having an early night. Before he went to bed, he traipsed to Kate's room and knocked on the door. There was no reply. Oh, well, he just had to hope that he would see her at the conference the following morning.

• • ● • •

"Where the fuck is she?" Grant Leftly was plainly annoyed. "It's about the only event on the news calendar this weekend except for the May Day Bank Holiday traffic jams. It's conference time and she hasn't rung in. Are you sure you've tried everything to get hold of her?"

"I've rung her hotel. There's no answer from her room," said his deputy Lane Bradford. "I've rung her mobile and been put through to voicemail. I've emailed her. Short of chasing off down to Brighton and scouring the sea front I can't think of anything else I could do."

"Well, she's going to get the most almighty bollocking when she does surface," said Leftly. "I never wanted to give her this job in the first place. She's too scatty for a serious job on a serious newspaper."

"She'll turn up," said Bradford, raising his eyebrows at his boss' last remark.

"I might be able to help," said Geoff Stevens, the number three on the newsdesk that day. "I probably know her a bit better than you do."

"You mean you've been into her knickers?" barked Leftly.

"I'll ignore that," said Stevens frostily.

"But you're not denying it." It was a statement of fact from Leftly, not another question.

Stevens shot a sideways glance at Leftly. He wondered inside why Leftly kept on trying to rev everybody up. ."I just happen to know she has a sister down in Brighton," he said adopting a rather pained tone. "She may have gone to visit her."

"Do you have her number?"

"Yes."

"Why?"

"Does that matter?" asked Stevens wearily.

"Probably not. Just seems further proof of what I was saying."

"If you must know I was invited round to her house for a meal a couple of months ago when Kate and I were down in Brighton for a weekend."

"See, you are into ...."Leftly stopped himself, surprisingly – in the view of Bradford – realising that his aggressive tone was not helping them to track down their lost reporter.

"I'll try the number," said Stevens. After a couple of rings, someone picked up the phone. "Barbara?" he asked.

"Yes," came the reply.

"I don't know whether you remember me. Geoff Stevens from the Globe."

"Yes, you came round to supper with Kate a couple of months ago. What can I do for you?"

"Is Kate with you?"

"No."

"It's just that she's down at a conference in Brighton covering it for us and we seem to have lost track of her. It's a bit worrying because she's normally very good at keeping in touch." Leftly snorted but luckily Barbara Williams couldn't hear it at her end of the phone.

"Yes, I knew she was down for the weekend. She said she might get in touch with me on the Saturday."

"And she didn't?"

"No. I tried her mobile a couple of times but it just switched on to ansafone.

Geoff remained silent. He had drawn a blank and couldn't think of anything else to try.

"Are you worried, Geoff?"

"I'm sure there's a logical explanation," he said reassuringly. For the life of him, though, he could not think what it was.

"Do you think we should call the police?"

"No," he said. "Perhaps we should give it a bit longer."

"Okay."

He put down the phone, thought for a moment and then said: "She's right. We should call the police."

"Oh, for fuck's sake, I'm not going to waste my time worrying about a little shit like that going missing," said Leftly.

Stevens reached for the receiver again. "Well, I am," he said.

CHAPTER TWO

Barbara Williams thought for a moment. Kate was always the feisty one. Getting into trouble. Arriving home late from parties when she was a teenager. The fact that she was missing after a night out was hardly surprising.

Yet she was professional. And it was unlike her to have no contact with her newspaper when she was on a job. She felt she should do something to try and find out what had happened. She resolved to go down to the conference centre in Brighton and see if she could chat to some of her colleagues and ask them if they could shed any light on her sister's disappearance.

She put on her coat and strolled down the road. It was about a fifteen minute walk to the conference centre from her home. As she began the trek, she thought about other scrapes that Kate had got herself into. There was the time she had had to pick her up from the police station when she had thrown a brick through the window of a local curry house after its staff had refused to serve her. It was late in the evening and Kate would later own up to having been a little the worse for wear at the time. She didn't seem to think she had done anything wrong. There was the time when she had telephoned at four o'clock in the morning and asked her to come and get her from a party because her boyfriend had dumped her after catching her flirting with another man. Flirting, Barbara had found out later, was a polite way of putting it. Kate had had her tongue down the other guy's throat. In the bedroom where her boyfriend had found them, she was also lying on the bed with her blouse unbuttoned to the waist. The man she was with, yes, Kate admitted, was unbuttoning his trousers. Her boyfriend had done a bit more than dump her. He had pulled the man off her and then slapped her round the fact before storming off. Then there was the time…. She decided not to go down that road any more.

On arrival at the conference centre, she did not know quite what to do. She approached the reception desk. "I wanted to contact a journalist who's covering this conference," she said. "I'm her sister."

The receptionist put her through to the press room, dialling the extension and then handing the receiver to Barbara.

"Hallo," a male voice replied.

"I'm trying to contact my sister. Kate Williams from the *Globe*."

"Ah," came the reply. It was Mark Elliott. "I'm afraid she's not here."

"I knew that," she confessed, "but I was hoping somebody might know something which would help me to try and find her."

"I'll come down," Mark volunteered. It would have made sense if Roy had gone down to see her, he thought, but his colleague was in the conference hall listening to a crucial debate on exam reform. Roy would be expected to write a detailed piece on what happened for his paper the following day. Mark, though, could get away with just picking up one or two quotes when the debate finished. He reflected, though, that Roy's demeanour had changed since the previous evening when had shown signs of being worried about Kate's fate. He had now buried himself in his work. Typical Roy, thought Mark. Once work reared its ugly head, all thoughts of any personal drama in his life seemed to go out of his head. He was, as they say, focussed.

Mark slowly descended the stairs to the reception area. He could see a woman standing there but did not automatically put two and two together and identify her as Kate's sister. For a start, this woman looked quite plain. She was dressed in sensible shoes and sported a green anorak. Her hair had a somewhat mousy look about it – totally unlike Kate.

"Yes, I am Kate's sister," she said. Her tone seemed to denote that people she said this to, often needed a little convincing that was so. "I know, we don't look alike," she added.

"I'm not sure what I can do to help you," said Mark.

"It's just that I had a call from her newspaper," she said. "They can't seem to find her."

"No," said Mark. "She didn't turn up to the conference yesterday – or to the drinks do that was arranged for us last night." This, the tone of his voice denoted, was a more heinous act than missing the conference.

"Do you know why?"

"No, we tried to get hold of her but couldn't. She'd had a pretty late night the previous evening. Went to a night club."

"Were you there?"

"No, she was with one of my colleagues, Roy Faulkner. He left her there." Mark swallowed. He felt he should not have said that or could have phrased it a little better. "I believe he offered to walk her back to the hotel," he added, "but she declined. She was having too good a time, she said."

"That sounds like Kate," her sister said ruefully.

Mark smiled. He was beginning to think something must have happened to Kate. He could feel her sister's anxiety. He had to get back to the conference, though. "Is there anything else I can help you with?" he asked.

Barbara thought for a while. "Yes, the name of the night club?" she asked.

Mark scratched his head. "It's just at the back of the hotel where we're staying," he said. "I think it's called the Lucky Star or something like that."

"Yes, I know it," she said. With that, she thanked him and turned on her heels and made her way out of the conference centre. The night club was only about another ten to fifteen minutes' walk away. She resolved to see if it could do anything to clear up the mystery of her sister's disappearance. She was just about to continue her walk when she stopped and thought for a moment. She took a scrap of paper from her pocket. On it she wrote: "Kate – last seen with Roy Faulkner at the Lucky Star night club early on Saturday morning."

• • • • •

Roy was on his mobile phone when Mark returned upstairs. He finished the call. "They seem interested," he said. By 'they' Mark knew he meant the newsdesk. It was, though, of supreme indifference to Roy's tabloid colleague after his meeting with Kate's sister.

"Roy, I've just been talking to Kate Williams' sister," he said. "She seems very worried about what's happened to Kate. I can see it will only be a matter of time before the police are called in to look for her if she doesn't turn up."

A frown came over Roy's face. "Yes," he said. "I can see that – but I can't see there's anything we can do."

"Tell me about Friday night," said Mark.

"There's nothing much to tell." began Roy.

"Come on, you're a journalist," said Mark. "There must be something to tell."

"Well." Roy began to think. "We had a very nice meal at an Italian restaurant in the Lanes." It was a popular area of the town – both for eating and for shopping.

"Goodness – you sound like an official communique from some top level government discussions. Think, man. I mean, you looked a little worried last night. I wondered whether you were holding something back."

"No," said Roy thoughtfully. He paused for a moment for thought. "If you must know, I was feeling a bit guilty."

"Why?"

"Well, I wondered if I should have left her alone in that night club. She was a little the worse for wear and it was 2.30 in the morning but then I'm not her keeper. I wasn't her boyfriend. She's a big girl and quite capable of making her own decisions," he said. He paused.

"But?"

"But nothing." Roy screwed up his face as if in deep thought. "Well, there was a guy who had latched on to us earlier in the evening," he went on. "I don't think it was because he was attracted to me," he added wryly. Roy had a habit of making self-deprecating comments about himself at awkward moments. "It was a warm evening and we were standing outside," Roy continued. "I remember he drew up in a white van. He got out and had a look inside the club and then went back to the van. He came back a few minutes later on foot – I assume he must have parked the van in a car park."

"Yes?"

"Well, he went inside and got a drink and then joined us and starting talking to us. I thought he was a bit odd. He started telling us he was divorced – and that his former wife was trying to screw some money out of him. It wasn't the kind of small talk you'd expect from someone you'd just struck up a conversation with in a pub – especially if, as I suspected, he was angling to chat up Kate."

"Was he still there when you left?"

"I don't know," said Roy. "I mean, he wasn't talking to us by then. We'd had a bit of difficulty shaking him off. I mean, he was boring. I think he then decided he wasn't getting anywhere or possibly erroneously thought I was Kate's boyfriend or partner. Anyhow, he went into the bar. We didn't feel any compunction to go and see where he was after escaping from him. He could have been somewhere else in the club, I suppose."

"Did he make a play for Kate?"

"Not really. He hung around us for quite a bit, though."

"Did he talk about anything else other than his divorce?"

"He seemed interested when we said we were both working

for newspapers. I think the *Globe* impressed him more than my newspaper did." Roy reflected for a moment. "The *Glob*e or Kate," he added.

"Did she show any interest in him?" asked Mark.

"No," said Roy. "In fact, when he left us to go to the bar she said 'thank goodness, we've got rid of that creep'."

"What was creepy about him?"

Roy thought for a moment. "Well, the way he just hung around after it was obvious conversation had dried up between us," he said.

"Can you remember anything else about him?" asked Mark.

"His name was Les. He wasn't particularly well dressed. Jeans and a leather jacket. Oh, and he said, he came from Newhaven. His wife had left him. He was still living in the family home. He had rented out the spare room because he needed the cash. To a woman. He had a stubble. Not a real beard."

"Designer stubble?" asked Mark.

"There was nothing designer about him," said Roy forcefully. Then he added earnestly: "What do you think happened to Kate, then, Mark?"

"I don't know. I wasn't there. Was Kate talking to anybody else when you left?"

"No. She was just a bit drunk."

"So she was last seen at 2.30 am. She'd been talking to a guy who was a bit creepy. She'd hardly be likely to have gone off with him, then. I think we should go back to the hotel and find out whether she got back to her room on Friday night or not."

"I haven't got time," protested Roy.

"I think you should make time."

Roy shrugged his shoulders and the two of them left the press room together to go back to the hotel. Once back at the reception area, they asked to see the manager.

"We're a bit worried about a colleague of ours," said Mark, taking the lead in the absence of any initiative by Roy. "Kate

Williams. She's been missing for a couple of days. I wondered if it would be possible to have a look in her room to see if there's any clue as to where she might have gone."

The manager looked at them both intently. "I would have thought – if you were worried about a missing person – the appropriate thing to do would be to go and call in the police," he said. "I don't think I can sanction you ferreting about in her room on your own."

"We'd be happy for you to accompany us," said Roy.

"I'm sorry, sir, but I think the course of action I have outlined is the appropriate one."

"We'll think about it," said Roy. The two of them decided there was little they could do and left the hotel to go back to the conference centre.

"What do you think?" asked Roy. "I'm a bit reluctant to involve the police just yet. She could just turn up."

"And pigs might fly. I think it'll come down to a police investigation eventually," said Mark.

• • ● • •

From the outside, it looked as if there was no-one in at the Lucky Star night club. It was, after all, only just midday and it didn't look as if the place was the type to serve lunches. Barbara pressed her face against the window. She could see there was someone in the bar area. She tapped gently on the window. He looked up and came to the door, shaking his head as he walked towards it.

"We're not open," he said as he got within earshot of her.

"I can see that," said Barbara. "I just wanted a word."

He opened the door. "What is it?" he asked snappily as if he was exasperated by her presence.

"I was looking for my sister."

"Well, she's not here," he snapped. "There's no-one here

except me and I'm busy clearing up after last night."

Barbara nodded. "I know she's not here," she said – a trifle frostily, "but she was here on Friday night and she hasn't been seen since."

As she spoke, she could see another man emerging into the bar area. In contrast to the man she was talking to he was wearing a sharp blue suit and what could only be described as a rather flashy tie. He made his way over to the door where the two of them were talking.

"Can I help?" he asked. "I'm the manager. Pete Sheldon."

Barbara emitted a sigh of relief. "Yes, I hope you can," she said, "My sister, Kate, came here on Friday evening and she hasn't been seen since. I was trying to find out what had happened to her."

Sheldon frowned. "I was here on Friday night," he said. "I wasn't aware of anything untoward happening."

"She's a quite stunning blonde," said Barbara. "Much prettier than me and (she blushed) well endowed."

Sheldon smiled. "I think I do remember her," he said.

"She was with a man," Barbara went on. "He left her, I understand, to go back to his hotel. It would have been in the early hours of the morning."

"I stayed until about midnight," volunteered Sheldon. "I left my deputy in charge but he didn't report anything out of the ordinary happening. I don't really see what we can do to help you. She obviously left here."

"I was trying to find out if she was in anybody's company," said Barbara.

"I wouldn't know," said Sheldon. "Look, if it helps I could have a word with my deputy to see if he knows anything but – if she went off with a man – I don't think there's anything I can do about that."

"Of course not," said Barbara. "I'm sorry to disturb you."

"No problem," said Sheldon smiling.

Barbara was convinced he was not trying to hide anything but she was equally convinced that having a word with his deputy would not help the situation either. The bar staff really didn't concern themselves with what their customers got up to unless there was a suggestion of violence, she thought to herself. As she left the night club, she was convinced the only sensible solution was to put the matter in the hands of the police. Before she did so, though, she decided to make a call on her mobile to Geoff Stevens to see if Kate had been in contact with her paper since she had last spoken to him. The answer came back that she had not.

· · ● · ·

It was Francesca Manners' turn to be the detective on duty that Sunday. It was again quiet so when the desk sergeant rang her to say someone had arrived in the front office to report a missing person – and that there could be something suspicious about it – she was only too happy to go downstairs to meet Barbara. She took the woman into an interview room so she could hear what she had to say in more privacy.

"I can see you're worried about your sister," she said when Barbara had finished telling her story. "I'll pass the details on and we'll look out for her."

Barbara appeared deflated. "That sounds a little like patting me on the head and telling me not to worry," she said. "Look, my sister is sometimes not the most organised person in the world but her job means a lot to her. She wouldn't just abandon it and go off without telling her bosses anything. Something must have happened to her."

"Well, they don't seem overly concerned about her. They haven't registered her as a missing person."

"She's not their kith and kin. They're a busy newspaper office. They haven't got the time to make enquiries like I have."

Francesca nodded. She looked at Barbara carefully. There was something about her that told the detective she was not the type to panic. "Has she ever done anything like this before?" she asked.

"I told you – she wouldn't let her newspaper down like this," said Barbara. "It was her big break getting a job on the Globe".

"Would it be out of character, though, for her to go off with somebody without telling anyone?"

The hesitation before Barbara responded spoke volumes. "She has done it before," admitted Barbara, "but not in these circumstances."

"Right." Francesca thought for a moment before continuing. "Have you got a photograph of her?" she asked.

"Not on me," said Barbara, "but I can easily go home and get one."

"Great – just give me the main details again." Barbara explained about how Kate had gone out for a meal with a colleague, Roy Faulkner, that evening and then on to a night club. Faulkner had left her at the night club – and then it appeared that she had just vanished off the face of the earth. It was just as Francesca was finishing writing down the details that there was a knock on the door. The desk sergeant popped his head round the door.

"I've got Detective Chief Inspector Barton on the line," he said. "Wants to know if there's anything going on."

Barbara looked up from her seat as Francesca got up to go to the phone. "I'll have a word with him," she said. Barbara heaved a sigh of relief. It looked from Francesca's response as if she thought there was something worth investigating. "Would you excuse me for a moment?" she asked Barbara politely. Barbara nodded. Francesca picked up the extension on the desk.

"Nick?" she asked. Back came the reply in the affirmative. "I don't know how significant this is," she said, "but a girl has gone missing after visiting a night club in the Lanes on Friday evening."

"Tell me more," said Nick.

"Kate Williams, a reporter on the *Globe*. She went to the Lucky Star night club in the company of another reporter on Friday night. He left her there and she's never been seen since. She was supposed to be covering the headteachers' conference at the conference centre today – but her newsdesk haven't heard a word from her."

"And what makes you think this is not an ordinary missing person's case?"

"Intuition – and the way her sister has described events to me."

Nick remained silent for a moment. As a rule, he trusted his deputy's instincts. "Why did this other reporter dump her?" he asked.

"It wasn't really a question of dumping her. They weren't an item – apparently. It was just a question of him wanting to go back to the hotel to bed and her wanting to carry on partying."

"What was his name?"

Francesca looked at her notes. "Roy Faulkner," she said.

Nick was silent for a moment. "Roy Faulkner?" he asked. He sounded surprised.

"Yes, do you know him?"

"Oh, yes, I know him." Something in his voice told Francesca that there had been bad blood between the two of them in the past.

"Right," said Nick. "First stop – Roy Faulkner. Let's get this investigation under way. Find out where he's staying and we'll get down there to talk to him straight away."

Francesca turned to Barbara. "I think my superior's taking this very seriously indeed," she said. She neglected to tell her of her boss' reaction to the name of Roy Faulkner in case it worried her unduly. She made a note, though, to question her superior as to why the name had given him such a surprise.

• • • • •

"You've combed your hair," observed Nikki as she came into Rivers' living room. It was a good sign – as was the fact that he was up and dressed by the time she had arrived at his flat that morning. There were also no half empty bottles of wine on what would euphemistically have been described as a coffee table.

Rivers smiled. If truth be known, he had enjoyed his trip to the pictures to see 'To Kill a Mocking Bird'. He had seen the film quite a few times before – but, as he had suspected, he found Gregory Peck's performance was worth watching again.

There had been no suggestion of Nikki staying the night after they had returned from the cinema. She had actually made it clear herself that she needed to go home to catch up on some chores after the film was over. Whether they were imaginary or actually existed he did not know – or seek to ask. It had been more than twenty years since a relationship had existed between the two of them – and it could not be rekindled after one night at the cinema.

"What brings you back here?" Rivers asked her.

"You," she said directly. "I wanted to see if you were all right."

"And what's your verdict?" he asked.

"I'm impressed. You were still lying in bed when I arrived at this time yesterday. And I'm not sure if you even combed your hair before we went out to the cinema."

"Probably not," he said. "You know – yesterday was the first time I'd been out with anybody since..." His voice faltered.

"Say it," said Nikki.

"Since Joanna's death," he said. "It was nice to go out with somebody who put no pressure on me relationship-wise."

"You're learning," she said. "You see – it is possible to enjoy yourself by going out with somebody that you're not having sex with."

"I know," said Rivers. "I have done it before."

"I'm not going to crowd you, Philip," said Nikki. "I really did only come round to see you if you were okay."

"Stay a bit," said Rivers. "Have a cup of tea. Otherwise I'll be all on my own for the rest of the day. I haven't got anything planned."

"Okay," she said, "but you've got to start doing things for yourself again soon. How about indulging in a spot of work?"

"I think I'm ready to start the long haul back," he said. He paused for a moment as if to ponder the words he had just uttered. Then he touched her hand. "Thanks," he said, "for at least getting me to that state."

Nikki wanted to kiss him – but thought the better of it. After all, he had just said the one thing he valued from spending the day together had been the fact that she had put no pressure on him to start a relationship.

• • ● • •

Nick was still staring at the telephone when Charlotte came downstairs from having tidied the washing away. She was startled by the look on his face."

"You look as if you've seen a ghost," she said.

"Roy Faulkner," he said.

It was Charlotte's turn to adopt a note of astonishment. "What about Roy Faulkner?" she asked.

"He's here. In Brighton. He's involved in a case I'm working on."

"Are you going to have to see him?"

"Are you joking? Of course, I am."

"I'm sorry. I...." Her voice tailed off. Charlotte definitely did not want to prolong any discussion about Roy Faulkner. The name just brought back too many memories, Painful memories.

"I'm sorry," she said – repeating herself. "I have some more washing to do."

Nick nodded. It was as if he could not hear her, though,

His mind had already drifted off. He was thinking of that day – more than thirty years ago now when he had arrived at Roy's house for the first session of the group they were setting up. He had arrived with his then girl-friend, Gillian Bird.

"They're upstairs," Mrs Faulkner had said. Gillian helped him carry his drum kit up the stairs. Roy met him at the top. Full of bonhomie. "We're all here now," said Roy. Roy took a look round the room. Graeme McAndrew was twanging away on his guitar. He looked up and smiled as he saw Nick. "Welcome to the band," he said. Graeme was playing an old Beach Boys' number from the 1960's – something that did not surprise Nick. Graeme always seemed to be playing an old Beach Boys number. This time it was 'Barbara Ann'.

Graeme was sporting a pair of jeans and a denim jacket. Two years ago his attire would have been described as smart casual – but it was now two years old. Graeme had not really bought anything much over the past two years. He had been a bit down on his luck – he had left school to take a job in a recording studio but had been fired from the job after being caught nicking a tape. His bosses thought he was planning to make a bootleg version of the latest recording by one of their artists and there was no dissuading them from this tack. Smart casual it was no more. Faded casual best summed it up.

Barrie Read was sitting on the sofa plucking away at his bass guitar. His clothes were loud – striped trousers and a satin polo-necked jumper. He and Graeme were chalk and cheese – certainly in the way they dressed. Barrie did have some money, too. He was working as a clerk in an office. Roy did not know for sure but he believed much of that money went on drugs. Barrie was only in the band because neither Graeme nor Roy knew anybody else who could play bass guitar.

It was a similar story with Nick – he was the only drummer they knew. He was an odd choice for a pop group, really, short back and sides, rather sticky out ears and most of the drumming experience he had gained had come from playing in the Boy Scouts band. Barrie had once said the best they could do with Nick was to dress him in a twinset and pearls and pretend he was their version of the piano player in the 1960's band, Thunderclap Newman. (She was rather a matronly figure.) Either that or get him to grow a moustache so he resembled a Hitler lookalike in the fashion of the pianist with the 70's rock band, Sparks.

At any rate, it was Graeme and Roy that had held the band together. Roy was the lead singer and, for that reason, the band was known as Roy and the Rivettes. They had played at a number of youth club dances – but now they were planning to broaden their horizons.

"I don't think you know Johnnie Simons," Roy said to Nick, pointing to a slightly wizened looking teenager sitting at an organ that had been set up in Roy's by now rather overcrowded spare room. "He plays the organ," he said. It was a rather superfluous statement to make, he thought to himself afterwards.

"Hallo," said Nick offering Johnnie a formal handshake which the latter seized upon. Nick then retreated to behind his drums and had a quick thrash on them. It elicited a smile from Gillian who was sitting on the arm of a settee next to where he had set them up. Nick frowned at her. The pose that she had adopted on the settee revealed a little more of her thighs than he would have liked. He could not make up his mind whether this was deliberate or accidental.

"There's a new number I'd like us to try," said Roy. "It's a wistful ballad."

"So another chance for you to do your pouting Mick Jagger impersonation," interrupted Barrie. It was a matter of fact statement rather than a question. Roy gave a rather sheepish smile. Jagger was a hero of his and he had tried to adopt some of the singer's poses when the group had performed another number formerly done by the Stones, 'You'd Better Move On', about a working class hero trying to warn a rich kid away from making a move on his girl. The pout – as Barrie called it – had served him well. He had made it that night with an exceptionally striking redhead at the youth club, as a result of it. Sadly the relationship had not lasted. He was really not in her league. Daddy was an oil millionaire – originally from America.

Roy handed out the music sheets of the new song, 'Like I Did', a ballad recorded as the B side of a single by a group called Wayne Fontana and the Mindbenders again in the 1960's. Roy and the Rivettes specialised in sixties' music – Roy found it more exciting and down to earth than the music of the decade they were in now – the 1980's.

The band did a passable interpretation of it – Nick switching to a tambourine for a softer backing for the song. There was little for Johnnie to do on the organ. "Your time will come," Graeme said to him reassuringly.

"Do you think we're ready to launch it tonight?" asked Roy. The band was playing at a dance at the youth club.

"You'd like the answer to be 'yes'," said Graeme. "That redhead is going to be there."

"How do you know?"

"I went out with her sister last night." It was the next best thing, Graeme had decided. She was not a bad looker herself if a bit toothy. He had had to make do with second best quite a few times in his life since the incident of the tape. He didn't have that enough money to go around splashing it out on classy girls – so had to put up with someone whose tastes were not so expensive.

The band practised another couple of songs before Nick got up and made as if to leave. "I've got a Boy Scouts practice session," he said.

"You don't have to practise being a Boy Scout," said Barrie cuttingly.

Nick gave him a long, hard stare. He turned to Gillian. "Are you coming?" he asked.

"No," she said. "I think I'll stay here. No point in going home before the youth club." She turned to Roy. "If that's all right?"

"Yes, by all means," he replied. Barrie gave a half chuckle. He was thinking the Jagger pout had already worked its miracle on her. He turned to Graeme. "Do you fancy going to get a burger?" he asked. "My treat." He winked at the guitarist as he spoke.

"Sound," replied Graeme. Nick looked uneasy. If Barrie and Graeme were going out for a burger, it left Gillian alone in Roy's company – or almost. He had forgotten about Johnnie. He knew Gillian could detect he was uneasy about the situation but – if he said something – he had the feeling it might make matters worse.

Back in the present, Nick winced at the memories he had conjured up. He didn't, of course, know what had happened while he was away at band practice. All he could remember is that Gillian had adopted quite a cold stance towards him when they were re-united at the youth club that evening.

He tried to remember as much as he could of what had gone on. He had seen Barrie and Graeme muttering together as he arrived.

"Oh well," said Graeme. "At least he's taken his scout uniform off for the gig."

"Should have kept it on," said Barrie. "That would at least have given us something unique to offer folks."

They did their standard ballads 'Like I Did' and 'You'd Better Move On'. When the session ended, Roy asked the assembled company if they fancied a drink down at the pub since there was still an hour to go before closing time. Johnnie declined. "I've got a ways to go before I get home," he said. He packed his organ into the back of his transit van and was gone.

"Seems like a nice guy," said Graeme.

"He's probably the most talented musician amongst us," said Roy, "but he's got a place at Cambridge to study English so I don't know how much more we'll be seeing of him. He just expressed an interest in coming along tonight and seeing what he could do. Are you game for the pub?"

"Count me in," said Graeme.

Nick did not want to – but when he saw there was no persuading Gillian to accompany him on his way back home he decided he would do – much against his better instincts. "Mine's a shandy," he said as Roy asked him what he would like to drink. His choice of drink appeared to disgust Barrie.

He did accompany Gillian home that night after the visit to the pub – but their walk took place in an almost stony silence.

Nick reflected. That evening had been the first time that a burning resentment of Roy had welled up inside him. It had welled up even further a few months later after the beating he had taken – a beating he was sure Roy was partly responsible for. It was still there under the surface or – if truth be known – not buried too deeply. Roy Faulkner, I am charging you with the murder of Kate Williams. The words were already forming in his head. He sat back in his armchair – as satisfied with himself as he had been at any other time of the day.

CHAPTER THREE

Revenge is a dish best served cold, Nick thought to himself as he drove down to the police station to pick Francesca up before they went to the Metropole Hotel to question Roy.

"You suddenly seemed to become interested when you heard the name Roy Faulkner," said Francesca – inviting a response.

"I know him."

Ah, thought Francesca, is that all I'm going to get from you? "And….?" she continued.

"And nothing," said Nick. "It's a long time since I've seen him."

Somehow Francesca thought that – whatever their relationship had been in the past – this was going to be no champagne reunion between the two of them. The steely look in his eyes told her there was more to their previous relationship than he was prepared to let on.

The two of them soon arrived at the hotel and – as luck would have it – Roy was in. "Tell him we'll come up," said Nick to the desk clerk. He knocked sharply on the door when he got to Roy's room. The journalist answered his call and a glint of recognition came over his face as he opened the door.

"Detective Chief Inspector Nick Barton," he said holding out his badge for Roy to see. "And this is Detective Sergeant Francesca Manners."

"Nick," said Roy slowly. He proffered a hand to the detective. His gesture was not taken up. "Nick Barton, of course." Or Big Ears as we knew you way back then, he thought under his breath. Indeed, that was the first thing that Roy had noticed about the former drummer. He was still making no attempt to hide them by growing his hair a bit longer. He thought it would be impolitic to bring up his nickname in front of his subordinate. "I didn't know you had entered the police force," he added. "Do come in."

"This is not a social visit," said Nick, stepping into the room. His voice sounded cold. "We've come to question you over a missing woman."

"Kate Williams," nodded Roy. "What do you think's happened to her?"

"I was hoping you might be able to tell me," said Nick. "You were, as I understand, the last person to see her alive."

A frown came over Roy's face. It seemed an odd way of describing the situation – after all, as far as he was concerned, it was still only a missing person's case. Mark Elliott's words came flooding back to him. He had exhorted Kate on Saturday night to ring in as soon as possible because Roy "thinks he might have killed you". He looked at Nick's stony face. This was no time for levity, he concluded.

"You think she's dead?" he asked.

"Is she?" retorted Nick.

"The last time I saw her she was very much alive," said Roy. "It was in the Lucky Star night club. It must have been about 2.30 in the morning. I had to go back to the hotel because I had to work in the morning. She wanted to party on."

"How was she at that time?"

"I suppose you could say she was a little bit the worse for wear."

"Drunk?"

"A little bit the worse for wear," he repeated with a little more emphasis on the words.

"So she was drunk – 'a little bit the worse for wear'," said Nick sneeringly, putting his own emphasis on Roy's words. "Vulnerable to any Tom, Dick and Harry and you deserted her – your date – in the middle of the night club. Very gallant of you, I'm sure."

"Hold on a minute." Roy was beginning to get not a little irritated by the detective's tone. "She was not my date – any more than Detective Sergeant Manners is your date by accompanying you here to talk to me. We were two journalists on an assignment who went out to dinner together."

Tell that to the jury, thought Nick – warming to his task of interrogating Roy. He decided against making his thoughts public, though. "What do you think happened to her?" he asked.

"I... er ... I don't know," replied Roy.

"Were you not in the slightest bit worried about her?"

"Yes, of course I was."

"But not enough to call the police and report her missing. Presumably you hoped it would all blow over and go away."

"What would blow over and go away? I just hoped she would turn up – as anybody else would have done in my situation."

"Instead you left it until her newspaper became so concerned they tried to track her down and rang her sister."

Roy scoffed at him. "I doubt whether her newspaper was that concerned," he said. He knew Grant Leftly, Kate's news editor, and had worked with him. The memory was still vivid enough to send a cold shiver down Roy's spine if ever he bumped into him at any event.

"Taking this a bit flippantly, aren't you?" said Nick, pressing his face up against Roy's. "This is not a beauty contest about who's most concerned about Kate Williams' disappearance."

"No, of course not," said Roy. He decided to try being nice to Nick and see if that managed to draw some of the sting from him. "Look, if this is going to take some time, would you like to sit down?" he asked.

"No thank you, I prefer to stand. As I told you before, this is no social occasion."

Roy smiled. "So I'm not supposed to ask you what you've been doing since Roy and the Rivettes?"

A look of astonishment came over Francesca's face. It was as if she suddenly saw her boss in a new light. Nick seemed a little bit ruffled at the mention of the group.

"I wouldn't have thought you'd have wanted to bring that up," he said.

"No, it wasn't our finest hour, I'd agree."

"Did you have a relationship with this woman?" Nick went on, trying to bring the situation back to the matter he had come to discuss.

"No."

"Yet you were happy to drink with her and flirt with her until 2.30am? My memory of you is you don't have a reputation as a tease. In fact, quite the opposite. Quite a ladies' man? Or perhaps the word 'lady' isn't quite the right one to define some of your conquests." Francesca's jaw dropped at this point. She wondered again what on earth had gone on between them when they were teenagers.

Roy swallowed, Nick was thinking of Gillian Bird, he thought. Or perhaps he was thinking of Charlotte. He would have been wrong on the latter score – but then he had been prone to jumping to conclusions as a teenager. Perhaps it was a trait that had followed him into the police force, Roy surmised.

"Perhaps we shouldn't go into people's attitudes towards women," he said. "You never know what might come up."

Francesca was becoming more and more riveted by the conversation by the minute. A sixth sense told her not to intervene, though. Not that she could have done. After all, she was not aware of what was happening between them. Only that at some point in their earlier lives there had been some friction between the two of them – probably as a result of a relationship problem.

"I'll ignore that remark," said Nick. "Have you ever dated Miss Williams before?"

"I didn't date her. We've been to conferences together before and, yes, I have taken her for a drink before."

"Taken her – as in an invite?"

"Sorry, wrong choice of words...."

"And you a respected journalist. Surely you don't make a wrong choice of words." It was said as a statement rather than a question.

"I have been out for a drink with her before."

"And to bed with her?"

"No," said Roy firmly. He was getting exasperated now. He turned to Francesca.

"Do you speak?" he asked curtly.

"I'm sorry?"

"Well, your boss has been hurling insults at me for the past few minutes. I just wondered what you thought of what he's been doing."

"You would be advised to answer his questions – rather than try and make mischief between the two of us."

"But that's it, they're not questions, are they? You're not finding out anything more about Kate Williams – where she is or who she was with at the night club after I left. Are you?"

"It seems," said Nick, "that you cannot – or will not -throw much light on what happened."

"On that, the cannot, we can both agree – at last," sighed Roy.

"So I propose we end this conversation now. We will be back with some further questions later, doubtless. You're not proposing to leave Brighton, are you?"

"The conference ends tomorrow – and then I'm going back to London," said Roy.

"We shall see," and with that Nick and Francesca took their leave. Roy immediately turned to the telephone and dialled Mark's room number. "I need a drink, old boy," he said mimicking his friend's mode of speech.

Once outside, Francesca turned to her boss. "Roy and the Rivettes eh, who were they?" she asked.

"Mind your own business," he snapped.

• • • • •

"He was on a mission," said Roy as Mark came back from the bar with two pints of Harvey's ale. "Whatever I said it was 'boom, boom – what have you done to her?'."

Mark nodded. "I think, old chap, we've got to be prepared for the worst. I don't think there's much likelihood of Kate waltzing back into the press room and saying 'hey, guys, what's all the fuss about?'"

"You're right, I'm sure," said Roy as he sipped his beer thoughtfully. "Trouble is I feel so useless. I feel I ought to be trying to find Kate. Nobody else seems to be doing so."

"We have to come to terms with the fact that there may be no Kate to be found," said Mark.

"What? You mean?"

"That you really were the last person to see her alive. Yes. The longer this goes on, the more likely it is that she has been killed."

"Oh, lord. And I become prime suspect. In Nick's eyes?"

"What's with this familiarity?"

"We grew up together." He chuckled. The memory seemed so inappropriate.

"We were in a rock band together. Fascinated by the music of the 1960's."

"What were you?"

"I was the singer. Roy and the Rivettes. We didn't get very far. Played a few youth club gigs. Then we all entered the world of work or went to university."

Mark smiled. Some of the late night carousing they had done at conference venues fitted into place. Roy also had had a penchant for soulful versions of old pop hits – especially at three o'clock in the morning. The later the hour the more soulful they became. Mark himself was not a pop aficionado but he could tell from the late night sessions that Roy had some raw singing talent.

"You had a falling out?" Mark ventured.

"I suppose we did. It was over a girl. I didn't think much of it but maybe Nick…."

"....has held a grudge against you ever since? You've not seen him since those days?"

"No, I didn't even know he'd gone into the police force. I would have thought he was a little bit namby-pamby for a career like that."

"Namby-pamby?" queried Mark.

"Well, weak, lacking backbone. Barrie, one of the members of the band, was constantly goading him. It seemed to get to him."

"A sensitive soul, then?"

"Anything but if his performance today is something to go on."

Mark nodded. "You're in trouble, mate," he said. "We have to think about what we should do about that."

"Find Kate Williams – or what happened to her."

Mark nodded again. "I have an idea," he added.

● ● ● ● ●

Roy reflected after Mark had gone. His mind went back to the day when he had first introduced Johnnie Simons to the band – the day which, he could now see, had probably sowed the seeds of friction between him and Nick.

Nick's body language had made it quite clear that he resented Gillian's decision to stay with Roy until the youth club dance that evening – rather than allow him to accompany her home. Roy was unmoved, though. Nick was a law unto himself. It was almost as if he had become middle-aged before he had finished his teens. Worse than that, some middle aged people still had a sense of fun. Nick did not. He looked at Gillian, still sitting provocatively on the arm of the settee after Nick had gone. She had a sense of fun, he was sure.

Gillian and he had history. They were only fourteen at the time but at the end of a youth club outing to the countryside for a picnic they had found themselves sitting next to each other on the coach for the return journey. One thing led to another and they had ended up in an almighty snogging session before the coach returned home. It had just been fun. He had not pursued it afterwards. Nor had she. Both had had a number of different relationships in the intervening period and – as far as he was aware – had never given what had happened between them a second thought.

Now they were thrust in the same room together again. Not quite alone. Johnnie Simons was busy packing his organ up.

"You and Nick, then?" asked Roy in an attempt to tease more about their relationship out of her.

Gillian crossed her legs to reveal a little bit more of her thigh. "Oh, Nick," she said – a note of exasperation registering in her voice. "He's so – there's an old fashioned term that sums him up – so square."

"And he's got big ears." It was out before Roy could stop himself. "Honestly, if I had ears that big I'd grow my hair longer to cover them up. You kind of get the feeling if he flapped them he would take off and fly." Gillian giggled. "But I mustn't be beastly about Nick," he carried on. "He's a good drummer and we don't know another one."

Gillian patted the settee next to her as if to motion Roy to sit down next to her. Johnnie became a little more deliberate in packing his organ away – as if stretching the exercise out to see how the rapport between Roy and Gillian developed. As for Roy, he was recalling the coach journey back from the youth club picnic. Maybe, just maybe, it was time to repeat that experience – even if it had been four years ago.

"I'll just put my organ in the van." said Johnnie. Roy burst out laughing and Gillian giggled again. The words seemed to have a double entendre. It also seemed unnecessary for Johnnie to draw attention to what he was doing. If he had just left the room., it would have been obvious that was what he was about to do.

After Johnnie had left the room, Roy took up Gillian's

invitation to sit by her. "So what's with you and Nick?" he asked.

"I don't really think it's going anywhere. He's not my type."

No, thought Roy. Nick was hardly a Casanova. He would have been far too embarrassed about the consequences to his reputation to have snogged Gillian in the coach. To quote another song from the 1960's that Roy had unsuccessfully tried to introduce into the Rivettes' set: 'He's a well-respected man about town doing the best things so conservatively'. Gillian, though, had a wild streak in her.

"So who is your type?" he asked.

"That would be telling," she said with a glint in her eyes. She leaned forward from her position on the arm of the settee to give Roy a peck on the cheek. He puts his arms around her whereupon she almost toppled off her perch landing half on top of him and half beside him on the settee.

"I think I'm beginning to get the idea of who that might be," he said, kissing her firmly on the lips. She responded by allowing him to French kiss her. She was wearing the kind of dress that flared up to reveal an even bigger expanse of her leg and also her knickers as she engaged in a passionate embrace with Roy. He put his right hand on her leg and slowly moved it upwards. It was then that they both heard a polite tapping on the door.

"I've put my organ away," came Johnnie's voice from the hall landing. They both burst out laughing again. "I was just about to get mine out," Roy whispered to Gillian. "Are you free at all this week?" he asked her as they dusted themselves down from their warm embrace. "We could go to the pictures."

"I'm free Tuesday or Wednesday night."

"Great. Tuesday it is. I'll have a scout round and see what's on and pick you up about seven. We could go for a drink if the film starts later."

"Look forward to it," she said while she managed to greet Johnnie's return to the room with a smile.

It was then that Roy's mother popped her head round the door asking them all if they wanted a cup of tea.

"Thank goodness you arrived back before her," Roy whispered to Johnnie. "She wouldn't have bothered to knock." Gillian went downstairs to help Mrs Faulkner with the teas.

"She wouldn't have known what was likely to be going on in the room. What have I gotten myself in to?" sighed Johnnie.

"What do you mean?"

"Jealousies. You can't go knocking around with Nick's girl without it having some impact on the band."

"You saw Nick. He's not exactly her type."

"Mark my words. It'll all end in tears."

In the present day Roy reflected. Perhaps it was going to do so now.

• • • • •

"I'll join you back at the police station," Nick said to Francesca as they made their way back to the hotel reception. "There's just one or two things I want to do first."

"Okay," said Francesca. "Anything you want me to do?"

"No, I think the next step is to have a word with the people at the night club but we'll see about that when I get back. Do a bit of digging. Anything you can find out about Roy Faulkner and Kate Williams that might help us with our enquiries."

"Not sure I can find out anything about Roy Faulkner that you don't already know," she replied jovially.

This time Nick did allow a smile to crease his lips. "Do your best," he added. As she departed from the hotel, he made his way to the reception desk.

"I wonder," he asked, "could I have the key to the missing girl's room?"

"Certainly, sir." The receptionist came back with it a moment later. Nick scanned the reception and bar area. He could see that Roy had arrived in the bar with a rather thickset middle-aged man. They were both drinking pints. It told Nick that they would be in the bar area for a few minutes yet. He made his way up to Kate Williams' room, taking some driving gloves out of his pocket on the way. He put them on.

Once inside, he could see the room was clean. He opened the wardrobe door. Some of her clothes were still hanging up in there. Underwear and tights were in the top drawer of the desk under the window. Even her laptop lay undisturbed on the floor. Not the signs he would have expected to see if the woman had suddenly decided she had had enough of this conference and her working life and walked away to make a new start.

He went into the bathroom and spied a hairbrush by the side of the sink. He paused for thought for a moment. There was a toiletries bag next to it. Instinctively, he picked the hairbrush up and put it in the bag and made his way back downstairs again. Roy and his friend were still ensconced in conversation in the bar area and were just about to start sipping their second pints. They seemed oblivious to his – or anybody else's presence. He smiled and rang for the receptionist. "I now need the key to Roy Faulkner's room," he said.

"He's just over there," said the receptionist, pointing at Roy and Mark. "I'll go and call him over if you like."

"No," said Nick. "This is a police investigation. I'm looking for something." He knew he was taking a gamble. She could decide that he needed a warrant before going into a guest's room on his own. A more senior person might well have done that. She didn't seem to want to query his request, though, and handed it over.

"By the way, does he have a car here?" Nick asked.

"I'll have a look." She brought out his registration form. "Yes, it's in the car park."

"I'll probably have to search that as well. Can you give me the number?"

She read it out to him and he wrote it down. "He's left the key with us," she added. "Do you want it?"

Nick thought for a moment. "Not necessary, yet," he said. He smiled and made his way back up in the lift to Roy's room. Once inside, he took some hairs from Kate's hairbrush and sprinkled them on Roy's bed and then moved to the bathroom to place some more by the sink.

Once he had completed this task, he made good his exit. As he walked down the corridor, he could hear voices coming from the lift round the corridor. One of them sounded like Roy's. He spotted a fire exit and swiftly hid himself on the other side of the door to it.

"I'll just get my jacket and then we'll be off," said Roy.

"The Lanes it is," said his companion. "You don't fancy going on to the Lucky Star for a night-cap afterwards?"

"No way."

"Just a thought, old boy."

Nick emerged from the fire escape and carried on with his journey back to the reception area. He saw the signs to the car park area and followed them. Once there, it took him a good fifteen minutes to find Roy's car. He had a set of master keys which he always carried around in his overcoat pocket and was confident he would be able to open the boot. His confidence was not misplaced. He took the hairbrush out of his pocket and sprinkled one or two of Kate's hairs in the boot. Job done, he said to himself. Not quite. He had to return the hairbrush to Kate's room. He still had the key so that was easy. Then there was Roy's room. He had put some of Kate's DNA on the bed and in the bathroom by the sink. That, though, would only explain that Kate had been in his room – not how he had smuggled her body out of the hotel to his car. He needed to place some of her DNA in Roy's suitcase to explain that. He looked at the hairbrush and wondered if there was enough DNA left to pick up her presence from a further deposit. He would have a look round Kate's room to see if there was anything else he could use. He would definitely be able to find something, he was sure. And time was on his side. Roy and his companion had obviously gone out for a meal and would not be back for some time.

He set off in the direction of the hotel reception again. He noted that he was sweating now. It was not usually a problem for him but really the shirt underneath his armpits was quite soggy. Keep calm and cool, he told himself. Remember: revenge is a dish best served cold.

• • ● • •

Mark looked in his address book when he got back to the hotel following the meal with Roy. Yes, he had Philip Rivers' telephone number. The private detective lived in the same block of flats as he did and they had become friends at the annual Magdalene Court barbecue the previous year. They had both been a bit cynical of the jolly hockey sticks kind of attitude that seemed to prevail amongst the organisers of the barbecue. The highlight of the evening was dancing round the patio to the tune of 'Tie a Yellow Ribbon Round the Old Oak Tree' (and singing the song for all their worth). It had seemed to Mark and Rivers to sum up the assembled crowd. Middle class and with appalling taste in music. Joanna had been there. A very fine looking woman, Mark observed, running his eye over her until he got a reproachful look from Mrs Elliott. He had heard about Joanna's death and regretted he had not been on hand enough to provide Rivers with some company and solace in the following weeks. He sat back on his hotel bed and dialled Rivers' number.

"Hullo." The voice on the other end of the telephone sounded startled. Mark glanced at his watch. 10.30pm. Perhaps it was too late to be calling the private detective.

"Oh, hi, Philip – it's Mark. Mark Elliott from down the hallway."

"Oh, why don't you come round?"

Mark relaxed. Rivers didn't seem to mind him calling. "Well, I'm in Brighton actually. I think I might have got some work for you. Are you in the market?"

"Yes, I'm being told it would be a good idea to take some on to take me out of myself and help me get over Joanna's death."

"Yes, I'm really sorry about that, Philip. I feel I should have done more to help."

"You came to the funeral, Mark. There's not much more you could have done – other than watch me sleep and drink my life away. Hopefully, you won't have to do that now."

"A friend of mine is in a spot of bother," Mark began tentatively. He recounted the story of Kate Williams' disappearance. "And there's this really aggressive police officer, a Detective Chief Inspector Barton. He knows my colleague from years back and appears to harbour a grudge against him."

"What do you think's happened to this girl?" Rivers asked.

"I don't know but I'm damned sure of one thing. Whatever happened to her, Roy Faulkner didn't have anything to do with it."

"Right. So you want me to find her?"

Mark grimaced. "Not sure it'll come to that," he said. "If she was still alive, I think she'd have turned up by now."

"Hmmm. You may be right. When do you want me to start?"

"Soon as poss. After the grilling he received this evening, Roy doesn't think the police are going to let up in their hostility."

Rivers thought for a moment. "Are we all right on pay?" he asked. "I'm not a charity and I need the money. I haven't had too much coming in during the past few months." That was an understatement. In fact, he had earned precisely nothing since Joanna's death.

"I think needs must," said Mark. "I haven't talked it over with Roy but he needs help – and he's not exactly poorly paid. He's down here until tomorrow afternoon – and the police have made noises about not wanting him to leave Brighton."

"Right, I could get down there tomorrow morning." If I get up in time, thought Rivers. It would be a challenge, he thought. "I'll be there by 10am – £200 a day, five days a week, that's what I charge."

"OK. I'll make sure Roy is ready for you."

Rivers replaced the receiver. Nikki would be proud of him, he reflected. Little more than twenty-four hours after she had come round to tell him politely to pull his socks up, he was working on his first case for six months. He reflected. Strange – for some unknown reason, it seemed to matter to him that Nikki would be proud of him. He recalled the relationship they had had and picked up the receiver to call her number. It diverted to ansafone.

"Nikki, I'm on the road again," he told her voicemail. "I'm off to Brighton tomorrow morning to investigate the disappearance of a missing woman."

● ● ● ● ●

"Right," said Nick as he summoned his team together. "I want you, Francesca, to go down to the Lucky Star and find out what you can about what happened on Friday night. Then first thing tomorrow morning, we'll do a bit of DNA testing in Faulkner and Miss Williams' rooms at the hotel and in his car to see what it throws up."

"Fine. What are you going to do, sir?" asked Francesca.

"Never you mind. I've got a couple of lines of inquiry that I want to follow up."

"OK." With that Francesca left him to his own devices. He flipped through his notebook to where he had jotted down Barbara Williams' number and called her.

"Oh, inspector, have you found her?" she asked after he had identified himself to her.

"No, I'm afraid not."

"It's only that it's so late I thought it must have been important."

"No." He paused. He felt no need to apologise for working late on her sister's case. "It just shows you the seriousness with which we're investigating the case," he said. "I was wondering – I remember you saying it was the *Globe* that contacted you about her going missing, a friend of Kate's, I believe?"

"Yes. Geoff Stevens."

"Do you have a number for him? I expect he'll have left the *Globe* by now."

"I think I've got a mobile number for him." She looked through her address book. "Yes, here it is." She read it out to him.

"Thanks." He was about to replace the receiver when he added: "Oh, and we'll keep you in touch with any further developments."

"Thank you, inspector."

Nick thought for a moment before ringing Geoff Stevens. The fact that he was ringing him so late might impress upon him how seriously he viewed the situation, he thought.

"Mr Stevens?" he asked as the journalist answered his mobile phone. He could hear the sound of chatter and clinking glasses in the background.

"Yes. Who is it?"

"Detective Chief Inspector Nick Barton from Brighton police station. It's about Kate Williams. I gather you were the person who alerted her sister to the fact that she'd gone missing. I thought you might like an update on how our inquiries are progressing."

"Thank you," said Geoff. It was unlike the police to be so helpful on a case – especially when the *Globe* had not yet reported her disappearance. "Shouldn't you be telling her sister this, though?" he asked.

"I already have done. That's how I got your number." Nick paused for a moment.

"I have to say that as time goes by I am becoming less hopeful of a successful outcome to this inquiry."

"Are you saying?"

"That's she dead, Mr Stevens. I can't really go that far now but it's certainly a possibility. Rest assured we're leaving no stone unturned in our efforts to try and find her – or what happened to her."

"And what stones have you turned up so far?"

"We have been questioning a man who was the last person to see her. He's a journalist – like yourself – his name's Roy Faulkner."

Geoff Stevens was almost stunned into silence. Police were always reluctant to release details of whom they were questioning unless they were really sure they had something to do with the crime under investigation. Come to think of it, was there a crime under investigation? "Was that on or off the record, chief inspector?" he asked.

"I'm sorry? Look, I have to go now. I've got a call coming in on another line." With that, he was gone."

Geoff put his phone in his pocket. "You look thoughtful," said Grant Leftly, his drinking companion for that evening. It was not a process with which the news editor was that familiar, thought Stevens.

"It was the police," he said slowly as if trying to comprehend the information he had just been give. "They're questioning a journalist about Kate Williams' disappearance. Roy Faulkner."

"Fuck," said Leftly. "Blonde bombshell slain by toff hack. That's a great story." He glanced at his watch. "We can get it in for our London editions."

"She's not been slain," said Geoff cautiously.

"All right, top hack quizzed over mystery disappearance of blonde bombshell. We've got byline photos of Kate. That'll help to sell the story."

"Okay," said Geoff Stevens cautiously. "I suppose he wouldn't have given me the name if he hadn't wanted me to use it."

"Don't worry about that," said Leftly.

The two of them had repaired to the pub by the office after

putting the first edition to press. It was but a short walk back to the office to put this late running story together. Geoff, though, was nothing if not thorough. He surmised Roy Faulkner would be staying at the Metropole and put in a call to him. There was no reply – he had probably fallen asleep. He put in a call to the night newsdesk of Roy's newspaper but there was no comment from there either. The night news editor said he would have to put in a call to the editor but back came the reply that whatever had happened was nothing to do with the paper and so there would be no comment from anybody.

• • ● • •

Francesca was surprised at how few people there were in the Lucky Star when she arrived to start her enquiries that evening. She soon found herself being bustled into the manager Pete Sheldon's office.

"I've already told that woman I don't know anything," He seemed a little bit irritated at having to give up some of his time to deal with the police.

"That woman?" asked Francesca.

"The girl's sister."

"Somebody must have seen her that evening, though," persisted Francesca. "Are there any staff here tonight who would have been on duty late Friday night?"

Sheldon thought for a moment. "Carlton and Miguel, I suppose," he said.

"Can you bring them in here? They're not exactly rushed off their feet in the bar," said Francesca.

"No sweat," said Sheldon, He left Francesca on her own while he went outside to look for them, returning a few moments later with a barman in tow.

"This is Miguel," he said. "I can't find Carlton. He must have gone home."

"Is he due off shift?"

"Not for a while – but it's so quiet I do encourage staff to go home if they're not needed here. Nice boss syndrome," he said smiling.

The detective ignored his last comment. "Do you know why we're here?" Francesca asked Miguel.

"Something about a missing girl."

"Yes, her name's Kate Williams. A very attractive blonde. We know she was here in the early hours of Saturday morning – possibly a little the worse for wear."

"I do remember her. I think," he said with a heavily laced Spanish accent.

"Was she with anybody?"

"She came with a guy." The description he gave was that of Roy. "I don't think she left with him."

"You don't. What makes you say that?"

"I have a vague recollection of her stumbling around the bar area. I don't think she stayed long after he'd gone."

"Did she leave with anybody?"

"I don't think so – but I'm not sure. I don't keep tabs on all the customers. I'm too busy serving behind the bar."

"Do you think your colleague would be able to remember anything more?" asked Francesca.

Miguel was silent for a moment. He shot a glance over in Sheldon's direction. The manager's face gave no clue as to his reaction. "No," he said, "I don't think so."

"Is that all, then, Detective Sergeant?" asked Sheldon.

"Yes, I'll be on my way," said Francesca, "but we may need to interview your other barman, Carlton. Can you give us a home address for him?"

"Sure," said Sheldon. He reached for his desk drawer and opened it, bringing out a file. He thumbed through it for a moment before coming to rest on a page. "Here you are," he said. He wrote it down on a separate sheet of paper and handed it to Francesca. She then left.

"Where is Carlton?" Sheldon asked Miguel.

"I don't know," the barman replied. "He just left immediately the police were ushered into your office."

Sheldon frowned. "I hope he hasn't got anything to do with the girl's disappearance. We could do without the bad publicity," he said.

Once outside, Francesca gathered her thoughts. They were not telling her the whole truth, she surmised. She looked at the address in her hand and resolved to go and try to find Carlton. The place was a back street in a rundown part of Brighton. Number 23, the number Sheldon had given them, looked as if it was divided into four flats. One of the buzzers had the name C. Mendonca on it. Francesca pressed it – but to no avail. She looked up. Most of the flats were in darkness but one had a light on. She pressed all the other three buzzers. One replied. "I'm looking for a Carlton Mendonca," she said.

"If he didn't reply, he isn't here," said a voice.

"Do you know anything about him?" she asked. It was too late. The man had gone.

• • **•** • •

Roy Faulkner was aware of a red flashing light emanating from his bedside telephone as he awoke in his hotel bed the following morning. The late night call, he discovered, was from the *Globe*. Its author told him that they were planning to run a story linking him to the disappearance of Kate Williams. No prize for guessing who had given them that tip-off, he thought. He wondered whether they had run the story when he heard the heavy thud of newspapers outside his bedroom door. As with any journalist covering a conference, he had ordered a full set that morning to keep abreast of what they had all been saying about the conference. He swiftly put on his dressing room and brought them inside. Sure enough, there was a story about him in the *Globe*. It described him as an award-winning journalist for a heavyweight newspaper. That bit was true, he had won awards before now. There was a picture of Kate to accompany the story. He, the article said, was "not available for comment last night". He got up and prepared to face the day.

Do I go to the conference, he thought to himself. It would be a bit embarrassing. The paper in front of him was all but suggesting that he could have been involved in the murder of Kate Williams. He felt, however, that he should go carry on as if nothing had happened and show everybody it was business as usual.

His thoughts, though, were interrupted by a knock on the door. It was Mark.

"Have you seen the papers?" Roy asked.

"You mean the *Globe*," said Mark. "Well, it is one of their reporters. You can understand them wanting to lay it on with a trowel."

"They always lay everything on with a trowel," retorted Roy.

"Anyhow, I did something for you last night," said Mark. "I've got someone coming to see you this morning. His name's Philip Rivers. He's a private detective."

Roy's first thought was to question whether he needed a private detective. On reflection, though, he probably did. He was convinced the police would be coming back to interview him again at some time today. That would lessen the time he himself had of trying to find out what happened to Kate. "Right," said Roy. "I suppose I'll have to pay him."

"£200 a day, Five days a week," said Mark, repeating what Rivers had told him the previous evening. "He'll be here in a minute."

Sure enough, half an hour later the two of them were sitting in the same bedroom with a newly arrived Philip Rivers. Rivers had managed to dust down a suit for the occasion and actually looked smarter than Roy who was just beginning to show the tell-tale signs of stress over his ordeal. He looked bleary-eyed – as if he had not slept well the night before.

"I'll just get off to the conference now Philip's arrived," said Mark. "I'll tell you if anything happens. Probably better if you don't show your face after all the publicity. They'll be a bit embarrassed." With that, he left.

"How do you know Mark?" Roy asked Rivers.

"Next door neighbours. But I'm not here for a social chit-chat. I gather you're in a spot of bother?"

Roy showed Rivers the paper. "That just about sums up what's happening to me," he said, "and I'm facing a detective chief inspector who wants my guts for garters. I know it sounds pathetic but he thinks I stole his girlfriend about thirty years ago. He appears still to be sore about it."

"Things can rankle with people," said Rivers.

"I didn't do it," said Roy. "I mean, have any involvement with Kate Williams' disappearance. I may have stolen his girl – although that's debatable. She had some free will in the matter and she didn't want Nick. They'd never have been happy together."

"I don't think I need to bother myself with that," said Rivers curtly.

"No," said Roy, "and I'm sorry – I don't want you to think I'm taking it flippantly. I suppose it's my typically British defence mechanism."

"So what do you think happened to her?"

"I don't know," he said. He told Rivers about leaving her in the night club at 2.30 in the morning, that she had been a bit tipsy and that he wished he had insisted to her that she left with him. She would probably have misconstrued that, though, as an attempt to get her into bed and – besides – he was not responsible for her in any way.

"Was she with anybody when you left?" asked Rivers.

"No, she had moved into the main body of the night club but she didn't appear to be talking to anybody else. There was this one guy earlier on in the evening. White van man. He latched on to us and kept on talking about his divorce. I don't think it was me he was interested in."

"Was he there when you left?"

"I don't know. We had shaken him off by then but I suppose he could still have been around."

"Can you remember anything else about him?"

"He was younger than me. I would have put him in his mid-thirties. Mousy brown hair. Slightly curly. He was wearing jeans and a bomber jacket. I thought he'd be a bit hot in that but it was nothing to do with me."

"Did he tell you what he did for a living or anything like that?"

"No. I got the feeling he used his white van for work. Making deliveries or something like that."

"Right."

"Oh, and his name was Les and he came from Newhaven. I've just remembered that."

Great, thought Rivers. Not the easiest of assignments for my first day back at work. All I need to do is find a man called Les in Newhaven who drives a white van. The words needles and haystacks came to his mind.

CHAPTER FOUR

The knocking on the door was quite furious. "Hold on, hold on," came a woman's voice from inside the house. "What the devil's the matter?"

"Open up, Marie. It's Rufus."

The door opened. A large black woman stood in the doorway rubbing sleep from her eyes.

"What's the matter?" she repeated. "I'm on a cleaning shift early in the morning. I need my beauty sleep."

"I need somewhere to hide away," said the man who had been knocking on the door. "The police – they came to the night club tonight. I had to get away."

"Were they looking for you?"

"I didn't stay to find out."

The woman sighed. "Stupid man," she said. "They will be now." She stood back from the doorway. "You'd better come in."

Some of the tensions in Rufus' body eased.

"Thank you, Marie," he said as she stepped aside to allow him into the flat. As she did so, a door opened down the corridor. A face peeped out.

"It's all right," said Marie to the face -that of the young woman in the next flat. "My cousin." Then she turned to Rufus giving him a severe look. "So I'm now a party to obstructing a police investigation – or whatever the words are they have for that crime. Hindering the police in the carrying out of their duties or whatever."

"I'm sorry," mumbled Rufus.

"Can I have that in writing when they put me away?" she said tersely. "Why did you come to me?"

"Why do you think?" asked Rufus. He reached out with his hand to touch her arm. She recoiled and pulled away. "I'm sorry," he said again.

"You're very good at saying that. I need to know more. Have you done anything?"

"What? You mean apart from being an illegal immigrant and stealing a dead man's identity? I guess Carlton Mendonca really is dead and buried now."

They were in the living room now. Marie turned on the lights. Rufus looked worried. He was, thought Marie, still a fine figure of a man. Six foot five, quite slimly built. In more placid times he had always had a twinkle in his eye. It had won her over when he had turned up in the pub where she had been working behind the bar. Marie had a number of odd jobs to help her make ends meet and earn enough money to bring up her twelve-year-old son who, surprisingly, appeared to have slept through Rufus' arrival and all his knocking.

He had been honest with her. He had a criminal record and was wanted for a robbery in Jamaica – and had decided it best to leave the country and try and put his past behind him. He had flown over to the UK on a false passport – manufactured for him by a friend. He had seized the opportunity when Carlton Mendonca, a tenant in the block of flats where Marie had then lived, died and taken his passport. Mendonca had tried to call Marie to get help when he suffered a heart attack but it was soon obvious any help would be too late. There was a rough resemblance between Rufus and Mendonca. Whether it would convince anyone in authority that he was Mendonca had not yet been put to the test.

"I'm not proud of myself," said Rufus, "but I was earning an honest living at the night club. I reckon I could do that again – with another identity."

"What do you mean? There ain't anybody else round here likely to die of a heart attack soon – except me if you stay here.

62

And I don't think that would help your cause," she said, allowing a smile to form on her lips for the first time since their encounter.

Rufus smiled, too. "No, I don't suppose it would," he said.

"So tell me. What were the police after? It wasn't a raid for illegal immigrants?"

"No. I don't really know. As I said, I didn't stay around long enough to find out. They mentioned something about a missing woman. Someone who had gone missing after being at the night club."

"Brilliant," said Marie. "So we may be at the centre of a murder investigation."

"What do you mean?"

"Police don't investigate ordinary missing persons unless they think something's happened," she said. "Do you know who this girl was?"

"No, but..." He stopped as if trying to rack his brains to come up with something. "There was this girl."

"Rufus, I have heard so many men say that. What did you do with her?"

Rufus smiled. "No, nothing like that," he said. "She was a bit drunk. It was well into the morning. She was with a man. He kind of bundled her into a car – or a van, I think. I couldn't tell whether he was helping her into it because she was drunk – or pushing her in. At any rate, she didn't seem to be resisting him."

"So you could have key information to help the police with their investigation? Great. If you'd just told them that, it would probably have been an end to the matter. They wouldn't have investigated your past."

"It's too late now, though," said Rufus. "I can't go to the police."

• • • • •

Nick was poring over some papers in his office when Francesca arrived for work that morning. "It's all here," he said smiling. "They've done a grand job."

"What?"

"I organised a search this morning. Kate's room, Roy's room, Roy's car. Guess what?" Francesca could tell what was coming by the look – rather like that of a Cheshire cat – on his face. "Kate's DNA in Roy's room, in the bathroom and on the bed. Kate's DNA in his suitcase. Kate's DNA in the boot of his car. All of which, I would say, is conclusive proof that he's done away with her. Didn't find anything in Kate's room but presumably they didn't go back there. I feel it in my bones. I've got him."

"Before you get too carried away ,"Francesca began.

"What?" said Nick, a puzzled look dawning on his face. It was as if he didn't want anything to muddy the waters and pour cold water on his theory that Roy Faulkner was bang to rights on this one.

"My visit to the night club last night."

"Oh yes?"It was as if Nick was trying to feign interest.

"One of the bar staff did a runner."

"So?"

"Well, he could have been connected with Kate's disappearance."

"Look, we have an open and shut case against Roy Faulkner. Let's try and work on that and not complicate matters.Your bar staff fellow – I take it that it was a fellow?" Francesca nodded. "Well, he could have been involved with some other crime and not want to get involved with the police."

"So, if you agree he's a criminal, we should investigate that and then rule him out of our enquiries into Kate Williams' disappearance. I went round to his home address last night to try and interview him and he seemed to have done a runner from there, too."

"But right now we have more pressing business on our hands. Roy Faulkner." He almost spat the words out of the side of his mouth. "Let's have a think for a moment. What happened? He took Kate back to his hotel room on Saturday morning."

"The guy behind the bar at the Lucky Star doesn't think they left together. The guy that didn't do a runner," she hastily added as she saw Nick raising an eyebrow.

"What precisely did he say?"

She took a notebook from her pocket and quickly thumbed through the pages. "He said he didn't think they left together, that she was drunk and left a little bit later."

"All sorts of things could have happened. He could have waited for her outside. He could have returned for her when the barman wasn't looking. She could have decided to go to Roy's room – changing her mind about going with him."

Going with him, thought Francesca. What a quaint phrase to describe what would have been a drunken romp early in the morning. "Yes," she said, "but it's our job to find out exactly what did happen."

"However she got there the two of them did end up in Roy's room together. We know that. She must have changed her mind. He got angry. The fact that her DNA is in his suitcase probably means he put her body in it and the fact it then appears in the boot of his car means he must have put the suitcase in the boot of the car and then dumped the body."

"No signs of a struggle, though."

"No." Nick thought for a moment. "Maybe he didn't mean to kill her. Maybe it was an accident. Until we find the body we won't know how she died but I think we can safely say one thing. She did die – and died at his hands."

Francesca had to admit the evidence – such as it was – pointed in that direction. Nick's obvious relish at pursuing a conviction of Roy Faulkner rankled with her, though. If she had been leading the investigation, she would have wanted to be a bit more even handed about things – and followed up all other leads.

Nick did not pick up on her misgivings. "Only one thing to do now," he said. "Bring Roy Faulkner in for questioning."

"Nice pint of bitter," beamed Nikki as she and Rivers sat down in the pub.

"Harvey's." said Rivers as if that was proof of excellence.

In truth, it was the nicest thing that had happened to them that morning. They had started off by trying to ascertain how many people named Les there were in Newhaven through the electoral register. There were forty-seven of them. It was now a question of – as Rivers would have said in his former police days – "eliminating forty-six of them from their enquiries". It was an easy thing to do. They just had to turn up on the doorstep and find out whether that particular Les was the owner of a white van. They had spilt up to try and make it easier and arranged to meet in the pub at lunchtime.

"Any luck?" asked Rivers.

Nikki beamed again. That rotund face of hers was beginning to look appealing to him again. He could see what he had seen in her all those years ago when they had lived together for a while. The fact that she had come down to Newhaven to help him with his needle in a haystack earned her another couple of Brownie points in his book.

Nikki, for her part, was glad to be involved. She had worried about whether he would be able to go out on the road again. After all, interviewing someone who patently wanted his help in a hotel room like Roy Faulkner was one kettle of fish. Going out on the streets to track down someone who – who knew? – was a potential killer was something entirely different. Also, she didn't know whether he had the stamina to go ahead with a whole day of enquiries. Most of his days in recent months had been spent staring at an empty bottle or food that needed to be cleared away – on those days when he had summoned up the energy to prepare some. This was his first real day 'back at the office'.

"Well," she said warily. "I found two Les' with white vans."

"That's two more than me. What did you do?"

"The first was in a very smart house – almost a mansion on

the outskirts of Newhaven. Turned out the white van was owned by Les' wife to do deliveries for her florist's business. Les himself was an accountant in the City. Very well off."

"Doesn't really fit the description that Roy gave of the man he met in the nightclub."

"I thought that," said Nikki, smiling and warming to the fact that the two of them were working together. "Also he very obviously wasn't going through a messy divorce."

"Did you see him?"

"No, I only spoke to her – but she was so plummy I can't imagine that: one, she was making up the fact that her husband was working in the city and; two, was covering up the fact that they were going through a messy divorce. I don't think they were the types."

Rivers winced. "You have to be a bit more methodical than that," he said. She looked a bit upset and he mentally reproached himself for his comment. She deserved a bit of praise for her work – not criticism, he thought. "But you're probably right," he added. "What about the second one?"

"Much better proposition," said Nikki, beaming again. Rivers felt a mad desire to kiss her face as it beamed but he thought the better of it. Getting over depression by starting to work again was probably a big enough step at the moment. Starting a relationship with someone you'd known for nearly thirty years and had lived with for five of them was quite another thing. Instead, he just nodded – encouraging her to continue.

"He was a window cleaner", she began.

"Does that make him more likely to be a killer?" asked Rivers with a note of sarcasm in his voice.

"No, of course not," said Nikki. She was not thrown off her stride by his manner. "I was just starting off by giving you the facts. He just seemed a bit evasive when I asked him what he was doing on Friday night/Saturday morning."

"Who did you say you were?"

"Oh, I just said I was trying to find a friend who had gone missing – and had last been seen in the company of a man called Les who drove a white van."

Rivers replied."I wouldn't have been that direct with him,"he said. "Remember we could be dealing with a killer here. Sorry to lecture – but I'm just a bit worried about your safety. What did he say?"

"Mind your own business." Rivers looked at her askance at what he at first thought was a rebuke."No, that's what he said," she continued, giggling.

"Just one thing. You said he was a window cleaner?"

"Yes."

"Did he have the name of his business on the side of his van?"

"Yes, he did."

"It couldn't have been him, then," said Rivers. "Roy talked of seeing a man in a white van – but he didn't make any mention of the van having any distinguishing marks on the side. I think it was just a plain ordinary white van. We'll keep a note of this guy and check it out with Roy but I don't think you've discovered our culprit this morning."

Nikki took another sip of her pint of bitter."So where does that leave us?"she asked.

Rivers looked at their two sheets of paper and started counting. "I reckon we've covered thirteen Les' this morning. We're just over a quarter of the way there,"he said.

"We'd better get cracking then,"she said finishing off her pint of bitter in haste.

He looked at her. A thought was emerging in his head. In his mind's eye, he could see the sign on the office door; Hofmeyr and Rivers – private inquiry agents. It looked good. Nikki, though, was quite successful in her own job, though. Would she really want to give that up to go into what today to her must have seemed a very unglamorous job he wondered?

• • • • •

Roy arrived at the police station flanked by Nick Barton and Francesca Manners. He looked grim faced. He had asked Francesca whether he was under arrest and – on being told that he was merely being asked to help the police with their enquiries – had consented to getting in the police car and being driven down to the station. The journey was conducted in complete silence. It was obvious that – if Nick had been on his own on in being unfriendly at their first meeting – he wasn't now. Francesca was equally as sullen.

He was ushered into an interview room. Francesca sat down opposite him. Nick had disappeared for the moment. There was no offer of a cup of tea or coffee or even glass of water. Eventually, Nick entered the room, carrying some papers and with a furrowed brow. He had, thought Roy, the look of a headmaster about to cane a child who was about to say: "This is going to hurt me far more than it is going to hurt you." Nick sat down.

"Nick , you don't really believe I killed this woman, do you?" Roy asked.

"Detective Chief Inspector Barton to you," snapped Nick.

No, thought Roy, you are still Nick – who doubled up playing with the Rivettes and the Boy Scouts Band and who had big ears. He declined to say it but kept that image in his mind – a move which made the whole affair feel less threatening. He was reminded of the words of a fellow woman reporter who had been with him when he had been working on a right-wing tabloid evening newspaper. It had an aggressive newsdesk. The woman had said to him: "Imagine them in their underpants – they seem less threatening." It hadn't quite worked for Roy then. He had tried it for a day but the thought was so unappealing that he had decided to drop it and instead develop a thicker skin. It might have been better had there been some women on the newsdesk. Not because it would have been nicer to imagine them in their knickers. No, they could have brought a bit more humanity to the operation. His mind came back to the present. This time, though, he thought he would conjure up an image of Nick with his short back and sides banging away on his drums. OK, Big Ears, he thought, do your worst.

"We have some more information about Kate Williams' disappearance," said Nick soberly.

"As you know, we mounted a thorough search of your room, her room and your car. It now appears she was both in your room – and the boot of your car. Can you explain that?"

"What?" Roy was incredulous.

"I think you heard what I said," said Nick icily.

"Yes, I did but I didn't believe it."

"DNA doesn't lie," said Nick. "We can trace DNA of her to your bathroom and to your bed. She was in your room."

"No, she wasn't."

"This is getting us nowhere, Roy," he said.

So he was allowed to call him Roy but he was not allowed to call him Nick, thought Roy. "I can see that but I'm telling you the truth."

"You went to the night club with her on Friday night. You both had a lot to drink. Initially you decided to leave the night club without her but you must have thought this was too good an opportunity to miss. She was drunk. You have a reputation as a womaniser. You either waited for her outside or went back inside and persuade her to leave with you."

"No."

"Once back in your room, she must have had second thoughts. She wasn't quite as drunk as you thought she was. At some stage while you were making advances to her, she said 'no'. At that moment you lost your rag and killed her."

"You've got no proof."

"DNA dear boy. DNA. It doesn't lie."

"It doesn't lie – but it's a question of how it got there."

"What are you saying?"

"Someone must have planted it there."

"That's a very serious accusation."

"So is accusing me of murder." He thought for a moment. "You should have cautioned me. You are treating me as if I was a murder suspect." At this stage, Francesca looked a little uncomfortable. It appeared she agreed with him.

"We have not charged you. You came here voluntarily to answer some questions. If at any time you wish to have a solicitor present, you only have to ask."

Roy reflected for a moment. "No, not yet," he said. He wanted to see where Nick's questioning would ultimately lead. "So after I killed her what did I do?"

"You are admitting you killed her?"

"No, I'm hypothesizing. Anyhow, if I was, you couldn't use it. You haven't cautioned me yet."

Nick ignored his last comments "You then placed her body in your suitcase and took it out to your car. At some stage you disposed of the body taking it out of the suitcase. That was your first real mistake. By doing that, you allowed DNA samples from Kate to be found in your car boot and in your suitcase – which you returned to the hotel. If you hadn't done that, all we would have had was evidence she had been in your room. Enough to cast suspicion on you – but not enough, I think, to charge and convict you."

"Wouldn't I have looked a bit suspicious wandering round with a heavy suitcase early in the morning – lugging a dead body through reception?"

"Nevertheless, that is what you did."

Francesca intervened at this point. "If you had delayed until breakfast time, a hotel has any number of people wandering around with suitcases. It wouldn't have looked untoward."

"Not many would have contained dead bodies," said Roy in a dead-pan voice. "I would have been struggling to get it through the lobby."

"No matter what time you transported the body, there is telling evidence that you did transport it and put it in the boot of your car."

"Whereupon I was spotted on CCTV unloading the suitcase into the boot, I suppose?" There was silence from Nick and Francesca. "Ah," said Roy, picking up on the atmosphere. "So I wasn't?"

Nick ignored his intervention. "The body was in the boot of the car," he said. "It was also in your suitcase."

"Whoever planted the DNA in my room could have also planted it in the boot and the suitcase," said Roy. He thought he saw a flicker of unease cross Francesca's face at this juncture.

"As I said, that is a serious allegation to make and – if you wish to pursue it – you should make a complaint in writing to the Chief Constable. In the meantime, let us continue with our questioning."

"It's not really questioning," protested Roy. "You just hurl a load of allegations against me and I say 'no' and that's it."

"I agree we are not making any headway. I now have to consider whether I have enough evidence to charge you with murder. Francesca, would you go and fetch a constable to take Mr Faulkner to the cells." Roy winced as the Detective Sergeant got up and did his bidding.

"I repeat, Nick," Roy said when Francesca was out of earshot, "do you really think I'm capable of murder?" Nick remained silent. "And do you really hate me that much? Christ, it was thirty years ago when we last met." Again Nick remained silent. "And why did I kill her? Just because she wouldn't have sex with me? Come on. I have no history of violence."

Nick eyed his prey up and down. "That's debatable," he said, stroking his chin. He could almost feel the pain of the beating he had taken so many years ago. Then he brought his thoughts round to the present again and added: "I will concede that you might not have meant to kill her – that it could have been an accident. But that doesn't matter really. The fact is you did."

"No, no, no, a thousand times no."

Nick was not listening, though. He was thinking to himself again: revenge really is a dish best served cold.

• • ● • •

After Roy had been transferred to a police cell, Nick called Francesca into his office.

"I really think we do have enough to charge him," he said.

"It seemed strange to me that he didn't wipe the DNA evidence away from his car and his suitcase," she said. "He seems to have thought it all out otherwise."

"People trip up," said Nick. "He may have thought he didn't have any in the car."

"But the suitcase – why didn't he just throw it away with the body in it?"

"He's not a calculating murderer. He probably didn't think."

"Nick," she said suddenly becoming earnest. "I want to follow up on this Carlton Mendonca thing. I think we really should leave no stone unturned."

Nick's brow furrowed. "If you must," he said. "I'm going to have a word with the Crown Prosecution Service and see if they agree we've got enough evidence to charge him."

With that, Nick picked up the telephone while Francesca walked out the room. She thought for a moment about Roy's allegation that someone had planted the DNA evidence. She had worked with Nick for a long time and could not bring herself to believe that he would do that. And, if he hadn't, who else would have had the motive and opportunity to do so? The thought did not linger long, though, as she made her way back to Carlton Mendonca's address to carry on with her enquiries. It was now 5.30 pm and perhaps some of the people in the other flats in the block might be home from work by now.

Once at the address, she knocked on Carlton's door again. There was no reply. Satisfied that he was not in, she moved to next door. A woman, half-undressed and just wearing a T-shirt over her knickers answered the door. She looked disappointed when she saw Francesca.

"Yes," she said aggressively, "what is it?" She had a heavy Spanish accent.

Francesca showed her her warrant card. "Detective Sergeant Francesca Manners," she said. "I'm trying to contact your next door neighbour."

"Carlton?"

"You know him?"

"Yes. I think he's left. I heard a lot of noise yesterday evening. He seemed in a hurry. He usually goes out to work at about 7pm – so if you don't catch him now you won't later."

"Do you know anything about him?"

"He works in the Lucky Star night club."

"Does he live alone?"

"He has no partner, if that's what you mean," she said. She sniggered. "He's not so lonely, though."

"What do you mean?"

"He often brings girls from the night club home with him. He's good looking. Big man. Well endowed," she said, pointing towards her nether region. She sniggered again. "Well over six feet tall."

"Did you hear him bring anybody home in the early hours of Saturday morning?"

"I would have been asleep. I mostly see them going away in the morning."

"And on Saturday morning?"

"I didn't see anything."

"What type of man was he?" asked Francesca.

"He was – how do you say it? – a wide boy. Into scams, I would think. That kind of thing." Francesca nodded and became aware of a man behind her approaching the woman's door.

"Sorry," she said. "I have a client. I must go."

The man squeezed past Francesca. He looked away as if he did not want to be recognised. Carlton's next door neighbour was a prostitute, Francesca thought to herself. What the hell, she thought. It was a rundown part of town. She should have predicted it. "You don't know where he might have gone?" asked Francesca as she was about to leave. The Spanish woman shook her head and – once her client was inside – shut the door firmly. Francesca tried the other two flats in the house – the man in one professed not to know anything about Carlton and there was no reply from the other.

Francesca decided to make her way back to the police station. She did not think there was any point in knocking on any other doors in the neighbourhood. It did not seem as if it was the kind of place where people knew much about each other. No sherry parties with the residents' association here, she thought, as was the case in the block of flats where she lived.

She decided to go straight to Nick's office to report her findings to him.

"He's gone out," said the desk sergeant after she had found his office empty. "I think he went to the pub."

Francesca smiled and decided she would join him. She opened the door to the pub and saw Nick standing there – a beaming smile on his face. He was almost unrecognisable from the cold fish she had worked with for years.

"I've just arrested Roy Faulkner on suspicion of murder," he said. "That's as far as the Crown Prosecution Service wanted us to go. We'll get there, though."

"I take it, then, that you don't want to hear Carlton Mendonca is a serial womaniser?" Nick looked at her as if she had just arrived from another planet. Nothing, it seemed, was going to be allowed to spoil his day.

• • • • •

Later that night Nick was alone at home. Charlotte had gone out with a girl friend to see a film. His thoughts turned to Roy Faulkner – the Roy Faulkner he had known as a teenager in Roy and the Rivettes. He was at the youth club. Neither Gillian Bird nor Roy Faulkner were there. He thought they must have gone out together that evening. He had gone round to Gillian's house one day the previous week and had been told by her mother that she had gone out to see a film with Roy. It was nine o'clock at night then. He reckoned they would be back around 10.30pm. He decided to go for a drink and then return. He didn't want to confront them. He just wanted to find out whether they were just friends or whether there was something going on between them. As he drove back to her street, he could see them walking along the pavement. They stopped outside Gillian's house. He parked on the other side of the road and wound down his window to try and hear what they were saying. They seemed oblivious to anything else around them and did not spot him.

"I hope you don't think I'm throwing myself at you," Gillian said to Roy.

"As far as I'm concerned, you can throw yourself at me as much as you like," he replied.

She smiled and moved closer to him – her mouth approaching his as if expecting a kiss. Her expectations were not in vain. They embraced.

"Do you have to go in now?" asked Roy.

No, thought Nick. Your parents are quite lax. You never have to. You never did with me either.

"No," said Gillian, smiling.

"Then I think I know a place where we can go," said Roy and with that he clasped her hand. They turned round and set off up the road in the direction of the cricket club. It was midweek. The bar would be closed. Nobody would be there. They stopped a couple of times for an embrace and then disappeared through the trees into the grounds of the cricket club. Nick decided not to follow them. He knew well enough what was about to happen. Instead he banged his steering wheel with his fist – only stopping for a few moments to shake it to try and get rid of the pain before he drove off.

His mind then returned to the youth club and the night Roy and Gillian were not there. "Hello," said a voice. "On your own?" It was Charlotte Woods. Charlotte was an attractive girl. A nice girl. One that his mother would have approved of. She was kind, caring. She did not dress to kill in the same way as Gillian did. She did not need to. She was wearing jeans and a check shirt with a cardigan and – he noticed – sensible shoes. Not the high heeled monstrosities that Gillian sported. She was intelligent, thought Nick. Destined to go to university. Not the maternity ward which was where Gillian was probably heading for one day. He racked his memory again. A couple of years later Gillian did become pregnant and – as one member of the youth club had put it: "We were all relieved when Josh (a lad from another youth club) put his hand up and admitted he was responsible."

"Yes, I am on my own," said Nick. "It didn't work out with Gillian."

"Oh, I am sorry."

"Don't be," said Nick. "She wasn't really my type."

"No," said Charlotte.

"No? You mean you always thought that?"

"I didn't really think until now," said Charlotte. "I don't think it's a good idea to spend much time thinking about other people's business."

"Very wise."

They had chatted to each other for quite some time that evening – so much so that, when Nick offered to get Charlotte a cup of coffee, Graeme had ambled over to him, saying: "You don't waste much time, Big Ears." Nick recoiled. He hated that nickname which had also coincidentally been given to him by the Scouts.

"Cut it out," he said tersely to Graeme "You know I don't like that name."

"Sorry, Big Ears," said Graeme and he sidled off. Nick scowled after him. As he came back with the coffee, he noticed that Roy had arrived at the youth club – apparently without Gillian – and had immediately walked over to Charlotte and started chatting to her. Not again, thought Nick. He handed Charlotte the coffee and then said pointedly to Roy: "Actually we were having a private conversation."

"I don't think Charlotte thinks you were," said Roy.

"It's all right, Roy," said Charlotte. "I'll talk to you later."

"Touchy bloke," said Graeme as Roy came over to talk to him.

Roy's thoughts also turned back to his youth club days that evening as he sat alone in his police cell. Nick had looked as if he was really enjoying arresting him. No fuss. No extraneous words. He just read the words and then clicked on his heels and went on his way – saying an interview would be set up for the following morning.

Roy recalled the evening he had received quite a distressing telephone call from Gillian Bird soon after he had started going out with her.

"Roy," she had started – her voice sounding frail. "I'm worried about Nick."

Worried, he thought. In what way? Worried that he might be feeling bad about being jilted. So worried that you're contemplating going back to him?

"Oh," he said non-committedly – hoping that she would expand on her fears..

"I've just come back from the shops," she said. It was not what he had been expecting to her to say. "I reached the zebra crossing and a car beckoned to me to cross. I did and as I stepped on to the crossing it drove full-pelt at me. I had to throw myself to the ground. Then, as I began to get up, it reversed back at me. I just managed to literally roll out of the way. It was Nick's."

"Are you sure?"

"I wouldn't make up something like that," she said. She started sobbing in the other end of the telephone.

"You ought to report it."

"Report it? Who to?"

"The police."

Gillian thought for a moment. "No," she said. "I treated him badly."

"So that makes it OK for him to try and run you over on a zebra crossing. Makes it OK for him to try and kill you?"

"He might have been trying just to scare me," she said. "I think if he'd wanted to hit me he would have been able to."

"That still doesn't make it all right. Do you want me to go round and have a word with him?"

"That might only make matters worse. Escalate it."

"So we let him get away with it – scot free?" Gillian was silent on the other end of the telephone. The sobbing had subsided, though.

"So why did you phone me?" Roy asked.

"I just want you to come round and give me a hug."

"That I can do," he said. Roy remembered replacing the receiver and thinking he wished he had been a bit more insistent with Gillian that she report the incident.

Nick should not have been allowed to get away with it.

Back in his cell, he thought to himself: If only I had gone to the police that day, I could have given Nick a criminal record – and then he would never have made it into the force and I would not have been in the predicament that I am today.

He reflected a bit further. Had the incident with Gillian Bird shown the true side of Nick's character? Did he have a bad streak – a dark side – to him? Could, therefore, he have been motivated to try and falsify evidence against him? Planted the DNA samples in his hotel room, suitcase and car? It was a proposition that he decided he would put to Philip Rivers the next time they met.

CHAPTER FIVE

"I think I've done a terrible thing," said Rufus as Marie brought his breakfast in that morning. She planted the bacon and eggs down on the table.

"What do you mean?" she asked.

"That missing girl...." His voice trailed off. He hung his head and made no move to start tucking in to his food. It was not like him.

"Go on, Rufus. You've started now. If there's something you want to get off your chest."

"No, I shouldn't have mentioned it," he said. It was obvious that he was now regretting his first statement. He toyed with the bacon and eggs on the plate.

Marie decided to be blunt. "Did you kill her?" she asked.

Rufus looked up from the table. A quizzical look came into his eyes. It was as if he was thinking "how could you believe that?"

He swallowed hard. "I wasn't quite honest with you when I told you what had happened on the night she disappeared," he began. He paused.

"Go on," she said. It was like getting blood out of a stone but Marie persevered. She genuinely thought Rufus – he had abandoned any idea of still being known as Carlton Mendonca – would feel better if he talked through what had happened.

"Well," he said tentatively. "I said I saw her getting into a van and that she was a bit tipsy and this guy sort of shoved her into it." He swallowed hard again. "Well, it wasn't quite like that," he continued. "She seemed a bit limp – and he called me over. Said she was drunk and he was having a bit of trouble getting her to go home with him. He asked if I could help get her into the van. I did help him and together we got her strapped into the front passenger seat. I remember thinking ...." He tailed off again.

Marie still believed patience should be the order of the day. "Thinking what?"

"Thinking perhaps it wasn't just the drink that had caused her to be in that state. I wondered if she had been drugged – or taken some sort of drug or something."

"Why did you think that?"

"No reason, really. No evidence, really. Just something didn't quite seem right."

"So why did you help him?"

"I just didn't think. Didn't seem wrong at first."

Marie swallowed. "You know, this could be important," she said. "I think you ought to tell the police."

"No," he said firmly.

"But Rufus."

"No buts, Marie," he said. "I'm wanted for robbery in Jamaica, I'm an illegal immigrant, I've been working here under a false name. What's going to happen if I get involved with the police?" There was no reply. "Well, I'll tell you," he said. "I'll be deported. Sent back to Jamaica – and then sent back to prison."

"I know, but I still think you should tell. You could have vital evidence which could help trap a murderer." She paused for a moment for thought. "And maybe – just maybe – if you co-operate with the police they'll go easy with you on everything else."

"Pigs might fly," he scoffed. "Since when have you heard of the law going easy on an illegal immigrant facing a robbery charge?"

"Think about it," she said. "Think about her." She looked at her watch. "I've got to go to work now. I've got a lunchtime shift cleaning at the factory. We'll talk about it again when I get back."

Rufus did not seem comforted by this, she could tell. She

went into the hallway to pick up her raincoat, "Promise me one thing?" he asked. She did not respond. "Promise me you won't say anything to anyone else about this until we've talked about this." he said.

She shook her head. He did not know what to make of her response – but it left him worrying about the potential outcome as she left the flat to go to work. He started pacing up and down the room – deep in thought about what to do.

• • • • •

Rivers had had no success in his afternoon searches for Les' with white vans and nor had Nikki. Between them they had got through well over half of the forty-seven people named Les on the electoral register. The following day he returned to Newhaven – without Nikki in tow this time (she was working). Hope did not spring eternal in his chest. All very well getting back to work as good therapy, he thought, but. God, it's boring.

The morning had produced no fruit. He had got round about thirty Les'by then. He stopped for a snack in a cafe before vowing to resume his task in earnest. The next address on his list was an attractive semi-detached house in one of the more affluent suburbs of Newhaven – 38, Acacia Avenue. It even sounded middle-class. It sounded as if it was a little upmarket for the Les Roy Faulkner had described, he thought, but no stone should remain unturned. He rang the doorbell. An attractive woman – possibly in her mid-thirties – answered his call. She was wearing jeans and a smart blue denim shirt with the top two buttons undone. She had long blonde hair which was slightly curly at the ends. Rivers smiled. His powers of detection – or rather the ability to sum up a person's appearance within a moment of meeting them – had not vanished in the aftermath of Joanna's death and his ensuing depression. Here was a good looking woman with whom he would enjoy striking up a conversation.

"Good morning," he said. He showed her his card – which seemed to take her aback.

"I'm looking for someone," he added.

"Aren't we all, darling?" she replied flippantly. It stopped him in his tracks and it was a moment before he could continue.

"Not in that way," he said, smiling. Although with you, he began thinking but then put the thought out of his mind. "As you can see I'm a private detective. I'm trying to find someone who I think could help me trace a missing person. His name is Les and he owns a white van."

The woman smiled. "Then you've come to the right place. But he's not here anymore. He moved out a few weeks ago. He was back at the weekend but I haven't seen him since Friday night."

Rivers sifted the information through his brain. It sounded promising. "Do you have a forwarding address for him?" he asked. "Was he your partner or husband? Sorry to be so probing but it would help me to know."

"Good Lord, no. I'm just a tenant. He didn't give me a forwarding address. I just pay the rent monthly into his bank account."

Rivers thought for a moment. It was obvious to him that he should try and gain the confidence of this woman but he did not believe he would be best served by firing questions to her on the doorstep.

"I wonder if you'd mind me coming in for a moment," he said. "I could explain what it is I'm trying to do." The woman looked at him. It seemed almost as if she was eyeing him up. To her eyes, she saw a man with a slightly faded elegance. Rivers had tried his best to dress smartly for work as a private detective but the effect had been slightly spoiled by spilling some milk on his trousers while trying to put it on the cereal he had had for breakfast. It had left a stain. In addition, he had not shaved that morning – although to the woman's eyes that looked like quite an attractive case of designer stubble.

"Okay," she said. With that, she moved inside. He followed her into the living-room. It had seen better days – to be honest. There were one or two stains on the carpet and the furniture had a jaded look about it. The covers to the settee were fraying at the edges. "Sit down," she said. "Could I make you a cup of coffee?"

Rivers realised he was getting his feet under the table. He did not like coffee that much but decided it was best to say yes. When she had made it and sat down with him, he began to tell her about Kate Williams, how his client had been to a night club with her and that she had disappeared off the face of the earth after he had left her and gone back to his hotel to bed.

"Nobody seems to know what happened after that," he said. "The only clue we have is that – earlier in the evening – they were both speaking to a man who said he was named Les and came from Newhaven and who was the owner of a white van.

"According to my client, he wasn't exactly dressed up for his night out. He thinks his prime interest was in Kate but he didn't seem to have a good line in chat up. Kept going on about his divorce."

"That could be Les," said the woman. "By the way, my name's Sian."

"Rivers," he said, then adding as he felt he was being too formal: "Philip Rivers."

They shook hands formally at that and Sian took up the narrative of how she had become involved with Les. "It was because he got divorced he was looking for someone to share the costs of his house," she said. "He decided to let it to a tenant and that was me." She blushed a little. "I had just been through a divorce and lost my family home – and needed somewhere to stay."

"What was he like?" said Rivers, deciding not to probe Sian about her own private life.

"To be honest, I didn't have much to do with him. I was a bit worried, you know. Sharing a house with a man who had just become divorced. I thought he might be looking for someone to make a play at. But he never did."

Rivers nodded. "You say the last time you saw him was last Friday night?"

"Yes."

"How did he seem?"

Sian thought for a moment and smiled. "Les didn't 'seem'," she said. "He was always boring straightforward old Les. Never gave a clue as to what he was thinking – or emotions or anything the like. Me, I'm, but then you haven't come here to discuss me."

"Maybe we'll get round to that later," smiled Rivers. It seemed as if his slight attempt at a flirtation had gone down well with her. At any rate, she blushed.

"He did say he was going to a night club and might be back late," she volunteered, "but he never returned."

"What did he do?" asked Rivers. "For work, I mean."

"I never really asked him. I think he was a handyman, electrician, that sort of thing. He certainly didn't have an office job."

"And he no longer lives here?"

"No, I think he's got a cottage up north somewhere. He did say once – but I've forgotten where. It could have been Scotland," She paused and then sounded a little alarmed.

"What do you think he's done?" she asked. "You don't think he's killed this woman, do you?" She shuddered at the thought. "If that's the case, I've been sharing a house with a murderer. Goodness."

"I'm not saying that," said Rivers, "but the police obviously think she's been killed. My client's been arrested on suspicion of murder."

"And he didn't do it?"

"And he didn't do it," Rivers affirmed. "If he has a cottage in the north and also this house, he must have some money," he said, turning the spotlight back on Les.

"Yes, I suppose so. I didn't really ask. He was worried that his wife would get her hands on it. Of that, I'm sure."

"Do you know where she lives?" Rivers asked.

"No, I've never seen her. I think he did say something about Hampshire – the New Forest way but I'm not really sure."

Rivers nodded. "Do you remember the registration number of his van?"

Sian thought for a moment. Then she shook her head. "No, I'm afraid not," she said. "I'm not being very helpful, am I?"

"Oh, I wouldn't say that," said Rivers. He could see she looked a little worried. She was strumming with her fingers on the side of the settee and he took it to mean she was a touch anxious about something. He had nearly exhausted his list of questions and realised that what he needed to do next was to search the house. He thought it might help if he put her more at her ease first. "Last question," he said. "What was his surname?"

It was unnecessary. He could have referred back to the electoral register to find the answer but he thought it might buck her up if she thought she was being helpful.

"Craven," she said. "Les Craven."

"Thanks," he said. He got up as if to go then added as if as an afterthought: "What I've told you must have come as a bit of a shock. I don't really want to leave you on your own to worry. Could I offer you a drink at that pub down the road before I go as a way of thanks for your help?"

She needed no second bidding. "Thanks," she said and – with that – she got up quickly from the settee and went to fetch a jacket that was hanging in the hallway.

• • • • •

The plane from Barbados touched down at London Gatwick at about 6.30 in the morning. It had been a long flight and Angela was not looking at her best. Her hair was a bit straggly. She did not look like the 'flamed haired temptress' Roy Faulkner had once described her as. She had managed to dress for Britain in early May – with a jacket and jumper – rather than retain her Barbadian attire. That was because she intended to drop off at her office before returning home. Angela did not live with Roy – she had a flat a couple of miles away from where he lived in Finchley. She was an organised woman and wanted to get things straight at work before resuming any social life. She took the Gatwick Express straight to Victoria and then a taxi to her office in New Bond Street. It was a solicitor's office. She was the head of administration in the firm.

"Anything happened while I've been away?" she asked.

Penny, one of the secretaries replied: "Have you seen the Globe this morning?"

"What kind of question's that?" Angela retorted. "I don't read that kind of rubbish. You should know that."

"I think you ought to," Penny added. "And you'd better sit down before you do." She took a copy of the paper from her desk and handed it to Angela. "Look at page fourteen," she said.

A furrow crossed Angela's brow as she opened the paper. There, on page fourteen, was a short follow-up to its previous story about the disappearance of Kate Williams. It said Roy was being questioned about her murder. "What?" she cried. She reached into her pocket for mobile phone and dialled Roy's number immediately. It was, of course, not surprisingly on ansafone. Roy was languishing in custody at Her Majesty's expense.

Angela immediately went into over-drive. "What was the name of that friend of his?" Unsurprisingly, the secretary did not answer. "Prunella, that's it," she said suddenly. "Married to Mark Elliott, Roy's journalist friend. I must get hold of him. He'll know what's happened." To her relief she actually had Mark's number in her mobile phone and rang it immediately. He replied.

"Mark, what's been happening? I hear Roy's been arrested," she said.

"Yes," he confirmed.

"Why didn't anybody ring me to tell me?"

"Well, it all happened so quickly I don't think Roy had time," he faltered. In his mind's eye he was imaging the conversation they might have had if Roy had telephoned her.

("Are you having a nice time in Barbados, darling?"

"Yes."

"Well, I've got some bad news for you – I've just been arrested over the murder of a leggy blonde I went to a nightclub with the other evening.")

He would have been in trouble for going to the nightclub with the leggy blonde. Who knows how the conversation would have gone after that, mused Mark. Instead, Mark told her about hiring Rivers to help try and find out what had happened to Kate.

"I assume he didn't do it," said Angela.

"You assume correctly," said Mark, a trifle irritated that she should even ask.

"What was he doing with this blonde in the night club?"

Mark winced. He gave a faltering defence of his colleague. He realised he should have anticipated the question. "It was the evening before the conference started," he said. "A table had been booked for six journalists but only Roy and Kate turned up. I think he thought that going out for an expenses paid meal with her was a better bet than just going back to his hotel room and ordering room service."

"And the night club?"

"Somewhere to go to end off the evening. He left her there when he realised it was getting late and he had to work in the morning."

"I must see him." Mark told her where he was being held.

"Has he got a solicitor?" she then asked.

"No, I don't think so. It wasn't until yesterday that we realised how serious the situation was."

"Right," said Angela with a tone in her voice which seemed to indicate she believed everybody had reacted inadequately to the situation. Mark had detected it in her before. She put the telephone down and then marched off down the corridor to the office of one of the firm's senior solicitors, Patrick Saunders.

"Have you got much on at the moment?" she asked. It was said in the sort of tone that indicated he was not expected to reply yes to the question. He took the hint and dutifully replied: "No."

"Then can we book an appointment to see my partner Roy in prison as soon as possible?"

That question did demand the answer yes.

• • ● • •

Rufus stopped his pacing up and down the room. He sat down at the table to try and think things out and banged his fist down on it in frustration. He had started afresh once before. He had got a false passport to get over to England, had found himself a job. He could do it again.

All he had to do was just leave. Marie could not be trusted. He was sure she would go to the police with what she knew. She was a decent sort, though, so she might not do that until she had talked things through with him. That gave him until the evening to get away. He packed his modest belongings and left the flat. He had a friend in north London whom he had not seen for weeks whom he had known from the old days back in Jamaica. He had been involved in quite a few of the scams that were going on back there. He would never insist on going to the police about anything. He was working as a labourer in Kilburn. Perhaps he could get him a job. No questions asked. It wouldn't be as good as serving behind the bar at the night club. There would be no women to chat up at the end of the evening. But hey – beggars could not be choosers. Also, Marie did not know about him. If she went to the police, she would never be able to give them a forwarding address. These things were still buzzing through his mind as he made his way across the road to the station. He never saw the van coming round the corner. Neither did it see him until it was too late. He was knocked flying. The van was obviously going too fast. That was probably why it did not stop. In its defence, though, it may not have seen him. It would not have been expecting anyone to cross the road at that point.

Somebody who did see what happened was Marie. She had been troubled at work by what Rufus had said that morning and had asked if she could take some time off to sort out a family problem. She was a respected and diligent employee at the firm where she cleaned. Requests for time off from her were few and far between. It was granted. She was coming round the bend on the same side of the road as the van when she saw it hit Rufus. He was lifted off the ground like a sack of potatoes and was unconscious by the time she got there. She immediately took her mobile phone out of her pocket and dialled 999. A couple of other bystanders had done the same thing. The ambulance arrived within minutes.

"Are you a relative?" one of the ambulance men asked.

"I'm the nearest thing he's got to a relative," she replied.

"Hop in the back with him then and we'll take you to hospital," he said.

Rufus was on a drip by this time. One of the ambulance men told her he had detected faint signs of life. She hung on to this for comfort but by the time they got Rufus to hospital it was too late. He was pronounced dead on arrival.

A policeman came up to take a statement from her about the accident. As she looked at him, she realised she was now the only person who knew what had gone at that night club the previous Friday evening. She had to tell him.

"Rufus was distracted," she told the policeman. "He probably crossed the road without looking. I didn't see the accident but Rufus was distracted."

The PC stopped taking notes. It wasn't the kind of thing he had expected her to say. He thought she would just give him a straightforward account of how the accident had happened.

"What about the van? Did you see the van? Was it going fast?" he asked.

"Yes, I saw the van," she said almost in an irritated fashion. "But Rufus was distracted. He's not a bad man."

The PC gave up on his line of questioning and decided to follow up on what she had been saying. "How do you mean – distracted?" he asked.

"There was this girl. She went missing. Rufus saw what happened. He blamed himself for what happened."

"What missing girl?"

"In Brighton. She went to a night club on Friday night and has never been seen since. Rufus helped a man bundle her into a van. She could have been murdered."

The PC took notes of what she was saying, asked a few peremptory questions about the van again and then shut his notebook for a moment. There was something puzzling him, though. "You called him Rufus?" he asked. "Yet he had a passport in his possession which said his name was Carlton Mendonca."

"Rufus was not a bad man," Marie insisted.

"But...?"

"He was living here as Carlton Mendonca. You see." She paused – and a tear formed in her eye. At one stage when Rufus first arrived in England the two had briefly been lovers. It hadn't worked. He hadn't shared her Christian values. She wanted more commitment than he was prepared to give. He had left her to go down to Brighton after meeting a man in a pub who had said he thought he could swing a job in a night club for him. She still had a soft spot for him, though.

"He was an illegal immigrant," she said. "His real name was

Rufus Braithwaite."

"Thank you for your help, madam," said the PC. He took a note of Marie's address "just in case of further enquiries".

"What will you do with the information I've given you?" she asked.

"Well, I'll have to report it to my superiors."

"Will you pass it on to the Brighton police investigating that missing girl?"

"I'm sure they will be told about it," he reassured her.

She thanked him. She realised there was nothing further that she could do at the hospital and so trudged her weary way home.

· · ● · ·

Nick Barton had a morose look on his face as he made his way to the car park by Roy Faulkner's hotel that morning. He knew this was the weak link in the evidence he had compiled against the journalist he had grown up with. If Roy was not identified on the CCTV entering the car park with his suitcase that Saturday morning, then – a good defence lawyer would argue – he could not have disposed of Kate Williams' body via his car.

He had booked an appointment with Bruce Delgado, the manager of the car park, and shook him formally by the hand after making his way into the little office space at the back of the enquiries counter.

"Good morning, Mr Delgado," he said. "We can dispense with the formalities, I think. I'm investigating what we believe to be the murder of a girl who has been missing since Friday night – Kate Williams."

"So I read in the papers."

"The prime suspect, who is at present in custody, had his car parked here over the weekend and we believe he used it to dispose of the body."

"Right."

"I'd like to see your CCTV covering the third floor – block B," said Nick

Delgado refrained from answering for a minute. "I'm afraid that's going to be a bit difficult," he said finally. "Our CCTV conked out about a couple of weeks ago. I've been meaning to get it seen to but …." His voice trailed off.

To Nick, though, the news was manna from heaven. At least there would be no evidence to discount his theory that Faulkner had dumped the body in the suitcase. Of course, he could not show his pleasure but allowed a deep frown to develop on his forehead instead.

"That's a pity," he said slowly.

"Well, I thought just having the cameras in place would be enough of a deterrent," said Delgado. "I am planning to call somebody in next week," he added as if trying to be helpful.

"That doesn't really help me," Nick found himself saying.

"I might be able to help you, though," Delgado said tentatively.

"Yes?" Nick was not sure he was going to like what the car park manager was going to say.

"The CCTV at the entrance is on a different loop," he said. "It's still working. I could show you film of your suspect coming and going."

Thanks a lot, thought Nick. He realised he could not ignore the evidence. The defence would be bound to call for it if it strengthened their case. "I'll get someone to look through it," he said. Quick as a flash, he was on his mobile phone to the station telling them to get someone down to the car park as quickly as possible.

Francesca, meanwhile, had decided off her own bat to make another visit to the night club. She was still convinced that the missing Carlton Mendonca held the key to what had happened to Kate Williams and thought his fellow barman, Miguel, might know more than he was letting on about his role in her disappearance.

"I've not heard from him since that night you were here," he said. As they spoke the door opened to the manager's office and Pete Sheldon walked out.

"Interviewing my staff again, Detective Sergeant?" he asked. "I thought you already had a man in custody over this."

"We're still looking for more evidence," she said.

"I might be able to help you," he said. He turned to go back into his office and re-emerged with a mobile phone. "One of my cleaners found it outside. It was in those flowers we've got outside in the courtyard. I don't know whose it is – but nobody's come back to claim it."

"When was it found?"

"Not until Monday morning – but it could have been there for some time. It was hidden from view. The battery's flat so I haven't been able to find out who it belongs to."

"Why didn't you tell us about it beforehand?"

"There was nothing to connect it to the case you're investigating. I thought somebody might come and claim it. I'm only trying to be helpful."

"Yes, sir, and you are," said Francesca, reaching out to take it from him. "I'll take it back to the station." She turned to Miguel. "And if you do ever hear anything from Carlton Mendonca, be sure to come forward and tell us."

• • • • •

Back at the police station, Nick had a look of smug satisfaction on his face. He had just been told the PC who had gone to the car park had returned with information that Faulkner's car had been seen leaving the car park at midday – returning at two o'clock that same afternoon.

That could have been when he dumped the body, he thought to himself. Why do it in broad daylight, though, he mused.

It was at that moment that Francesca came back from her

visit to the night club. She went immediately into her office and began charging up the mobile phone that had been left outside it. Before long it had sprung back into life and it did not take Francesca long to realise it was Kate Williams' mobile – many of the emails were connected to journalism and there were some press releases from the headteachers' conference. There were also a few voicemail messages that she began to plough through. Some were obviously from friends – Geoff Stevens, her sister, trying to find her. One, though, made her sit up and take special note.

The voice simply said: "For goodness sake, Kate, ring either me – Mark Elliott – or Roy as soon as possible. The poor lad thinks he may have killed you."

She almost ran into Nick's office.

"Sir, sir," she said breathlessly. "I think I've found something you should listen to."

"Yes?"

"I've found Kate Williams' mobile phone and I think there's something you should hear on the messages." Nick accompanied her back to her office and listened to the voicemail. "Interesting," he said. "We'd better find this Mark Elliott and ask him what made him say that. Presumably Faulkner must have shown signs of feeling guilty about something to lead him to make a call like that. Also, what made her drop the mobile in those flowers? Was she being forced to do something against her will?"

"But surely, if it was Faulkner he would have just said 'let's go back to the hotel'?" mused Francesca. "Any trouble between them would probably have occurred when they got back there. If she was doing something against her will, doesn't it mean she was being taken somewhere else? Somewhere she didn't want to go?"

"Maybe she just dropped the phone because she was drunk," said Nick. He mentally kicked himself for opening up the possibility of an alternative scenario in Francesca's mind. "She may not have wanted to go back to the hotel with Faulkner, Whatever happened, though, it means we have an interesting lot of questions to put to him in the morning" he added.

• • • • •

Rivers turned away from the bar to look at Sian after going up to buy the second round of drinks. She was an attractive woman, quite bubbly, vivacious. It had been easy to chat to her. Easier than he imagined. Since Joanna's death, he had not been in the position of chatting up a woman. He stopped his thoughts in their tracks. Chatting up? Was he really chatting up a woman? They had gone to the pub – ostensibly so he could help her recover from the shocking thought that she may have been renting a room in the house of a murderer. Worse still, a man who had murdered a woman. In reality, he wanted to gain her confidence so she would let him poke around in the house to see what he could find out about her landlord, Les Craven. In reality, too, he was enjoying himself. Not many of his days since the death of Joanna had been filled with pleasant conversation. He walked back to the table where they were sitting.

"I wouldn't worry too much about Les Craven," he said as he placed a glass of dry white wine down in front of her. "I somehow don't think you're in danger from him." He began sipping his pint of bitter. "If he tried anything with you, it would so easily point back to him. He didn't know Kate. There was no connection between the two of them."

"Your client?" suggested Sian.

"Yes," said Rivers, taking a fresh sip from his bitter. "He made a mistake there. He shouldn't have mentioned his name when he was talking to Roy and Kate together. After all, if he hadn't, I'd just have been looking for a man driving a white van. The words needle and haystack wouldn't have come into it. It would have been far more difficult than that. It makes me think. Maybe what happened wasn't planned. It was a spur of the minute thing."He swallowed again.

"So what happens now if there's a disaster at the house? How do you get in touch with him?"he asked.

"He said he'd been in touch with me when he got a permanent new address. When I saw him at the weekend, he said he was still looking. He said the cottage he was in was just a short-term rental. As I said, he did say where it was. I think it was Scotland. To be honest, I haven't tried to get in touch with him – or find out where he is. There's been no need. I suppose I count myself as quite lucky. I've got to live in a decent sized house for the rent of a room in it. What's not to like?"

Rivers smiled. "No, I agree with you." He was silent for a moment."Look," he said eventually, "would you mind if I came back with you to the house? I'd like to have a look round to see if I can find out more about our friend Mr Craven."

"Not at all," she said. They finished their drinks and got up from the table. As they made their way outside back into the lane, Sian slipped her hand round Rivers' arm.

"Thanks for that," she said. "I really enjoyed it. My social life's not been great over the past few months."

"Nor mine," replied the private detective. He wondered whether to tell her about Joanna but thought there was no need really.

"You're single, too?" she asked. He realised she was not relaxing the grip on his arm.

"Yes, but I was living with someone. Unfortunately, she was taken ill and died of cancer last year."Last year, he thought, put the event sufficiently far in the past for her not to think he was still in a state of mourning for her.

"I am sorry,"she said."More tragic than me. I just had a pig of a husband who couldn't keep his hands off flashy young secretaries and – well, I suppose I wasn't exactly a nun, either." She thought for a moment. "Maybe it's best if I say we just weren't suited for each other," she added. They had arrived back at Les Craven's house and she opened the door and invited him in.

"What do you want to do now?" she asked.

She was standing in front of him now. He was fixated on her two top buttons which were still undone and showing signs that there was an ample breast underneath her shirt. He had a sudden desire to undo the next two to expose the breasts more clearly but managed to restrain himself. Instead, he kept things on a professional footing.

"Did Les Craven have a study?" he asked. "Somewhere where I might find documents – somewhere where I could find out more about him."

"Yes," she said, "It's upstairs. He converted what would have been a third bedroom into a study. I think he took most of his stuff with him, though." She took him upstairs and showed him into the room and left him to his own devices.

"Can I fix a drink for you while you're doing that?" she called back as she made her way down the stairs to the ground floor.

"That would be nice," said Rivers but he added: "It'll be getting to the stage where I won't be able to drive back home if I have another drink."

She cut in quickly. "You could always stay over," she said. "It's a massive house. Far too big for just one person to stay in." Rivers did not respond but sat down at the desk in the study only to find Sian returning upstairs with a drink. "Vodka and tonic," she said. "It's up to you whether you drink it but I won't have you saying that I'm not hospitable." With that, she gave a little laugh and turned on her heels again.

Rivers began sipping the drink. The accent seemed to have been placed on the vodka rather than the tonic. He smiled then got back to work. The drawers to the desk were locked and he sighed. If he had realised he would be involved in this kind of work, he would have brought his set of master keys with him which he was sure would have opened the drawers. As it was he did not feel confident enough about breaking open the drawers on his first visit. He rummaged around the desk but came up with nothing except a couple of old bills and receipts.

He went downstairs again. "I think I'm going to have to back another time," he said to Sian. "It's all under lock and key."

"I certainly wouldn't object to that," she said turning to face him. She looked into his eyes. "Another vodka and tonic?" she asked, "or would you prefer this?" She moved towards him and kissed him firmly on the lips.

"This," he replied firmly, responding with an equally passionate kiss. His hands went to the third button on her shirt and he started undoing it.

"You know," she said. "This may be a massive house – but that doesn't mean we have to be in separate rooms." She took him by the hand and started leading him upstairs. "We're not going to the study this time," she said, "and you can have that vodka and tonic a little later."

Once in her bedroom, she turned to him and said:

"You know, I don't make a habit of doing this."

"Nor do I," said Rivers. "In fact, it's the first time." He stopped. His mind went back to Joanna and he wondered what she would have thought of what he was doing. Her voice came into his head. He remembered Joanna saying just before she died: "I want you to enjoy yourself. Do what you want when it comes to forming new relationships. Just don't forget about me." He smiled as a tear welled in his eye. Fat chance, he thought.

"I don't believe that," said Sian.

"What?" Rivers responded as if he was not quite on her wavelength.

"That it's your first time."

Rivers grinned. "No," he said, "not quite, I meant the first time since I lost Joanna."

"It's the first time since I lost Shaun – my husband," said Sian, "but that was a cause for celebration not sadness."

She started tugging at his shirt buttons, undoing them slowly while giving him another passionate kiss on the mouth. They had set off for the bedroom early. It was still daylight. It was a long time, though, before Sian ventured downstairs to get that second vodka and tonic

• • ● • •

Nick had been just about to leave the office that night when fielded a call from Hendon police station. It was an inspector on the line telling him about the death of Rufus Braithwaite – or Carlton Mendonca as he had known him. He learnt that the man had told a friend about how he had helped get a tipsy girl into a car at the Lucky Star night club early on Saturday morning.

He was given the name and address of the woman who had given police this information.

Nick put the telephone down and got up to leave his office. He stopped as he approached the door and turned back to pick up his notebook from the table. He tore the page on which he had scrawled Marie's address on out of the notebook and very deliberately screwed it up and threw it in the waste paper bin.

CHAPTER SIX

Rivers' night of passion with Les Craven's lodger was still fresh in his mind as he drove away from her Newhaven home the following morning. For both of them it had been a release. For Rivers, following six months where he could hardly contemplate even talking to another woman – or human being, for that matter – let alone make love to her, it was a sign that his confidence and ability to cope was returning. For Sian, it was closing the door on months of heartache since the break-up from her husband and subsequent divorce.

In a sense neither of them was thinking of each other as they made love that evening. It was an animal instinct that had to be sated and that was probably why it ended up being so passionate a night. They must have made love five times at least during the course of the night. Okay, he thought Sian to be attractive and good company but it went no further than that. Would he see her again? Ah, he had to. He had to return with his master keys to see if he could unlock the drawers in Les Craven's study and find out more about the white van man.

His mind returned to the case at that juncture. What had he learned about Les Craven from the visit? Well, he seemed to be quite a secretive fellow – not giving Sian an address or telephone number to contact him on if anything went wrong with the house. Maybe he wanted to disappear from view when he left the house in Newhaven. Maybe he had been planning something – but what? If he had killed Kate Williams, would he have needed to vanish off the face of the earth? Rivers thought for a moment. Yes, he concluded, because of the encounter with Roy Faulkner in the night club. That meant there was somebody who would have recognised him. He could hardly have thought that Faulkner himself would become the main suspect.

All the time he was thinking about this, he was driving along the route to take him to his home in Finchley. It suddenly became clear to him. He had uncovered a whole load of evidence that the police had either ignored or failed to realise the significance of in their pursuit of Roy Faulkner. It was time to bring it to their attention, he thought. He turned in at the nearest service station and headed back to Brighton. As he drove, thoughts of Sian faded from his memory and he focussed on how he could convince Detective Chief Inspector Nick Barton that he should follow up on the lead that he had found.

He was lucky. Nick Barton was in when he called at the police station. He told the desk sergeant to usher Rivers in to his office.

"I don't normally have time for private detectives," said Barton stiffly, "but say what you've got to say."

The words hardly filled Rivers with confidence that he had a sympathetic ear.

"You've arrested my client on suspicion of murder," the private detective began.

"My goodness," sneered Barton. "No flies on you. I can see why you became a private detective."

Rivers decided not to rise to the bait. "There is, though, another explanation for what happened that night at the night club," he said.

"I'm all ears," said Barton. It was difficult for Rivers to hold back a smirk at this. Barton was right about this. He definitely was all ears and he – as had always been the case even when he was a teenager – made no attempt to cover up the size of his ears by growing his hair a bit longer. Rivers, like his client, thought that was odd. Barton still sported the kind of short back and sides haircut that had gone out of fashion in the 1950's. It was also not cropped with designer stubble as was the modern fashion. Just plain short back and sides.

"Where was I?" said Rivers, trying to regain some composure.

Barton looked at his watch. "You've already taken up ten minutes of my time," he snapped. "Don't waste any more."

It was then the two were interrupted by a knock at the door. It was Francesca Manners.

"Come in," said Barton. "You might like to listen to what this guy's got to say. Mr .... ?"

Barton remembered his name only too well but declined to use it.

"Rivers. Philip Rivers," the private detective said, getting up and offering a handshake to Francesca. She accepted it. If there was no piercing Barton's armour, thought Rivers, at least the sergeant did not seem to feel the necessity to score points off him at every opportunity. Rivers decided that – as a result – he would at least make sure he was civil to her.

"I'm a private detective and I'm representing Roy Faulkner," he said. "I believe my client told you of a conversation he'd had at the night club with a man driving a white van – at least a conversation both he and Kate Williams had with the man." He was looking at Francesca while he was speaking rather than Barton.

"Yes," she replied. Barton feigned lack of interest.

"Well, I've been trying to trace that man and I've made significant progress. His name is Les Craven. He lives in Newhaven – or should I say he lived in Newhaven. He has disappeared, too. On that Friday night\Saturday morning." He paused there for dramatic effect.

"Mr Rivers," began Barton but Francesca cut in. "How do you mean – disappeared?" she asked.

"He owned a house in Newhaven and rented out a room. His tenant last saw him on Friday night. So he goes to the night club on Friday night – and doesn't come back either."

"Are you sure that this man and the man Kate Williams and Roy Faulkner met in the night club are one and the same?"

"Yes." His mind went back to the fact that forty-seven people named Les living in Newhaven. Only one had fitted the bill – answering the description of the man his client had chatted to.

"Another thing," Rivers went on. "This Les Craven gave no forwarding address to his tenant for her to contact if anything went wrong with the house. Another suspicious sign, I would have thought. Seems as though, for some reason, he didn't want to be traced."

"Mr Rivers," said Barton seizing control of the situation again. "I don't go around questioning people about murder on a whim."

"No, but you did get a certain amount of satisfaction from questioning my client," said Rivers.

Barton feigned surprise. "What do you mean?" he asked.

"I mean there is bad blood between the two of you."

"And you think that has coloured my judgement?"

"Yes," said Rivers, staring intently at Francesca while he was speaking. Her face was impassive. He could not tell what she was thinking.

"That's a very serious allegation, Mr Rivers. I told you when we started this interview that I don't normally give the time of day to private detectives. Nothing you have said makes me think I should alter that stance. Indeed, I am now beginning to regret that I gave you an interview. We have an overwhelming amount of evidence stacking up against your client. I do not feel the necessity to outline it all to you. You'll find out about it all when it comes to court. Now, good-day Mr Rivers."

Rivers made no attempt to get up from his seat. Instead he reached into his pocket and took out a scrap of paper.

"I'm writing the address of Les Craven down for you should you see fit to investigate what I have told you." He put it down on the table nearer to Francesca than Barton – but the latter reached across, snatched it up and put it in his pocket.

"I said good day, Mr Rivers. I have pressing work commitments to attend to." Barton was not even looking at the private detective now. He picked up some loose papers from his desk and started ostentatiously reading them.

"I'll see myself out, shall I then?" said Rivers sarcastically. He was hoping that Francesca might take the opportunity to escort him from the room and back to the front office so he could have a word with her but it appeared that was too much to hope for. Whether or not she was critical of the way Barton was handling the case, he could not tell. What he did realise, though, was that she was not prepared to do anything that might be construed as an act of open defiance of her boss. As there was no move from Francesca, he did what he had suggested he should do and saw himself out. Before he left, though, he aimed one parting shot at Barton:

"You'll find you understand those papers better if you turn them the other way up."

Barton emitted an irritated grunt. He turned to Francesca once the private detective had gone and asked;

"What did you make of that?"

"Interesting," she said. "We have one or two unexplained things going on that night – or at least as a result of that night. White van man goes missing after going to the night club that evening and talking to Faulkner and Kate Williams. One of the bar staff does a runner the following evening when the police turn up to question him about events on the Friday night\ Saturday morning."

"And the man who was last definitely seen in her company has her DNA in his hotel bedroom, her DNA in his suitcase, her DNA in the boot of his car, has his closest friend making a mobile call saying he thinks he may have killed her and took a ride from the car park on the Saturday morning when arguably he should have working at the headteachers' conference. Spent two and a half hours away from the conference – enough time to dump the body virtually anywhere in the neighbourhood.

No, we've got a good case. Good enough to put to a jury. Good enough to convince a jury, I believe."

"So you don't propose to investigate Les Craven?"

"No, I don't think so. I don't see any need."

"We can be sure Philip Rivers will."

"Let him," said Barton in a tone that seemed to indicate he did not think anything the private detective came up with would throw his investigation off course.

• • • • •

"Darling, this is awful," said Angela when she finally got to talk to Roy on the telephone. "I don't know what to do."

That's a first, thought Roy mischievously. "There's nothing you can do. I'm in good hands. I'm sure Philip Rivers will come up with something."

"I've sent Patrick Saunders to see you. He's a sweetie."

"Good." Roy was not sure he wanted a 'sweetie' acting as his solicitor. Somebody who was hard as nails would be preferable. Or at least as hard as Nick Barton. "I've got to go now, love," said Roy. "I think your Patrick's arrived."

"Oh, give him my love," said Angela.

Roy replaced the receiver. One thing he liked about Angela was her boundless enthusiasm. She would throw herself into enjoying anything she took part in. He couldn't help thinking, though, that it was a little misplaced now. She seemed to be treating his meeting with Patrick Saunders as if it was some sort of social occasion – rather than an attempt to thrash out a strategy which would hopefully avoid him spending possibly the rest of his life in jail. He was not lying about Patrick in an attempt to end the call, though. His solicitor really had arrived.

"How are you keeping?" asked Patrick after they had got the introductions over. He looked a serious young man, shiny grey suit, short haircut, glasses adding a touch of gravitas to his appearance. Roy judged him to be in his late thirties or early forties.

"Fine, I suppose," said Roy. "The standard of accommodation is not the same as I received at the hotel I was staying in in Brighton a couple of nights ago, though." A couple of nights ago thought Roy. God, it seems an age.

"No, I don't suppose it is," said Patrick. "Look, I'll come to the point. If they charge you, you'll be up in court tomorrow morning. It's a formal thing. I can try making out a case for bail but – to be honest – we won't get anywhere with it. There would have to be very exceptional circumstances before they released someone charged with murder out on bail. I'm getting you the best defence lawyer I can. Angela said that money would be no object."

Roy grinned. That was very different from the Angela he knew and loved. She was always complaining about how everything was so expensive.

"Whose money is it, then?" he asked.

"Yours."

"I thought as much."

"Are you worried about that?"

Roy shook his head. "No," he said. "If it's got to be spent, it's best spent on getting me out of here."

"The police do think they have a strong case," Patrick began. He stopped as one of the prison warders came over to them.

"There's a Detective Chief Inspector Barton to see you, Faulkner," he said. "I'm to escort you to an interview room.

"And me," said Patrick.

"I have no instructions on that," said the prison warder.

"I am Mr Faulkner's solicitor. If the police want to interview him, he has a right to have a solicitor present." Patrick's tone was not argumentative. He was just stating facts. Roy appreciated his intervention.

The warder motioned over to one of his colleagues standing by the door of the visiting room. He accompanied them on the walk to the interview room.

"Two people have to be escorted by two people," said the first warder.

"You're worried that I might overpower you and do a runner with my client," said Patrick. "Well, one thing I'm a good six inches shorter than you and..." He eyed the warder up and down "... probably a good three stone lighter than you. I don't think I'd have much of a chance."

"Don't get funny with me, sir."

"Sorry," said Patrick. "I meant no offence. Just trying to lighten the tone."

The look on the warder's face seemed to indicate he did not understand what lightening the tone meant. In truth, Patrick was reacting in the way that he did because he was a little nervous. He did not have much experience in criminal cases. The foursome arrived at the interview room where Barton was waiting for them with Detective Sergeant Francesca Manners.

"Morning, Nick," said Roy.

The Detective did not deign to reply to this informal greeting but the stony look on his face appeared to indicate Roy was speaking out of turn in addressing him as Nick.

"I have one or two more pieces of evidence to put to you," he said as Francesca set up an interview tape. Once done, all four introduced themselves on the tape.

Roy then spoke. "As a journalist, I have always endorsed a policy of openness," he said. "I intend to answer your questions as openly and frankly as I can and not hide behind 'no comment'."

Barton ignored the remarks, Privately, he thought Roy was sounding a bit pompous.

"So," he said, "when we last spoke I informed you we had evidence of Kate Williams' DNA in your car, your hotel bedroom and in your suitcase. It led us to believe you had taken her back to your hotel bedroom that evening, killed her and then tried to smuggle her body out of the hotel to your car."

Saunders leaned forward to intervene. "Was there any evidence of a struggle in the bedroom?" he asked.

Barton ignored the remark again. "We can now prove that your car left the car-park for just over a couple of hours on Saturday morning, returning at about 2.30pm," he said.

"I don't deny it," said Roy.

"Why didn't you mention this to us before?"

"I didn't think it was that significant," said Roy. "I went for a drive up to Beachy Head. Had a quick drink and a sandwich and then returned to the conference."

"A bit suspicious that," said Barton. "Surely as a conscientious journalist you should have been covering the conference?"

Roy couldn't resist it. "You're not praising me for my journalistic integrity, are you, Nick?" he asked.

"I advise you to take matters seriously," came the reply. "Tell me – why did you desert your post and suddenly decide to drive off to Beachy Head."

"If you looked at the agenda of the conference, you'll find that they were in private session until 3pm. They had a quick open session at 10am but that ended at 11.30am so I was free for the next three hours."

"And you chose to go to Beachy Head – quite a substantial distance away?"

"Yes. My grandparents used to live in Eastbourne. When I went to stay with them they always used to take me for lunch at Beachy Head. The last time I was with them before they died was at Beachy Head. When I'm down here I often go up to Beachy Head just to bring back memories."

"Did you see anybody you knew at Beachy Head?"

"No."

"So no-one can corroborate the fact that you were there?"

"I'm glad you see it is a fact, Nick."

"A slip of the tongue," the detective replied. "You didn't get a receipt for your drink?"

"Do you when you go to the pub?"

"Or for your sandwich or whatever you had to eat?"

"No."

"Didn't you want to claim it on expenses?"

"That would have been tantamount to fraud, Nick. I wasn't entertaining anyone in the line of work. We're only allowed to claim expenses if we're entertaining a client."

Save me from this sanctimonious clap-trap, thought Barton. Journalists are always claiming things on expenses, aren't they?

"That fraud would have been a far less serious crime than the murder you committed," he carried on.

"I didn't."

"What about the bar staff? Would they remember you?"

"I doubt it. It's a busy place."

"We could take you up there under escort and find out," volunteered Francesca Manners.

"Yes, and if you take me up there and find no-one recognises me, it'll give you further ammunition to say I wasn't there but was busy dumping Kate Williams' body in a field. No thank you."

Barton allowed himself a smile of self-satisfaction at this. It was, he thought, a case of tails you lose, heads we win.

"Do you have any other questions you wish to put to my client?" asked Saunders, butting in.

"No," said Barton, "except we have now recovered Kate's mobile phone – and there is evidence on it that you were worried that you might have killed her. Why on earth you wouldn't know whether you'd killed her or not, I must say, though, baffles me."

Roy looked surprised at this turn of event. "Why do you say I was worried I might have killed her?" he asked.

"There's a voicemail to that effect from one of your colleagues."

"Oh, that. That's Mark Elliott trying to be funny." Barton moved as if to speak, "I know, I know," said Roy waving his arms to try and stop him from opening his mouth.

"It's not funny to joke about a murder. But then neither of us thought there had been a murder at that stage."

"You're right that it's not funny to joke about a murder," said Barton, "and I would differ in my interpretation of the words on the voicemail to you." He paused and then started shuffling his papers and gathering them up. "I think we're finished here," he added.

Francesca took the tape from the tape recorder while one of the two warders came in to unplug the tape. As Nick Barton reached the door, he turned back – a smile creasing over his face.

"You know," he said to Roy, "if your version of events is true I wish I had had someone tailing you on the Saturday. After staying in a night-club drinking until 2.30am and the shooting off to Beachy Head at lunchtime for another drink, I bet you would have failed the breathalyser. At least I'd be able to charge you with that." With that, he tapped the wall with his hand and was gone.

Patrick Saunders turned to Roy. "I suppose that's his attempt at humour," he said.

"No," said Roy, "it's proof he's determined to get me for something."

• • ● • •

Marie shook her head. An inspector had told her that he had passed the information about Rufus on to the Brighton police investigating the disappearance of the missing girl. He even told her the name of the detective in charge of the case – Nick Barton. Why then had she not heard back from them? She tried telephoning Brighton a couple of times but Detective Chief Inspector Nick Barton either would not take the call or was not there. In her frustration, she decided the only thing to day was to make a pilgrimage down to Brighton to meet him face to face.

It was quite a journey for Marie if the truth were known.

She was a large woman who moved with difficulty – ambling from side to side as she walked along the pavement outside her home to the tube station. It wasn't that there was anything wrong with her – other than the fact she was overweight. She was fit enough to hold down a cleaning job. It was just that she looked ungainly as she made her way down the street.

Eventually, after three and a half hours, she arrived at Brighton police station slightly out of puff.

"I want to see Detective Chief Inspector Barton," she said to the desk sergeant on arrival.

"He's not here," came the reply.

"But I've come all the way from London."

"You should have made an appointment."

"I've been trying to phone him but I never get put through to him."

Ah, thought the sergeant, here was an obvious example of a pain in the ass. Best protect the inspector from her. "Well, I'm sorry, he really isn't here," he said defiantly. "There's not a lot I can do to help you."

"I'll wait," she said.

"I really wouldn't," said the sergeant. "I can't guarantee he'll be back today – and there's nowhere here for you to sit."

It was at that moment that Francesca walked through the door to the police station to hear Marie ask: "Does he have a deputy?"

"I don't think there's anybody in the office," said the desk sergeant. Francesca raised an eyebrow at him as she passed him by but he shook his head firmly. It was meant as a signal to her that she really did not want to get involved with this woman. She initially interpreted it as the sergeant saying it was not her boss that the large lady in reception wanted to see,

"But I really do have some important information about that missing girl," Marie continued.

Francesca stopped in her tracks as she was going through

the door that led to her office. The desk sergeant tried to deliver another shake of the head in her direction but he was either too late – or Francesca did not want to receive the message. She walked over to Marie.

"Can I help?" she asked. "I'm Detective Sergeant Manners. I'm working on the case of a missing girl. It may be the one you're talking about."

"She went missing from a night club Friday night/Saturday morning? I'm a friend of Rufus' and just before he died he told me something important."

"Wait a minute," said Francesca. "Who is Rufus?"

"Rufus." Marie shook her head in exasperation. Of course to her Rufus was Rufus. However, she added: "You might have known him as Carlton Mendonca."

"Carlton Mendonca's dead?" said Francesca with a note of astonishment in her voice. She thought for a moment.

"I think it might be an idea if you came into my office for a chat," she said.

Marie smiled. A tear almost formed in her eye. "Thank you ma'am, thank you," she said. "I just want to do the right thing. Rufus would have done, too. He wasn't a bad man. I've come all the way from London." She was crying now.

To be met by rudeness at our reception, thought Francesca. She did not say anything but pointedly turned to the sergeant and said: "Would you get two teas or whatever this lady wants and bring them to my office." She fixed the sergeant with a stare which told him she disapproved of what he had done.

"Tea would be just fine," said Marie as she was ushered into Francesca's office. She emitted a sigh of relief as she sat down.

"Now tell me: how did Carlton Mendonca die?"

"You've been told," said Marie.

"I'm sorry but I haven't," came the reply.

"The police in London – they said they'd passed the information on to you."

"To me?"

"Your boss – Detective Chief Inspector Barton."

"Ah." Things were beginning to fall into shape. Maybe Nick had been told whatever information the woman had but had chosen to ignore it.

"Rufus was not a bad man," Marie said again. "He came to me on Sunday night. He'd run away from his job at the night club here. He was worried when the police turned up. He thought they might be looking for him."

"Why?"

"He was an illegal immigrant. He fled from Jamaica when the police wanted to question him about a robbery. He stole the identity of a man in our block of flats when he died – Carlton Mendonca."

"So what did he have to do with this missing girl?"

"He told me the morning that he died. He must have been distracted. That's why he wasn't looking when the van came round the corner. He didn't stand a chance. He said he thought he had done something very bad."

"Killed the girl?"

"No, no. I told you Rufus was not a bad man." She sobbed again as she remembered the man who had once been – albeit for a short time – her lover.

"He saw her with a man outside the night club. He was trying to get her into a van but she was either very drunk…"

"Yes?"

"Or drugged or something. He helped the man get her into the van."

"Was it white?"

Marie's train of thought was interrupted by Francesca's question. "I … er … I don't know," she said. "He didn't say."

"Why did he think he'd done something that was so bad?"

"He read the papers. He saw that you thought she had been murdered. He thought he had helped her killer kidnap her from the night club. With hindsight, he thought she had been drugged and – if she had been wide awake – maybe she would not have got into the van with the man."

"I see." Francesca got up from her desk. "I want to thank you for coming all the way down here to give us this vital bit of information," she said. It was at this juncture that the desk sergeant arrived with two mugs of tea.

"You took your time, didn't you?" Francesca snapped. The desk sergeant did not respond but just backed out of the room after putting them down on the table.

"Enjoy the tea – have a bit of a rest before you go," said Francesca. "Is there anything else that you think you need to tell us?"

"No," said Marie without hesitation. "So did Rufus do something bad by helping to get that girl into the van?"

"Not something bad," said Francesca. "He wasn't to know the consequences. I can understand him feeling bad when he read in the papers about it afterwards but he didn't do anything that would get him into trouble – more trouble, at any rate."

Marie smiled. Francesca could see her words of reassurance had gone a long way towards confirming Marie in her conviction that Rufus 'was not a bad man'.

"Just jot down your name and address on this piece of paper," said Francesca, pushing a notebook across the table to Marie. "I know we should have your details but it's best to be on the safe side – so that we can contact you again if we need to. And thanks again."

• • • • •

Mark Elliott looked the epitome of glumness as he sat opposite Nick Barton in the office kindly vacated by his deputy editor that morning. All the bonhomie that he usually showed towards people he met in the course of his job seemed to have drained out of him.

"Do I need a solicitor?" he asked. "Only I hear you've got a good line in fitting people up."

"I wouldn't adopt that tone with me," said Nick. "All I want to do is ask you a few very simple questions. I want you to listen to this." He played the voicemail message on Kate Williams' mobile with Mark's voice saying:

"For goodness sake, Kate, ring either me – Mark Elliott – or Roy as soon as possible. The poor lad thinks he may have killed you." "That's you," he said. It was more of a statement than a question.

"Yes."

"Why did you make that call?"

"We were worried about Kate. We wondered what had happened to her."

"We?"

"Me and Roy Faulkner."

"Why did you say Roy thought he might have killed her?"

"I don't know whether you understand this concept, Detective Chief Inspector," said Mark slowly, "but it was a joke."

"A joke in very poor taste."

"With hindsight, now we know Kate really is missing, I would agree with you. At the time, well we didn't really know what had happened to her. I thought she might have been suffering from a stupendous hangover and that was why she hadn't shown up on the Saturday."

"If we played that voicemail to a jury, what conclusions do you think they would draw from it, Mr Elliott?"

"I think they might think I was trying to get in touch with Kate," said Mark. "Think about it, Detective Chief Inspector, I obviously didn't think Roy has killed her. 'For goodness sake, Kate, ring me'. I wouldn't have said that if I thought she was dead."

"Yes, but Roy Faulkner was worried about what had happened to her. He thought he may have killed her."

"Wouldn't you be worried? You'd left a glamorous tipsy woman on her own in a night club at 2.30am in the morning – and she hasn't been seen since. You know, Roy might very well have been wrong in leaving Kate on her own and not insisting she return to the hotel. But that's a far cry from killing her."

"Thank you, Mr Elliott," said Nick, putting the tape with the voicemail away in his pocket. "I agree it's not conclusive proof that Faulkner may have harmed her – but it does show his state of mind." He walked to the door before turning round to speak to Mark again.

"And if he had killed her, he wouldn't have admitted it to you. He would have gone along with the attempt to find her. We'll be putting it before the jury."

"You'll be charging him with murder then?"

"Yes," said Nick. "The Crown Prosecution Service now thinks we have enough evidence."

"Will you be calling me as a witness then?" asked Mark.

"Oh, no. We'll be asking them to draw their own conclusions."

• • ● • •

Rivers arrived home at his Finchley flat that afternoon with two things on his mind. First, there was his interview with Nick Barton that morning. The only good thing that seemed to have emerged from it was a suspicion – well, more than a suspicion actually, of a difference of opinion between the Detective Chief Inspector and his deputy. He wondered how he could exploit that. Maybe he should try getting the Detective Sergeant on her own in future with any information he came up with.

Then there was the question of Sian. The more he thought about it, the less certain he became that he had been right to go to bed with her. Since he had begun to drag himself out of the stupor he had fallen into following the death of Joanna, it had been Nikki who had been his constant companion. Always there for him. Helping him take every step along the way to recovering his confidence. That afternoon they had gone to see 'To Kill a Mocking Bird' together. It still stuck out in his mind as one of the most enjoyable days he had spent during the last six months.

Nikki. Why was she still there? He had dumped her unceremoniously almost thirty years ago yet she was still there to help him pick up the pieces three decades later. A thought occurred to him. If the situation had been reversed, what would have happened? Say Nikki's partner, instead of cheating on her, had died from a terminal illness and Nikki had gone into a decline would he have gone round to make sure she was okay? He had to be honest. He did not think he would. Yet he had been delighted to see her when she had turned up unannounced that Saturday afternoon. A tear welled in his eye as he thought of her and as he reproached himself for the way he had treated her. She deserved better than him. She deserved someone who would always be there for her in the same way as she was always there for him. Sian – or Nikki? It was ridiculous to play the two off against one another. He had known Sian for one night. She was vivacious, attractive but – if he was honest – he would not care all that much if he never saw her again. Nikki? Before he could answer that question, there was a ring at the doorbell. "Who is it?" he asked.

"It's Nikki."

"Of course," he said, smiling as he let her in.

"I wanted to find out how you were," she said.

"I'm getting somewhere, "he said. It was a two-edged statement. He was getting somewhere in terms of trying to help out his client, Roy Faulkner. He was also getting somewhere in sorting out his emotions and his feelings for Nikki. Was he happy that she had come round to see him? Yes. Would he be happy if she continued to come round to see him – and made herself a more permanent fixture in his life? There was a moment's hesitation before the answer to this question came to him but – when it did – it was 'yes' again. "I'll make you some tea," he said.

"So – tell me more," she said as she accepted a mug from him.

"I've found white van man. Or at least I know who he is. Les Craven. He, too, vanished on Friday night not leaving a trace. He was having a difficult time – a tricky divorce from his wife. I spoke to his tenant. He left no forwarding address."

"So what can you do now?"

"Search his house."

"Don't you need a search warrant or something like that?"

"I don't think I'll have any difficulty in gaining access." He paused for a moment. He felt a little uneasy about his choice of words.

"Nikki, I've got something to confess to you," he began.

She gave him a surprised look. "What do you mean?"

"Well, the reason I know I'll gain access to Craven's house is that I slept with his tenant."

Dead silence. "Well," faltered Nikki. If she was upset, she was not showing it. "I don't know why you're telling me this," she said adopting a slightly haughty tone. "I mean, you're a completely free agent. There's nothing between us. No romantic attachment, I mean. We're just mates, aren't we?"

Her voice seemed to tail off a little at the end of her sentence. It was almost as if she needed confirmation of that. Or maybe she wanted confirmation of the opposite.

"That's just it," said Rivers. "I'm not sure we are just mates any more. I'm not going to say I did a foolish thing when we split up all those years ago but...."

It was his turn to falter now. "I'm so glad you had the perseverance to stick around. I mean to make sure I was okay."

"It's been no hardship, Philip. I always told myself I'd be there at the end of the day to pick up the pieces when Joanna died." She wiped a tear away. "I always would have been but the truth is that -over the last thirty years – there have been precious few pieces to pick up before Joanna."

"We got together too young," he said as he moved next to her on the sofa and put his arm around her."We're not too young now."

"No."Nikki's statement was emphatic."What do you mean?"

"I mean." Rivers moved towards her on the sofa. He kissed her firmly on the lips. Actions were speaking louder than words, he thought. Nikki responded by slowly unbuttoning her shirt and then moving her hand down to his thigh. He needed no second bidding. Within minutes they were naked on the sofa. They made love there and then – the first time they had been with each other for nearly thirty years. It was a different kind of loving to that between Rivers and Sian earlier in the day. They did care for each other. Rivers was anxious to please her. Nikki was anxious to please him. For a few moments afterwards, neither of them seemed to believe what had happened. They just looked at each other and smiled.

"Welcome back,"said Nikki as she moved his hands towards her thighs, indicating she wanted a second confirmation of his feelings towards her. He lost no time in obliging her. Afterwards, they sat side by side – neither of them saying very much.

"You know," said Nikki smiling, eventually. "You've got a dilemma now."

"What's that?"

"You said you had access to Les Craven's home through the tenant just now." She giggled as the words came out of her mouth."Do you have access to the tenant any more, I wonder?"

"I think I can get into the house," he said, "but thereafter I might have to make use of an old journalistic phrase and make my excuses and leave."

Nikki squeezed his hand as they sat there naked on the sofa. "Are we an item?"she asked.

"Yes," he said definitely, allowing her to cuddle up to him again.

She placed a hand on his thigh again and then moved it up to touch his penis. "You know, you're going to be a tired man tonight," she said.

• • ● • •

"Did you want to see me?" said Nick as he became aware of Francesca hovering in the doorway.

"Yes."

"Well?"

"I'm not that happy with the way we've been handling the case."

"By we you mean me?" said Nick.

Francesca nodded. "Yes, I suppose I do. You've tended to operate as if we have an open and shut case against Roy Faulkner and you don't want anything to cloud your vision of that," she said.

"Yes?"

"Well, I think there is an alternative way of looking at things. I've just had a woman from London come to see me. She's was a friend of Rufus Braithwaite – Carlton Mendonca as was. He was killed in a road traffic accident the other day."

"Yes, I know."

"Well, he helped someone bundle Kate Williams into a car on the night she disappeared. It couldn't have been Roy Faulkner. He wouldn't have needed a car to take Kate back to the hotel. It's only a hundred yards away."

"Granted."

"We also have Rivers' evidence about the white van driver. That he's gone missing, too."

"And we have a watertight case against Roy Faulkner that I'm willing to trust any jury with. The CPS agrees with me and I have now charged him. What alternative evidence do we have? A landlord who doesn't live at his house in Newhaven visits it on Friday but hasn't been back since. He hasn't disappeared. He's just gone back to wherever he does live." Francesca moved to interrupt him.

"And before you say anything else – consider this about him not leaving a forwarding address. Maybe he hasn't sorted out a new forwarding address. Maybe he doesn't want to be pestered by her. Maybe he's getting an agent to manage the renting of his home but hasn't quite set it up. There are all sorts of innocent explanations but there are no innocent explanations for Kate's DNA being found, in particular, in the boot of Roy Faulkner's car and in his suitcase."

"And Marie Coombs?"

"Second-hand evidence that an armed robber and illegal immigrant told her he helped bundle a woman into the back of a car. He can't positively identify that it was Kate Williams. He can't say it was Les Craven. Or that it was even a white van. He's dead. There could quite easily have been another woman leaving the night club at that time in the morning who was slightly tipsy who had a hangover in the morning but was all right to do the weekly shop by the afternoon."

"Quite a persuasive argument," Francesca had to admit but there was still something in the tone of her voice that made it clear to Nick that she was not happy about the turn of events.

"I'll tell you what," he said. "I'll go and have a word with this Marie Coombs just to satisfy myself that we haven't left a stone unturned."

"Thank you," said Francesca.

• • ● • •

Roy lay back in his cell that night. Tomorrow he was to appear before magistrates charged with the murder of Kate Williams. He could scarcely believe it was happening to him. He was convinced it would not have been had it not been for Nick

Barton. Nick Barton was desperate to prove him guilty. Nick Barton, he believed, was tampering with evidence to fit him up.

And why? A vendetta from his childhood days? Surely the loss of a girlfriend more than thirty years ago could not be rankling with him now. Admittedly, Roy had been a little obvious in making his move for Gillian Bird at a time when Nick thought he still had a relationship with her. But Nick and Gillian? Chalk and cheese. Nick with his clean white shirt, short back and sides haircut, shiny clean black shoes and nights spent drumming with the Boy Scouts Band. Gillian with her short skirts, provocatively sexy way of sitting on a sofa exposing a large amount of thigh, her love of pop music. God, he could recall the night when he had said she could throw herself at him as much as she liked. She had done. He could still remember the night at the cricket club as if it had been only yesterday. Nick and Gillian were just never meant to be and – if it had caused Nick a moment's heartbreak – it was worth reflecting that it was something that was going to happen sooner or later. Roy, on the other hand, liked to think he was considered a catch by Gillian. Singer in a pop band. That pouting stuff he did with songs like 'You'd Better Move On' and 'Like I Did'. He had been out with some of the best lookers from the youth club. He hung around with Graeme, who was also considered to be one of its sex symbols. Roy and Graeme were considered cool to be with. Nick, by comparison, could just dampen your enthusiasm for life. There was another side to Nick, though. You couldn't just dismiss him as a geek with big ears. What about the story Gillian Bird had told him? That Nick had sought to run her down – or maybe just frighten her – on that zebra crossing. He had never checked that out. Never done anything about it. He paused for thought. Actually, that was not strictly true. He had done something. That night he had gone round to Charlotte Woods' house. He had seen at the youth club evidence that Charlotte appeared to be taking up with Nick, He felt he should warn her about what he perceived to be Nick's dark side. In particular, he should tell her about the incident at the zebra crossing.

"Roy," said Charlotte, a genuine smile forming on her lips when she opened the door to him. She seemed pleased to see him.

"Come in." She ushered him into the living room. "What brings you here?"

"It's a bit difficult, Charlotte," he began.

"Would you like a drink? My parents are out but I'm sure they wouldn't mind me offering you one." He nodded and she poured both him and herself a glass of white wine from a bottle that had been left open in the fridge.

"Now tell me what it is that's on your mind," she said.

"It's Nick," he said. "Can I ask? Are you seeing him?"

Charlotte blushed. "I... er ... yes," she said. She wondered what he was going to say. Surely he was not going to make a play for her himself. He had seemed to be quite happy with Gillian Bird at the youth club during the past few weeks.

"There's something I feel I ought to tell you about him." He related the story about Gillian Bird and the zebra crossing. She listened attentively but at the end said:

"I can't believe Nick would do a thing like that," she said. "He's never shown an aggressive side of himself to me. In fact, quite the opposite."

"Charlotte," said Roy. "You could do better than Nick. You're an extremely attractive girl. And Nick? Where's he going to end up? Playing full time in the Boy Scouts Band?"

"That's not a very nice thing to say, Roy. Nick's a very nice boy, I'm sorry, Roy, I respect the fact that you mean well by what you've said but I just can't believe it. Have you asked Nick whether it's true?"

"No, I didn't see the point."

"And did Gillian take it any further? To the police or anything like that?"

"No, she seemed to think it was best to let bygones be bygones – and let it rest."

"Then I think you should do, too," said Charlotte firmly. "Let's talk about something else. How are you getting on with Gillian?"

"Oh," he grinned. "Fine"

"Good. Maybe we should make a foursome one night."

Fuck, no, thought Roy. Instead of giving vent to his emotions, though he just smiled and clinked glasses with her. Soon afterwards, he got up to go. As he was leaving the house, he gave Charlotte a kiss on the doorstep. Just a peck of friendship. Nothing more. He then walked to his car – not noticing the car parked on the other side of the road whose driver was drumming with knuckles on the dashboard. He looked angry. It was Nick Barton.

• • ● • •

Not for the first time in his life Nick felt the phrase "revenge is a dish best served cold" framing in his mind. Tomorrow Roy Faulkner would be appearing before magistrates charged with murder. If the case was proved at the end of the day, he would be sent down for life. The prospect appealed to Nick. He didn't want anything to get in the way of a conviction. True, he hadn't seen Roy Faulkner for decades – almost thirty years if the truth be known – but he had never forgotten him. Roy was the epitome of everything he had hated in his teenage years – lax morals, long hair, sex never far from his mind. A degenerate. In addition, he had now made a successful career out for himself, fooling around writing, while Nick had started off by pounding the beat and worked hard to get to the top of his profession.

Stealing Gillian Bird from him was bad enough but his mind went back to that evening when he had decided to go round unannounced to Charlotte's house and had found Roy Faulkner's car outside. At first it had taken him by surprise but then he wondered what Roy Faulkner was up to. Was he not happy with stealing one woman from him? Did he have to have a go at another? And what was that farewell kiss all about? Nick had been brought up in a family where you didn't show emotion. You would only kiss if you were involved in a relationship with someone. Was that the message that Nick was supposed to take from his chance discovery of Roy and Charlotte? He waited for Roy's car to disappear down the road and then got out and strode very determinedly over to Charlotte who had been looking down the road after the departing Roy and not seen him until he was virtually standing right in front of her.

"Nick," she said with a tone denoting surprise.

"Would you mind telling me what's going on?"

"What?"

He pushed her through the door and into the sitting room where he saw the two glasses of wine on the table. "What is going on, Charlotte?" He pointed to the two glasses of wine.

"Nothing."

"Nothing?" he almost shrieked. "Roy Faulkner who – only a few weeks ago – took Gillian Bird away from me sees me starting another relationship with you. He comes round here. Gets invited in. Poured a glass of wine and gets a kiss on the doorstep when he leaves. You look wistfully after his car as he drives away like some love-struck puppy. I suppose it's just as well I didn't come round half an hour ago – or else I'd have probably found the two of you had been cavorting naked on the floor and that you had hurriedly put your knickers back on as you came to see who was knocking on the door."

"Nick," she said. "It's not like that."

"Tell me, Charlotte. Did you have sex with that man?"

"No, Nick."

"Did you have sex with that man?" Before he could stop himself he brought his right hand back and slapped her with a backhander across the cheek.

Charlotte started to cry and nursed her bruised cheek. "Nick, I never would."

"Right, I want you to prove that you love me and not him?"

"How, Nick?"

He moved towards her and started unbuttoning her shirt.

"Nick, no. My parents."

"They are out and won't be back for an hour or so. Prove to me you love me and not him." By now he was unzipping her jeans.

"Please Nick."

There was no stopping him, though, and eventually she relented allowing him to have sex with her. She would not have called it making love even though he would refer to it in that way in the future. It was the night she became pregnant, which led Nick to propose to do "the decent thing" and marry her. Eventually she lost the baby due to a miscarriage but – by that time – Nick's profuse apologies for the way he had behaved that night had been accepted by Charlotte. He promised never to hit her again and had kept to his promise. Before they got married he was always attentive to her, kind, friendly. However, if truth be known, even he would acknowledge that he was sometimes a little too possessive towards her.

Nick reflected in the present. Did he regret marrying Charlotte? No. It hadn't quite worked out how he would have liked. He found it difficult to explain his actions to himself but it was almost as if he had to prove to himself that he could persuade someone to marry him – hence all the attention and kindness after that night. After they got married, he didn't feel the need to continue in that vein and gradually threw himself into his work. Yes, they had a child – the one conceived that night may have been the subject of a miscarriage but later they had a daughter who was now at university. Their relationship, though, was now like two ships passing in the night, exchanging pleasantries – or sometimes not even that. They were barely tolerating living under one roof with one another.

When he recalled the night he had found Roy leaving her house, he could still to this day muster up anger that she had invited him in and had shared a cosy glass of wine with him. He was also sure that – despite accepting Charlotte's protestations that nothing had happened between them on that night – that it had been Roy's intention to make a pass at her and destroy his relationship.

CHAPTER SEVEN

A small group had gathered outside the court house. Angela was very much to the fore. Prunella – Mark Elliott's wife – was there to support her. Mark had found it impossible to get away from the office. Rivers arrived a few moments later.

"How's it going?" said Angela, anxiously gripping Rivers' arm.

"I've got a number of leads I can pursue," he said. "To be honest, it's not helped by the attitude of Detective Chief Inspector Barton. He's turning a blind eye to any alternative evidence. He's got it fixed in his mind that Roy murdered Kate Williams."

At that juncture Nick and Francesca entered the courthouse. They stood a few feet away from Angela, Prunella and Rivers, chatting to their solicitor.

"That him?" said Angela. Rivers nodded. Angela made her way over to Nick.

"What the hell have you got against my Roy?" she said. "He wouldn't harm a flea and you know that." Nick tried to avoid her but Angela was a difficult person to ignore. "I'm talking to you," she said, jabbing him with her finger. "At least do me the courtesy of listening. My Roy did not kill this woman."

"All will be revealed in court, Mrs... Mrs Faulkner?" He did not know whether they were married or not. He assumed, though, that this woman with the striking red curly hair was Roy's partner,

"No, wrong again. Angela Hopkins, and let me tell you I won't rest until my Roy is freed, you disgusting piece of shit."

At this juncture a look of horror formed on Prunella's face. For a moment, she was worried that Angela might just go too far and assault Nick. She bustled over to her side. "Angela, dear," she said. "It's not worth it. You'll only get arrested and that won't help Roy."

"I would advise you not to use threatening language, Miss Hopkins," said Nick. "You could end up in court yourself. Listen to what your colleague is saying."

At that Angela let Prunella lay a restraining arm on her shoulder and move her slowly back to beside where Rivers was standing. Angela and Prunella looked an odd couple that day. Both of them were dressed up to the nines as if they were attending some kind of court social rather than a magistrates' hearing. Prunella even had a hat – the sort that would more commonly be found at Royal Ascot rather than Brighton magistrate's court.

"I think for the first time in my life I'm beginning to have a bit of sympathy for Faulkner," Nick confided to Francesca. "If that harridan is what he has to put up with at home, it's not surprising he wanted a night off with Kate Williams."

Francesca smiled. "She's just determined to support him," she said. "It must come as a great shock to have your partner accused of murder. Just don't have anything to do with her. Keep out of her space."

"I'm sorry," Angela said to Rivers when she had calmed down a bit. "I couldn't control myself."

"I could see that – but no need to apologise to me." He thought for a moment. He would also have relished the opportunity to tell Nick Barton what he thought of him.

At that stage they were called into court for the case to begin. The trio took their seats on the public benches. Roy had already been brought into court by a couple of warders and was sitting in the dock. As he looked round, Angela waved at him and blew him a kiss. The hearing only lasted a few minutes and Roy was remanded in custody for a week and led from the dock. Patrick Saunders, who had been representing Roy during the hearing, came over to the trio after Roy had left the court. "He's being transferred to Lewes," he said. "The case will be heard at the Crown Court."

"Will I be able to get to see him?" said Angela.

"I think it'll be easy while he's on remand," said Patrick.

"How's he shaping up?" she asked.

"Well," said Patrick. "He's convinced he's going to be found innocent."

"And you?"

Patrick sighed. "I'm convinced of his innocence," he said, Angela stared at him. He was aware that was different to saying that he would be found innocent. "I do believe the Crown have a strong case," he confessed.

Straight after the hearing, Nick Barton leapt into his car and drove off to London. He was aiming to do what he had promised Francesca he would do. Go and talk to Marie and see if her evidence would hold water. As luck would have it, he found her in when he knocked on the door in mid-afternoon armed with the address his colleague had given him.

"Been on the early shift this morning," she said. "Do come in. Thank you for coming all this way to see me. What can I do for you?"

"Detective Sergeant Manners has filled me in with the evidence you gave her about this missing girl," said Nick. "Did Rufus give you a description of the girl he helped to bundle into the van?"

"No," said Marie. "But it must be the same girl, mustn't it? There wouldn't be two girls going round in a haze at that time in the morning?"

Nick ignored her question. To his way of thinking, there could be any number of girls going around in a haze at 2.30am in a night club like the Lucky Star. "And he didn't describe the man who was bundling her into the van to you either, did he?"

"No."

"Or the van?"

"No, but Rufus was convinced it was the same girl. He had seen her earlier in the evening with this man who's accused of her murder. I'm sure he was convinced it was the same girl. He wouldn't have been so worried otherwise."

"Look, Mrs Coombs," said Nick, "or may I call you Marie?"

"Marie."

"There are one or two things I don't think you've taken into account," he said. "You do realise that – by coming forward – you will be acknowledging that you were harbouring an illegal immigrant? Rufus was in this country illegally. There could be charges."

Marie's jaw dropped. "Is that what you're investigating now?" she said. "I've only been trying to do my duty. I think you should know this girl may have been kidnapped."

"I appreciate that but I'm just telling you why it might not be in your best interest to come forward."

"What could happen to me?" Marie was genuinely worried.

"I can't really comment on that. It's not really my area of expertise but I would imagine your visa could be withdrawn – or you could face possible criminal charges and prison."

"Why on earth would anyone want to put me in prison? What good would that do?"

"It's not a question of what good it would do. The law is the law. I'm only telling you this for your own good. You don't want to draw attention to yourself."

"No," she mumbled. "And thank you."

Nick smiled inwardly. Here he was threatening her with awful consequences that might not come about if she went ahead with testifying but she had accepted his word that he was really doing her a favour. "No need to thank me," he said magnanimously.

Marie was still thinking about what he said. "But that other woman – the Detective Sergeant – why didn't she warn me about all this?" she asked

"She's a bit new to the job. Not so much experience," said Nick. "I suspect she didn't realise the difficulties you could get into. Anyhow, it's not really the police's job to warn you off if you could be prosecuted for a crime." Again Marie seemed to accept his argument.

"Oh, and another thing, I wouldn't tell anybody about what I said here today. I shouldn't really be saying what I have been saying – but I thought it only fair to warn you of what might happen if you went ahead with giving evidence."

"No, I won't," she said. "Thank you."

With that Nick was gone. As he got outside, he almost laughed at how easy it had been to persuade Marie not to pursue the evidence she had.

• • ● • •

As Rivers left the court that morning, he had an uneasy feeling in his stomach. Time was moving on and he realised he had to get cracking in his pursuit of Les Craven as soon as possible. That meant going back to the white van man's house and confronting Sian again. She was a nice woman but not for him. However, he hated the idea of letting her down. Too often in his past life he had been weak in terms of decision making over the women he had become involved with. It had left him in awkward situations. This was no time for squeamishness, though, he reflected. There was a real chance of a reconciliation with Nikki in a relationship that meant something. Now, he reflected, was not the time for any weakness or to let his loins rule his head.

He drove up and parked outside the Newhaven house. She answered his knock on the door and when she saw it was the private detective a beaming smile came over her face. It reminded him in an odd way of Nikki when she greeted him.

"Nice to see you," she said. She moved forward to give him a kiss on the lips.

"I'm afraid I'm just here on business," he said stiffly. He was aware it was not the best way to start a conversation which he hoped would lead to her allowing him access to Craven's personal effects – but he could not muster any enthusiasm for subterfuge.

"Oh," she said, withdrawing a pace.

"Look, I'd better be honest. What happened last time was nice."

"But you don't want to pursue it," she interjected. "I understand. I did wonder if I would ever see you again." She sighed and puffed out her chest. "So I'm not crestfallen," she added. "Someone else?"

"Someone I've known for a long time," he said. "Someone who was there for me as I tried to get over my partner's death."

"They're the best ones," said Sian ruefully. "Those that you've known for a long time. You get a feeling you can't let them down -and they won't let you down."

"Exactly," said Rivers, surprised that she was being so understanding about rejection. He assumed from the welcome he had received that she had been hoping they would continue with the relationship.

"So what is it you do want from me?"

"Well," he said thoughtfully. "Access to anything of Les Craven's that he's left behind would be a start. My client's already come up in court charged with the murder of that girl so I need to get my skates on."

Sian nodded and led Rivers into the room that acted as Les' study. Rivers took out his set of master keys as Sian left the room. He opened the cabinet. There were a series of letters in it which he started to read. They appeared to relate to Craven's separation from his wife. They were not letters from the wife herself but from a firm of solicitors based in Andover. She was seeking a divorce, they informed him, on the grounds of his 'unreasonable conduct'. That, thought Rivers, covered a multitude of sins. It could mean Craven had had an affair. Alternatively, it could mean he had been violent towards her – or had made unwanted sexual demands on her. Unsurprisingly, the letters did not elaborate on the nature of the conduct but they did indicate that the question of the divorce had not been settled. Surprisingly, though, the last letter was dated three months ago. What had happened in the interim period he wondered? He jotted down the address of the solicitors and made a mental note to go and visit them after he had finished at Craven's house. He began thinking about the letters and what kind of a picture they showed of Craven. He would bank on Craven making unacceptable sexual demands as being the reason the two of them had split up. That would fit in with a man who drugged and picked up a girl in a night-club and then murdered her. Wait a minute, though, he thought, suppose she's not dead? Suppose he's kidnapped her and is holding her somewhere? That, too, would fit in with the picture of Craven he was building up in his mind's eye.

Rivers rummaged through the rest of the drawers. There was nothing much else. A picture of a man with his arm around a woman on a beach. He surmised it was probably Craven and his wife and decided to take it to help him identify his suspect if it came to it. He could ask Sian whether it was him. There were a few odd coins, a pencil and a letter from the local police informing him he had incurred a speeding fine. It included the registration number of his van which Rivers also duly noted down. He shut the desk, locked it and returned to join Sian in the sitting room. He took the picture out of his pocket.

"Is that Les?" he asked.

"Yes," she replied after looking at it carefully.

"So that must be Mrs Les?"

"I don't know. I never saw her."

"Did he talk about her much?"

"Not really. When he did, he just talked about 'that money-grabbing bitch'." she said.

"She was divorcing him for 'unreasonable conduct'. Any idea what that was all about?"

Sian thought for a moment and then shook her head. "No," she said. "I wouldn't have thought it was another woman, though. There were no signs that he was having a relationship with anybody else."

"And he never tried it on with you?"

"Not like you, you mean." She couldn't resist having a dig at the private detective. Rivers showed no reaction, though. "No, he didn't."

"You don't sound like you think you were missing out on something."

"No," she said. "He was not an attractive man. To tell you the truth, I was a little uncomfortable sharing a house with him."

"Uncomfortable? In what way?"

"Oh, I never thought he was going to pounce on me or anything like that. I just didn't like him – and I don't think he liked me. I had a feeling that maybe he didn't like women."

Maybe he didn't, thought Rivers, and maybe that was as a result of his relationship with his wife. "Well," he said. "I've got quite a lot to do as a result of all this. I'd better be on my way."

"Yes," said Sian, "I'll show you to the door."

"It's all right. I can see myself out."

She nodded. "I don't suppose I'll be seeing you again," she said as he departed.

"No," he replied firmly. As he got outside, he relaxed. Sian was attractive but he told himself could not have lived with himself if he had been unfaithful to Nikki that day.

• • ● • •

"You have a visitor," said the prison officer as he opened the door to Roy Faulkner's cell.

"Good," said Roy. He was quite surprised when he found out the identity of the person who wanted to see him, though. It was Charlotte – Nick Barton's wife. He could not for the life of him think what she wanted to say to him but – well, prison was a boring place to be so any visit was to be preferred to none. He walked into the visitor's area and sat down at a table and waited for Charlotte to be sent over to him. To tell the truth, he did not quite know how to greet her. A kiss seemed inappropriate. He and her husband were sworn enemies and he had not seen her for thirty years.

"Well, you've worn well over all these years," she said as she sat down opposite him.

"Must be the prison food," he muttered. "You didn't come all this way to say that, though."

"No," she said. "I was horrified when I heard you'd been arrested for that girl's murder."

"You mean, you don't think I did it?"

"No, of course not," she replied.

"Would you mind telling your husband that?"

"Oh, Nick," she said.

"Oh, Nick. It's a damn sight worse than just 'oh, Nick'. He's trying to put me away for life."

"I know," she said. "He hates you."

"God, no," said Roy sarcastically, "and there was I going to invite him to come on holiday with me."

"Oh, Roy," she said. "I don't know if there's anything I can do but I came to offer you my support – for what it's worth."

He smiled. "It's worth a lot, Charlotte," he said, "especially if you go into the witness box and tell people of the vendetta Nick has against me."

"No, Roy," she said. "I don't think I can do that. He's my husband."

"Why, Charlotte? Why are you still with him?"

"I stayed with him because of our daughter," she said, "and after Sarah had grown up I suppose I thought I was too old to kick over the traces and start again."

"You're not too old. Not even now," he said. He thought for a moment about his own life. Angela had only been a recent acquisition as a lover.

"So why does he hate me so much? Surely he's got over Gillian Bird?"

Charlotte looked a little startled. "Yes, I'm sure he has," she said. "It's me."

"You?"

"You remember that night you came over to see me and warn me off him?"

"You didn't tell him about that, did you?"

"I didn't have to. He was parked outside the door when you left. He saw you going. He came in and saw two glasses of wine poured and jumped to the wrong conclusion."

"You mean he thought?"

"We'd made love."

Roy shook his head. "Incorrigible," he said – although, in his heart of hearts, he would admit to thinking that Charlotte was a fine, attractive woman and he would not have minded making love to her at some stage during his life. Perhaps that was the problem, he thought. Rival suitors could detect that instinct in him and feared the worst if their women were ever left in his company for too long.

"What did he do?"

"He asked me to prove I loved him by letting him make love to me. I thought he was going to rape me."

"And did he?"

"I let him make love to me," she said.

"But he would have done it." said Roy as a matter of fact

rather than as a question. "Jesus, Charlotte, why did you stick with him?" He waved his hand at her as she sought to reply. "No need to tell me. You said it earlier. It's your daughter."

"He was very nice to me."

He cut her short. "Hitler was nice to animals."

"He was very kind to me," she continued. "I got pregnant as a result of what happened that night and he promised to stick by me and marry me. He stood by his decision even when I had a miscarriage."

"And life has been honey and flowers ever since?"

"No," she said. "He seemed to lose interest after we got married – and work took over."

"He'd proved he could get someone and once he had got someone he had nothing to prove."

"It wasn't like that," she said.

"Anyhow, I don't want to dissect your marriage, Charlotte. I want to thank you for coming to see me."

"You know it's not just you he hated."

"And I'm supposed to feel better about that?"

"There was a beating he took. He thought it was from you, Graeme and Barrie. So he hates the rest of the band, too."

"I wasn't involved in that and he hasn't had the others arrested for murder."

"He can't," said Charlotte. She paused for a moment. "They're dead," she said.

Roy stopped in his tracks and stared at her. "What? All of them? How?"

"Graeme and Barrie. I don't think he felt strongly about that guy with the organ."

"Johnnie? No, he didn't know him. So what happened to Graeme and Barrie?"

"You know, it was sad about Graeme," said Charlotte. "He was a lovely guy. The last time that Nick and I saw him was at the Willow Tree – you know, the pub we used to go to – he was collecting the glasses. He was drunk and he was virtually begging us to get him a drink. Things didn't work out for him, I guess."

She paused for thought. "Well, a few days later I caught sight of a few paragraphs in the local paper. Apparently, Graeme had been the victim of a hit and run driver as he walked home from the pub. He was crossing the road from the green to the cricket club. They never found out who did it. I showed it to Nick. I thought he – like me – would be sorry to see it but his reaction, well, it was weird. He just nodded his head and said 'he had it coming'."

"What did he mean by that?"

"I asked him and he said 'you saw the way he was in the pub – he was an accident waiting to happen'."

"Except," said Roy, He donned an air of puzzlement. "I can't see a hit and run accident happening in that road. It doesn't lead anywhere. The only place you can get to is the cricket club – oh, and the deserted cottage on the right. It's a dead end. You wouldn't speed down there."

"Well, the police never found the driver, anyway," said Charlotte.

Roy nodded. He thought about the accident for a moment. A small nagging idea came to him. Perhaps someone had deliberately lain in wait for Graeme that night. It would have to have been someone who knew the route Graeme would take from the pub to his home. Someone who had a grudge against Graeme. Someone who thought he had had a hand in beating him up. He chided himself. Perhaps being locked up was causing him to fantasise. It couldn't be, he thought. But then Nick had tried to run Gillian Bird over or maybe scare her. Perhaps he had meant just to scare Graeme, too, and it had gone wrong.

"Tell me about Barrie," he said.

"There's not much to tell. We hadn't kept in touch," said Charlotte. Roy nodded. He had had no desire to keep in touch with Barrie either. The guy was a jerk. He could remember one dance he had been to, with Gillian Bird, ironically, and someone had made a pass at her and been rejected. The rejected suitor had cut up rough about it and – when he and Gillian had sought to leave – he was waiting in the car park for them with a few of his friends and a knife. Barrie had been just getting into his car but, when he and Gillian had gone over to him to ask him to get them out of there he just ignored them and drove off. Luckily, the roadie of the group who had been playing at the dance – whom Roy knew quite well – was also there. He was quite a threatening presence, too, and he escorted Roy and Gillian to his van and drove them to safety. It was the last but one time Roy had seen Barrie. He had had the decency to go round to Roy's home two nights later and ask if he was all right but Roy had just slammed the door in his face.

Roy came back to the present. "Tell me what you know," he said.

"Well, he moved into his own flat and – one day – was found dead from a drugs overdose," she said. "Apparently the drug had been diluted. The inquest recorded an open verdict. There was no suggestion that Barrie wanted to take his own life."

"No, but there would have been plenty of other people wanting to take it," said Roy.

"But there was one thing that was slightly odd about it," said Charlotte. "If you had diluted drugs on your patch, you would expect a number of incidences to have occurred. There weren't any others."

"And Nick's reaction to his death?"

"Absolute delight. We read about it in the local paper again. I remember him saying," she paused for a moment.

"Saying what?"

"Two down."

"As if there was one to go?" Charlotte nodded. "This should come out in court," he said. "Charlotte, will you at least think about giving evidence?"

"No, I can't, Roy," she said. "I only came here to tell you some people believe in you."

"Well, I thank you for that," he said. She got up to go. They shook hands and Roy sighed. She did not deserve to be living such an unfulfilled life, he thought.

As he was being escorted back to his cell, he thought about what she had said. Would it be worth asking Rivers to have a look into Graeme McAndrew's death? Had Nick already been a member of the police force at that stage? Barrie's death – even if it was murder – could easily be explained. He had crossed so many people in his life it was not beyond the realms of possibility to think any one of them could have been capable of killing him. Besides, Nick's reaction to seeing news of the death in the paper seemed to be one of a man who did not realise Barrie was dead before he had read the article. But Graeme's death. To Roy's mind, that was an entirely different state of affairs. He doubted whether Graeme had taken part in the beating Nick had received. He was too nice a bloke.

• • • • •

Priorities, priorities, thought Rivers. It would have been so easy in the days that his Bahamian boatman friend, Jo, had been working for him. One of them would have gone to Andover to check out the solicitor and try and find Craven's former wife. Actually, not so much of the former, thought Rivers. It seemed that their divorce had not gone through. The other would have followed up on Craven's car. Was it registered in Newhaven – or would it have another address which would give a clue to where Craven was living now? He would probably have gone to Andover while asking Jo to check out the car. Jo, though, was thousands of miles away – back in the Bahamas looking after his family.

As he left Craven's house, he was aware of a woman working

in the front garden of the house next door. She was pruning some flowers and looked about sixty – dressed for gardening. A thought occurred to him. She must have known Craven's wife. At least she would have done if she had been living there any length of time.

"Excuse me," he said. "I wonder if I might have a word."

"I don't talk to tradesmen," she said. Her accent was clipped. She would have been a cut above Craven and his wife, Rivers thought.

"Nor do I," said Rivers. "I'm a private investigator. I'm trying to find Les Craven."

"Oh?" By the tone of her voice Rivers thought she was trying to pretend she was not interested in why anyone should want to find her next door neighbour. It was not a good pretence, though.

"Why do you want to find him?"

Rivers thought he would lure her in with a little more bait. "I'm investigating a murder," he began. "I wondered if you knew him?"

"Not really."

"How long have you lived here?"

"Oh, about thirty years," she said. "We didn't really mix in the same social circles." It was obvious she was intimating that he was on a lower social strata to her.

"But you must have known his wife?"

"Same thing, really. We didn't really mix."

"Nevertheless, did you form any impression of them? Was theirs a happy marriage?"

"No," she said emphatically. "Who's been murdered? Not her?"

"Why should you think that?" Rivers asked.

"I wouldn't have put it past him. Creepy kind of guy. You hear things."

"Yes?

"Well, they were constantly arguing. On a couple of occasions, I couldn't be sure, I think he hit her. She had a weal on the side of her cheek. It wasn't long after that that she left."

"How long ago was that?"

"Oh, about nine months ago, I would have thought."

"Did she confide in you at all?"

"No, I told you – ours was not that kind of relationship."

"But you knew she had left?"

"She was just not around anymore. I didn't see her go but...."

"That was why you thought that I could have been investigating her murder."

"Yes, although he seemed a bit of a weedy type. I didn't think he would have it in him." It sounded as if his neighbour thought it would have almost been a plus factor if he had.

"He did hit her, though?"

"I think so."

Rivers felt he had exhausted the amount he could get out of her. "Thank you," he said. "You've been most helpful. Just one more thing, though – were they particularly friendly with anybody else in the road?"

"I don't really know. They're not my types." None of them thought Rivers. He suddenly felt sorry for the lady. She had obviously not made as much of her life as she had expected to and – as a result -had spent the last thirty years living in a street where there was no-one she felt able to socialise with. Tragic, he thought, but he only gave the matter a moment's thought. It was her loss – no-one else's – and she could have solved the problem if she had not been so much of a snob.

"Try the other side, Mrs Garside. They were continually having cups of tea together."

Rivers nodded. "Thank you," he said.

"What has he done?" she asked.

"It's a missing woman. He may be responsible for what happened to her."

"Why haven't the police been round here, then?" she asked.

Because they're pillocks, thought Rivers, but he judged that would not be the best answer to give her.

"They're pursuing another line of enquiry," he simply said. She was the type of character who would have had nothing but respect for the police. He strolled down the road and knocked at the door of the house on the other side of Craven's.

Kerry Garside was very different to the woman he had just been speaking. She was smoking a cigarette and had the trace of an Essex accent. He thought she was in her forties. Rivers thought she could make an interesting companion for Sian and wondered if the two socialised at all in which case he smiled, she might know of his liaison with her next door neighbour.

"Hallo, darling, what can I do for you?" she asked.

"I'm trying to find Les Craven," he began.

"Blimey, you must be the only bleeding sucker who is," she said.

Sadly, thought Rivers, that's true. There was no police interest in him, after all.

"I'm investigating a murder," he said.

"Oh, are you that private detective of Sian's?" She rolled her eyes. "I've heard all about you. Do come in."

Rivers was not quite sure what he was getting into – whether Kerry Garside thought that because he had had sex with her next door neighbour there was a chance he might repeat the experience with her. Once inside, he realised that assumption was a mistake. There were two children in the living room – aged about eight and ten. They were instantly dismissed to their bedrooms.

"You think Les done it?" she said.

"I'm investigating that possibility."

"Well, I wouldn't put it past him," she said. It was extraordinary that no-one seemed to have a nice word to say about Les

Craven. Worse still, they were all only too happy to have a go at him. "You know he hit his wife Natalie – at least twice as far as I know," she said. "I had her in here. Crying her eyes out. I told her. She should get out. I wouldn't stand for that. If my Kevin so much as raised a finger to me, me and the kids – we'd be out of here like a shot."

Rivers had a mental image of her Kevin – a small waspish kind of man – trying to raise a finger to her and thinking the better of it at the last moment.

"Don't blame you," he said in quite a disinterested fashion. "She took your advice, then?"

"Yes."

"Do you keep in touch?"

"Well, we did. You know, we'd have a natter on the phone. But I haven't heard from her for the last three months. She went to Andover, you know."

"Yes, I thought as much. Did she leave you an address?"

"No, I've got her mobile number, though. I've tried ringing it a couple of times but it just goes on to voicemail."

"Would you give it to me?" She did. "Thanks," he said. "Well, I don't think I need detain you any longer," he said. Then he thought he would try a parting shot. "I don't suppose you've been in touch with or seen Les Craven at all during the past few months?" he asked.

"Do me a favour," she said.

"So you have no idea where he might be?"

"He did talk about having a cottage in Scotland. He had it when he was with Natalie. It was a sort of holiday retreat for them. Maybe he's still got it?"

"Thanks." He got up to go.

"Pardon me for being nosy, but you and Sian going to make a thing of this?" she asked.

"I don't think so," he said candidly.

"Shame. She's a nice girl."

Yes, thought Rivers, she was a nice woman but his time in Newhaven was up now.

• • ● • •

"Do sit down." said Angela as Patrick Saunders entered the room."How do you think we're doing?"

"I've got Sir Joshua Partridge to appear for us. He's one of the best," said Patrick.

The name was familiar to Angela. He had appeared in one or two high profile murder cases – always for the defence. On one occasion, she remembered he had got a teenager off a murder charge when – to all intents and purposes after the prosecution's presentation of the case, it looked as if the police had got him bang to rights. It had been a gang killing and there was a question mark over who exactly had plunged the knife into the victim which Sir Joshua had exploited. Angela seemed to remember the teenager had gone on to commit another murder a few weeks after being cleared but had not been so fortunate the next time. Nor did he have Sir Joshua defending him. The barrister had weighed up his chances of winning and refused the case.

"It's good that he has taken on the case," said Patrick."There are a lot of pressures on his time."

"It's a high profile case," said Angela. "Respected journalist killing tabloid hack. Probably every crime correspondent on a national newspaper wants to cover it as well."

Patrick looked at Angela. There was something that was not quite right. Normally she was such a forceful character. She never allowed anything to stand in her way but – if he were to sum up her character today – he would have to say she seemed meek. As if anybody could walk all over her.

"What's the matter, Angela?" he asked.

"I'm worried," she confided in him."That Rivers doesn't seem to have come up with anything yet. Why are we paying him such a vast amount of money?"

"We're not," said Patrick, "and he is working hard. At least he's come up with an alternative explanation as to what happened to Kate Williams. It's just that he hasn't found his suspect yet. Give him time. He'll certainly be able to give Sir Joshua something to work with."

"I suppose," said Angela. "You know, I love Roy – but if I thought he was playing away from home." Her voice tailed off.

"Angela, what are you saying?" asked Patrick. "Don't you believe Roy's version of events?"

"Why did he go out to dinner with this woman in the first place – and then on to the night club?"

"The same reason that when you're abroad on a trip you go out with a client for a meal," said Patrick. "It's what journalists do. They go out for meals." He smiled. "You should take heart from the fact he left her on her own, drunk in a night club at 2.30am – when he probably could have had his wicked way with her."

"Yes," she said unconvincingly.

"And he's probably regretting that now. He'll be thinking if only he'd insisted she go back to the hotel with him, she would be alive now."

"And we'd be having a row now because he'd have been to bed with her."

"You don't know that, Angela."

"Experience, dear boy. It's what men are like."

"Look, he needs your support now, Angela, instead of you theorising about what appalling things he could have got up to. If you think you're having a hard time, try swopping roles with him – languishing in a prison cell charged with a murder you know you haven't committed. Go and visit him tomorrow. There's not a lot else you can do at the moment." He swallowed.

"Keep that anger you showed to Detective Chief Inspector Barton in the forefront of your mind," he said. "He's the one you should be thinking bad thoughts of. Not Roy."

"Right," said Angela,

•   •   ●   •   •

"That Marie woman," said Nick as Francesca came into the room. "We can't rely on her. She doesn't want to give evidence."

"I find that hard to believe," said Francesca. "There seemed to be something about her when she came all the way down here to speak to us. She seemed to want to do what she thought was her civic duty."

"Not anymore," said Nick.

"You went to see her, then?"

"Yes."

"And as a result of the visit, she decided not to give evidence. What did you say to her?"

"I just asked her about her story."

"No, you didn't. We all know where you're coming from on this one. You talked her out of it."

"I beg your pardon, Francesca. How dare you."

"I dare because it's been obvious that you want to pin this one on your old school friend."

"We didn't go to the same school. I went to the local comprehensive – he was educated privately." The tone of his words made it seem to Francesca that he was irked by this. It could, she thought, throw some light on why Nick detested him so much. He was the public schoolboy with a spoon in his mouth while Nick had had to battle for what he had got.

"I'm sorry, then, Nick. Your former band member friend, then."

"Band member is accurate. Friend? Not really. Anyhow, that's irrelevant. I wasn't too impressed by her story anyway.

We have the word of someone whose dead friend who was an illegal immigrant thinks he may have seen something on the night that Kate Williams disappeared from the night club. By the way, he was a bank robber, too. Or had that escaped you? On the other hand we have a suspect who had Kate Williams' DNA in his car boot, suitcase and bed – and who pulled out of a conference for two hours to drive up to Beachy Head ostensibly for no reason when, in fact, I'm damned sure he went there to dispose of the body. Pull yourself together, Francesca. Get behind me and support our open or shut case. Or ...."

"Or what?"

"Think of the consequences. If you don't support me, will I want to work with you again in future?"

"But then there's the evidence that Philip Rivers, the private detective, has uncovered. The white van man who also disappeared that night."

"He didn't disappear. He doesn't live around here. He just went back to where-ever it is he does live. Anyhow, I've been doing a little bit of digging about our Mr Rivers with the local constabulary where he lives. He hasn't been practising for the past six months. He needs to make a name for himself to get his private detective agency off the ground again."

"You've got an answer for everything."

"I have," said Nick firmly, "and it'll result in a conviction against Roy Faulkner when the case comes to court. You mark my words. Now go. Get on with your work."

Francesca went back to her office. She could see that Nick was making a strong case for Roy being guilty but she still felt that they should have explored other avenues in their investigation. It was put up or shut up time. If she really felt the investigation was faulty, she would have to raise it with her superior, Chief Superintendent Rimmer, in the morning. She resolved that she would do just that.

CHAPTER EIGHT

Angela reached over to touch Roy's hand – a move which seemed to be frowned upon by the nearby prison officer who made a gesture suggesting she should stop and move her hand away.

"Sorry, love," said Angela to Roy. "The rules and regulations – I'm not familiar with them."

"You never were one for rules and regulations, I seem to remember," replied Roy smiling. Angela noticed it was the first time during their meeting that the furrow had disappeared from his brow and said so. "I've been thinking," said Roy. "About the night Kate Williams disappeared. I should never have left her alone in the night club."

"There's no point in thinking that way now," said Angela.

"No, but it's so unlike me – I mean, I never like leaving you to make your way home on your own even though you're completely sober all the time." Angela would relax with just one drink sometimes when they went out in the evening – but never more than one.

"That sounds as if that's a criticism," interjected Angela.

"No, it's a statement of fact," said Roy, "and I can't help thinking that maybe I didn't leave her on her own at the night club that night."

"And you did what?" There was a certain coldness in Angela's tone. Inside she was wondering whether this meant she had been wrong to put all her eggs in one basket – and rush to the defence of her partner.

"This is going to be hard for you to take."

"Then maybe you shouldn't say it."

"No, I've been in here on my own for too long thinking thoughts. I need to talk about them."

"But perhaps not to me."

"I'm in too far – and you deserve to know what's going on in my mind if anybody does."

"Okay." She still did not seem to have relaxed her guard – or agree with him.

"Well, I can distinctly remember when I woke up the following morning reaching to my side or turning over wondering if I was alone in my bed. I felt relieved when I found out that I was – but supposing I had brought Kate back that night."

"And in a drunken state killed her. I've always told you drink can play funny tricks with your mind."

He ignored the lecture. "But, if that is the case, what did I do with the body? I know I didn't do what Nick says – and dump her body off Beachy Head later that morning. I mean her body wasn't lying around in the bedroom when I woke up that morning. I can remember what happened the following day, too, and – if I had made an early morning trip to Beachy Head to get rid of the body – you'd have thought that would have been triggered off in my mind when I went there at lunchtime. Also, the car's exit from the car park would have been caught on CCTV."

"So really this is the meanderings of a mind given too much time to be by itself and ruminate about what happened that night?" said Angela."

"Hold on to the fact that you can remember what happened on the Saturday and it doesn't fit in with what you think might have happened on the previous evening." She thought for a moment and then added:"And don't confide about your worries to anybody else."

"Probably not a good idea,"agreed Roy."Best if I don't ramble on about them in the witness box,"

"You don't really think there's the slightest chance that you killed Kate Williams, do you?"

Roy hesitated for a moment."No, not really,"he said.

"Oh, not really – that's great,"said Angela."Roy Faulkner, you are accused that – on the morning of May 2 – you did murder Kate Williams. How do you plead? Not really. That'll go down well."

Roy was beginning to get irritated. He had wanted someone with a more sympathetic tone to confide in. Angela seemed annoyed by his musings. He should have saved his thoughts for either Rivers or Mark when they visited, he thought.

"I've been thinking about Nick Barton, too,"he added.

"Goodness, you do know how to give yourself a hard time," said Angela,

"No, bear with me,"he said – reaching out to touch her arm but withdrawing when he remembered the gesture would be frowned on by the prison authorities."I had a visit from his wife, Charlotte, yesterday."

"How nice for you,"said Angela sarcastically.

"We grew up together,"said Roy."She told me a story."

"I hope it helped you get to sleep,"said Angela, bitterly.

Roy was beginning to get more than a little irritated by now. "No, listen,"he said."Graeme, one of the members of our group, is dead. Run over by a car – a hit and run driver. It happened just a few nights after he met Charlotte and Nick in the local pub. He had become an alcoholic. Was begging them for a drink."

"I can't quite see where this is leading,"said Angela.

"Graeme and Nick didn't see eye to eye."

"I'm beginning to like this Graeme."

"Graeme kept on disparaging Nick when he was in the band. It was only light-hearted banter but he kept on suggesting he should go back to the Boy Scouts band and leave the cutting edge pop music to those – well, I think we had a phrase for it – those who were more cool."

"Are you trying to say that Nick might have been responsible for the accident?"

"It was no accident," said Roy firmly. "That road. The one where it happened. You wouldn't race down there. It's a dead end. It only leads to the cricket club and a dilapidated empty cottage owned by monks."

He could see there was still a look of disbelief coming over Angela's face. "And it fits in with something Nick did earlier." Roy swallowed. "When I started going out with Gillian Bird and Nick maintained I'd stolen her from him he tried to run her over on a zebra crossing."

"But you have no proof for any of these assertions?" Angela asked, bringing Roy down to earth with a bump.

"No, I suppose not."

• • • • •

Francesca Manners had been nervous in submitting her request for a meeting with the Chief Superintendent. Charles Rimmer was known as a stickler for protocol but also had a reputation for not liking to hear of any dissent within his force. Everyone should pull together, that was his creed. Therefore the perpetrators of any dissent had better have some solid facts on their side before they approached him and asked him to step into any internal matter.

She was wearing her best suit (and not a trouser one) for the occasion. Rimmer also had the reputation for being nostalgic about the past. He had often stated a preference for the values of the 1950's. Whether he approved of high ranking women officers in the force was not known. He definitely favoured women being feminine, though, and wearing dresses to work. If he had prejudices beyond that, though, he was diplomatic enough to keep them hidden. Given his track record, Francesca was not overly confident of pursuing her case for a fresh look at the Kate Williams case but she felt she had to make the effort.

"I'll see if Chief Superintendent Rimmer is free to see you now," said his personal assistant whom – Francesca noticed –

was also wearing a sober suit (not trousered). She made her way over to Rimmer's office door and knocked a trifle tentatively.

"Yes?" came a voice from behind the closed door.

"Detective Sergeant Manners to see you, sir," she said.

"Come," barked the voice from behind the door and Francesca was led into his presence. He was sitting behind a large desk and did not bother to get up as she entered the room. Not that much of a traditionalist, thought Francesca. "Sit," he barked as if he was giving an order to his dog. He was a small man. Had he been standing, he would have been shown to be smaller than Francesca – about five foot six inches to her five foot nine. He was wearing his uniform as befitted his post but Francesca could not help but notice that his shirt seemed at least one size too big for him. As he spoke, his head made as if to disappear into the shirt – only to bob up again at the last minute. His Adam's apple was also constantly wobbling. She could not help but think he would not have cut a dashing figure in county or senior police circles but he had held his post for almost a decade and no-one had voiced any open hostility to the idea of him continuing in office. He was, she had heard Nick say on occasions, a safe pair of hands to use cricketing terminology – although whether he would be able to catch the ball in a real sporting game, Francesca doubted.

"Now, what can I do for you, young lady?" he asked, deigning to look up and remove his glasses and fix her with a stare.

"It's the Kate Williams case," she began.

"Where we have a man in custody awaiting trial on a murder charge even though we have not found a body yet. Jolly good work all round, I would have thought," he said.

His comments reinforced Francesca's feelings that she should not have embarked on the course that she had set her mind on. There was nothing for it now, though, but to press forward with conviction and hang the consequences, she mused. "Except he might be the wrong man," she said.

"Oh, does Detective Chief Inspector Barton share your views on this subject?" he asked.

"No, that's why I have come to you. The deceased, if indeed she is deceased, was seen chatting to another man on the night of her disappearance – a white van driver – and at least one witness has said she left the night club in his company. He has since disappeared, too, it seems."

"Does the fact this man was driving a white van in any way suggest he is guilty?"

"Er, no, sir, I merely mentioned it to help identify him."

"And this witness? Will he or she prove to be reliable in court?"

"Again, no, sir. She has told Detective Chief Inspector Barton she does not wish to give evidence. I believe he talked her out of it. She was only too willing to give evidence when she was talking to me. Indeed, she saw it as her duty."

"That's a very serious allegation, Detective Sergeant Manners. Nick is an experienced detective with a string of successful cases behind him. He believes he has got his man, then?" She noted he had dropped the formality of Detective Chief Inspector Barton now.

"He does, to the extent that he won't even...."

He cut across her. "In which case it is your duty to back him up and support him and help him to secure a conviction," he said firmly.

"I was going to say he won't even investigate any evidence contrary to the theory that the murder was committed by the suspect we have in prison." Francesca managed to complete her sentence despite the obvious hostility from the man across the table from her.

"But I thought you said he did investigate the claim of this witness and found that she no longer wanted to give evidence. Presumably when he saw her he realised what a flimsy witness she was and, as a result of his questioning, she decided to withdraw from the case. Sounds as if he's done justice a favour, Detective Sergeant Manners."

"It seems as if I'm wasting my time, sir." Francesca was beginning to think she could not wait to get out of the room.

"I'm not sure I like your tone, Detective Sergeant Manners." His head seemed to be bobbing up and down above his shirt more frantically than ever now. "As I said, it is your duty to work with Detective Inspector Barton and help him to secure a conviction in this case." He paused for a moment. "It is, of course, commendable that you should want to pursue every angle in a murder case but sometimes that can lead to you not being able to see the wood from the trees." He looked down at the papers on his desk. "Thank you, Detective Sergeant."

Francesca tried to think of something to say in reply but could not. Rimmer seemed to note the hesitation. "Thank you, Detective Sergeant," he repeated again enunciating his words more clearly.

$$\bullet \ \bullet \ \bullet \ \bullet \ \bullet$$

The solicitors' offices Rivers was looking for were in a converted residential mansion on the outskirts of Andover. He drove into the pebbled car park and took another look at the name of the solicitor who had been representing Craven's wife, Natalie, in her divorce from Les. Stephen Aymes. He walked over to the office door and rang the doorbell. Someone must have triggered a device inside the building because the door suddenly opened. Surprised, Rivers walked in.

"Not too hot on security here, then," he said to the girl behind the reception counter. She looked no more than a teenager.

"We looked at you on the screen," she said. "Decided you weren't a risk. Can I help you?"

"Yes, I've come to see Stephen Aymes."

"Do you have an appointment?"

"No, I just came here on the off chance. I think he may be able to help me in a murder investigation I'm pursuing." A man who had been doing some filing in the office just behind the reception area suddenly dropped his papers and looked up at Rivers. "Mr Aymes?" said Rivers.

"No, no," said the man, bending down to pick up his papers. "It's just that we don't usually get caught up in murder investigations. Divorces, wills, etcetera – but not murder."

"Well, maybe the word murder will intrigue Mr Aymes just as much as you," said Rivers. "Is he in?"

"I'll give him a call and see if he's free," said the receptionist. She turned away from Rivers as she made the call, turning round to say to him: "He'll see you now."

A rather rotund man suddenly appeared from a doorway by the side of the reception desk. Rivers noticed that he had extraordinarily rosy cheeks – perhaps the legacy of a long liquid lunch that day.

"Mr....?"

"Rivers. Philip Rivers. I'm a private detective. I was wondering if you could help me with a murder investigation I'm pursuing."

"Won't you come into my office?" His voice had a deep Hampshire burr. The man was in his thirties or early forties, Rivers surmised, but listening to him brought memories of being tuned in to Test Match Special on Radio Three in the early days of cricket commentary when bon viveur John Arlott was at the helm. It was the same mixture of Hampshire accent and good quality wine, thought Rivers.

"Who's been murdered, then?" asked Aymes when they were both seated in his office.

"I don't know whether the name will mean anything to you. Kate Williams." Aymes shook his head. "We're not sure she's been murdered. She went missing from a night club in Brighton and my client has been charged with her murder."

"So where do I come in?"

159

"My investigations lead me to believe that the man responsible for her disappearance may be familiar to you – Les Craven." Rivers was a past-master at releasing as little information as possible to his interviewee and then just sitting back and observing the reaction.

"Les Craven," said Aymes, thoughtful for a moment. "Yes, Natalie Craven's husband. I'm afraid I can't help you very much. I've never met him."

"No, I didn't suppose you had," said Rivers. "It's Natalie I'd like to meet. To find out more about him."

Aymes nodded. "Strange thing, though," he said. "She moved down here a few months ago and was keen as mustard to get divorce proceedings under way. Then suddenly not a peep from her. I thought that the break-up must have been fresh in her mind when she first moved in – but then she kind of got over it and was no longer giving it a priority. I haven't heard from her for three months now."

"Have you been round to see her?"

"Yes, but she wasn't in. I thought she might have gone away on holiday."

"Three months is a long time for a holiday," said Rivers.

"Yes, I suppose so," mused Aymes. His interest appeared to be rather half-hearted at this stage – now that he reasoned he was not exactly at the cutting edge of the murder investigation.

"Could you give me her address?" asked Rivers.

"Well, I'm not sure," said Aymes. "There is a bit of an issue of client confidentiality here."

"This is a murder investigation I'm pursuing. My client's future could depend on it. Then again, you say she hasn't been in so perhaps all I'll do is post a note through the letter box asking her to get in touch with me."

"All right," said Aymes. "I suppose it can't hurt." He opened one of the drawers to his desk, took out a letter and then jotted down an address on a scrap of paper which he handed to Rivers.

"Are we done, then?" he asked.

"Yes, and thank you for your help," said Rivers.

"Shame," said Aymes, leaving Rivers feeling that the solicitor would have liked to have a much wider involvement in the murder investigation he was pursuing.

Once outside, Rivers looked up directions on his mobile device and saw that Natalie Craven's cottage was only about five minutes' drive away. He decided to go over there immediately. What he saw seemed to confirm Aymes' impression that the occupant was not living there at the moment. The grass had grown – almost to an unkempt level. He thought he would go through the motions, though, and rang the doorbell. He was not surprised when there was no reply. He tried one or two of his master keys on the door – but to no avail. He walked round to the back of the house and took stock of the situation. There was a living room and a kitchen backing on to the garden. The living room had glass windows from top to bottom but he was loathe to smash them – a move which could have been the precursor to an investigation into breaking and entering. That could also have ended disastrously for him as Aymes the solicitor would be able to tell the police he had handed the address of the property on to him just before the break-in occurred. Instead, he looked to the kitchen window. There was a small glass panel above the main window which, he thought from the outside, had not been placed on the latch. With the judicious use of a pen-knife he managed to prise it open and then reach down with some string on the inside and open the main window frame. He brought over one of the garden chairs on the patio outside and stood on it. The gap he had created by opening the window was just enough for him to crawl through. It was touch and go – another occasion where he lamented the loss of his Bahamian boatman friend, Jo, who was extraordinarily slim and would have managed to get through the window without having a passing thought as to whether he might get stuck.

Once inside, he looked around him. The rooms had obviously not been dusted or cleaned for some time. It was a small cottage. A kitchen, living room and store room downstairs and a rickety staircase leading to two bedrooms upstairs. The store room did have a desk inside and his first instinct was to rifle through there and see if there was any correspondence or something like that which would give him a clue as to where Natalie Craven was. There were one or two holiday brochures – about inter-city breaks in the main although there was one extolling the virtues of rural France. Perhaps she had bought a retreat there and was relaxing in it even as he searched her UK home. He discounted that theory, though. Surely, if she had have purchased a property abroad, she would have used the services of Stephen Aymes to complete the purchase. The next thing he came across was an insurance certificate for her car and MOT test certificate. Interestingly enough, it had not been parked on the driveway when he arrived so he deduced that – where-ever she was – she must have driven there herself. It seemed to discount any theory that she had undergone a similar kind of disappearance to Kate Williams. The next thing he came across, though, was her passport – which disproved the French rural retreat or series of inter-city breaks theories. Where-ever she was, she was in the UK with her own car. He resolved to take a note of the licence number. You never knew when this kind of information would come in handy.

• • ● • •

Angela walked down the tree-lined road wondering whether she had done the right thing. She had looked in the local directory and found there was one McAndrew still living in the Barnet area and thought she would give it a go. She had taken on board Roy's criticism that she had not shown enough support for him and was now determined to offer him whatever help she could. If Roy's seemingly half-baked theories about Nick Barton's involvement in Graeme McAndrew's death had any weight to them, perhaps she could help shed some light on the situation. Ordinarily, she would have passed on the information she had received to Philip Rivers and asked him to investigate but she had not been able to get in touch with him. Secondly, she wanted to prove to Roy she could be helpful in his defence.

She came to a halt outside number 83 – the house where McAndrew, J.A, according to the directory, lived. It looked different to others in the street. The curtains were closed for a start even though it was the middle of the day and it did not look as if it had been shown much more than cursory lick of paint in the recent past. She rang the doorbell and a well-dressed woman – probably in her fifties – opened the door.

"Yes?" she asked.

"I'm sorry, I may be barking up the wrong tree – but did a Graeme McAndrew live here?" Angela asked.

"Yes," came the reply. The voice was slightly faint – as if perplexed by the question. "He's been dead for nearly thirty years, though," said the woman.

"I know," said Angela. "I'm the partner of a friend of his. Roy Faulkner."

A smile creased the lips of the woman at the door. "Oh, Roy, he was such a nice boy."

Boy, thought Angela. This woman, she would surmise, was a few years older than Roy. She might well have looked upon him as a boy thirty years ago when he and Graeme had been in the group together. "Very handsome," the woman added. "As was my Graeme."

The two seemed to be at an impasse with Angela not quite sure how to broach her enquiry.

"Look," she said, "would you mind if I came in? I've got a complicated story to tell which I believe you might be interested in."

"No, of course not," came the reply. "It would be nice to talk about Graeme again. My name's Jane, Jane McAndrew, Graeme's sister." She proffered a hand to Angela.

"Angela Hopkins," Angela replied accepting the handshake. Jane McAndrew ushered her into a hallway. Off to the left was what was probably the main living room in the house. Again Angela got the feeling it was stuck in a time warp and had not seen much in the way of a lick of paint for years. Jane asked her to sit down.

"I'm not sure what I've got to say will form the basis of a pleasant conversation," said Angela. "I really wanted to talk about Graeme's death."

"Yes." Jane thought for a moment. "I have to confess I've found it difficult to come to terms with it," she said. "I still miss my younger brother." Angela felt an overwhelming sense of sadness. Here was somebody who has been in mourning for nigh on thirty years, she felt. "I managed to continue with my career," she said. "I've been teaching at the local primary school. Still am. It's a fulfilling job. Nurturing the talent of tomorrow – the talent that didn't see the light of day in Graeme's case," There was silence for a moment. "Graeme's death, it was – it was so unreal," she said.

"Roy thought that," said Angela. "He said the stretch of road where he was killed, it was very unlikely to have been a hit and run driver."

"We thought that," said Jane quickly, "My parents were alive then. We thought the police should have mounted a more thorough enquiry into it. We even went to see a friend of Graeme's to see if he could help but ...." Her voice tailed off.

"A friend of Graeme's?" asked Angela.

"Yes, Nick Barton. Roy would know him. He, Graeme and Nick were in the same band. Nick had joined the police force and we thought he could open up one or two avenues for us. But he never got back to us."

"I'm not sure Nick was a friend of Graeme's," said Angela.

"What? Everybody like Graeme."

Angela sighed. She wondered if she had put her foot in it. An imaginary voice inside her wanted to scream out "everybody doesn't like anybody" but she thought the better of it. Instead, she tried another tack. "Would you say everybody liked Roy?"

Jane thought for a moment. "He was sexy," she finally came up with. "And a little dangerous. You should have heard him singing 'You'd Better Move On'. I tell you, I'd have moved on if I'd been the bloke in the song." Angela smiled. She didn't think it was the time to tell Jane she had heard Roy singing 'You'd Better Move On'. Several times – but always after he had had a bit to drink.

"Where is he now?" Jane asked innocently.

"He's in prison, awaiting trial on a murder charge," said Angela in a matter-of –fact way.

"Oh, my goodness," said Jane quite shocked.

"And Nick Barton is the detective who has charged him with murder. It was Nick's wife, Charlotte who first put the thought I should investigate Graeme's death into my mind."

"Not Charlotte Woods? She was a really nice girl. I knew they were going out together."

Angela was getting a bit sick of Jane McAndrew's rose-tinted memories of thirty years ago but, instead of commenting upon them, said through gritted teeth: "The very same." Then she added: "Anyway, she told Roy that Graeme had been run over just a few days after he had met Nick in the pub."

"Oh, Graeme never told me anything about that."

I doubt if he would have remembered it, darling, the gritted teeth thought again. Your brother was completely paralytic and probably wouldn't have been remembering much by that stage. "Charlotte said Nick had a very strange reaction to Graeme's death – saying that he had it coming or words to that effect. Tell me, was Nick a really nice boy?" Angela sat back to await Jane McAndrew's verdict.

The other woman was reflective for a moment. "Nick was in a time-warp," she said finally. "He didn't really fit in with the others. His clothes were – well, we had a word for it in those days. Square. He was also in the Boy Scouts Band. I don't think Graeme or Roy would have been seen dead there." She giggled – possibly at the thought of Graeme being in the Boy Scouts Band. Angela thought she had probably not giggled for years. Her face suddenly seemed different. She must have been an attractive woman all those years ago, she thought. Such a pity her countenance was so severe today and that her hair was tied up in a bun which almost seemed to be hurting her.

"You see, Roy thinks Nick is trying to stitch him up on this murder charge – and that he might have been the hit and run driver that killed Graeme, too," said Angela. "That may be why he didn't respond when you asked him for help over the hit and run."

"Oh my God," said Jane. Angela felt Jane was not the kind of person to take the Lord's name in vain often and was genuinely shocked by what she had just said. "What – what should we do about it?"

"I think I came here today to see if you had any evidence that would support Roy's theory," said Angela. "You don't, though, do you?"

"It would never have occurred to me in a million years," Jane said. Angela had anticipated the answer. Bad thoughts just didn't occur to Jane. She understood that. It must have been down to teaching in a primary school in what was probably a relatively affluent area, she thought.

"Two things," said Angela. "Roy has hired a private detective to help him prove his innocence. We can pass this information on to him and see what he makes of it. Secondly, we could try and goad Nick Barton into making some kind of admission or mistake."

"Wouldn't that be dangerous if he's already killed Graeme?" Jane asked.

"There is a third alternative," said Angela.

"Yes?"

"We sit back and do nothing, allow Nick to frame Roy for murder and ensure Graeme's death never gets investigated. It's not an attractive one."

"No," Jane agreed.

•   •   **•**   •   •

"Hello, old boy, how are you holding up?" Mark Elliott's genial voice immediately brought some comfort to Roy who had been worrying about what he had said to Angela.

"I'm as well as can be expected," came the reply, "after buggering up a visit from Angela by confiding there are moments that I wonder what I might have done on the night Kate Williams disappeared."

"And what might you have done?"

"He thinks he may have killed you," he said paraphrasing the words in Mark's message to Kate the night after her disappearance.

"God, I'm sorry I ever sent that," confessed Mark

"Well, you did – and it sent Nick Barton into an orgasm of delight but I'm not sure it proves anything," said Roy. "But, getting back to your original question, I wish I knew more of what's going on out there. What's Philip Rivers doing, for instance?"

Mark was silent. "I don't know," he said.

"But you do live in the same block of flats as him. Couldn't you just pop down the corridor and find out?"

"You know," said Mark. "I wouldn't pin too much hope on his investigations."

"But you were the one who introduced me to him in the first place. What do you mean?"

"He's had a bit of difficulty getting his life on track during the past few months after his partner died."

"Now you tell me."

"I'm sure he's trying his best but I think he's spending as much time sorting his own life out as he is yours. I've seen one of his former girlfriends during these last few days – she seems to be a constant visitor to his block of flats. I'm sure he's following up every lead he has but...."The journalist's voice tailed off.

"Mark," said Roy urgently, "There's some time pressure here. My trial's coming up soon. I need him to find white van man."

Mark winced. "Tell you what, old boy," he said. "I've got quite a lot of leave still owing to me. How about if I take a bit of time next week and either go and help Rivers or make one or two enquiries myself?"

"It would be great if you could,"

"Consider it done."

• • ● • •

Rivers looked at his mobile. The number of the caller was being witheld. Intrigued, he answered it.

"Detective Sergeant Manners here," came the voice down the line. "I wonder if we could meet up. There are one or two things I'd like to talk to you about."The call had been the precursor to Francesca arriving at Rivers' flat in Finchley about three hours later.

"I thought you lot thought I was persona non grata," said Rivers as he ushered her in through the door.

"I think we could help each other," said Francesca. "Let's put it this way – I'm not a hundred per cent comfortable with the way my superior has handled the case."

"Join the club."

"Trouble is, my superiors are. That's why I've come to you." She sat down in his living room – casting an eye around the room. It looked too organised for a man living on his own, she thought. "I was pursuing another line of inquiry to the conventional theory that Kate Williams was murdered by your client, Roy Faulkner."

"It's not a conventional theory to me," interrupted Rivers. "So what have you got?"

"A witness who says a friend helped a guy – presumably the white van man – bundle a woman fitting Kate Williams' description into a van."

"If that did happen, it would clear my client of the crime once and for all."

"Two snags. One, she won't testify and two, her friend has been killed in a road traffic accident." Rivers pricked his ears up. "Nothing to do with the case," said Francesca, moving swiftly to dampen any speculation that there could be another murder to investigate here. "The witness says he just wasn't concentrating on crossing the road – she thinks he was trying to work out in his mind whether he should come forward with the evidence he had. The upshot of all this is that I've not got anything concrete to go on – except a suspicion that there may be an alternative explanation as to what happened to Kate Williams. Oh, and my boss has refused to investigate the disappearance of the white van man that Roy Faulkner said he and Kate Williams had been talking to earlier in the evening."

"He hasn't been seen either since the night Kate Williams went missing," said Rivers. "I have the registration number of his van, though. Maybe you could find out where it was registered. Of course, it could be to his Newhaven address but apparently he's always had a retreat up in Scotland which his tenant has never had the address for." He took a piece of paper from his pocket and handed it to Francesca.

"I'll check that out immediately," she said and – with that – got up and took her mobile out of her pocket and got through to a colleague in the office to whom she passed the details.

"There's one other twist to this," Rivers continued. "Les Craven has separated from his wife and – by all accounts – they were involved in a bitter divorce battle up until three months ago when the wife went missing, too. I've been to her house. Her car's gone but her passport is still there. So she's disappeared somewhere into the ether in the UK with her car. I've got that registration number, too. Could you put out an alert to see if anyone can spot it in their travels?"

"I can try when I get back to the station," said Francesca. "It may be a bit more difficult. I've been told in no uncertain terms that I must get behind my superior and help him to secure a conviction against Roy Faulkner." At that moment her mobile started ringing and she answered the call. She took a notebook out of her pocket and started jotting some information down. When she had finished the call, she turned to Rivers.

"We're in luck," she said. "It's registered to a Scottish address – Loch Rannoch."

"Never heard of it," said Rivers, taking the piece of paper with the address on it from her, "but I've a feeling I soon will have." He frowned. "Which brings us to the elephant in the room," he said.

"Yes?"

"Nick Barton. Is he corrupt?"

"You mean?"

"I mean did he plant evidence against my client to secure a conviction?"

Francesca swallowed. "There's no evidence to suggest he did," she said.

"But – if you think it's still worth investigating alternative theories for Kate Williams' disappearance – it means there must be a suspicion that he did. You can't have it both ways. Either Nick's evidence is kosher in which case my client's guilty and all this stuff about white van man and a girl being bundled into a vehicle is lies or irrelevant- or Nick is lying through his teeth."

"I can see how you could come to that conclusion," said Francesca, speaking in measured tones. "I've worked with

Nick Barton for years and I've never suspected him of cutting corners, inventing evidence or anything like that. He's been a bit blinkered in some of his investigations – but he's got results. So I'm not going to tell you your friend…."

"Client," interrupted Rivers.

"Your client," Francesca corrected herself," has been stitched up by a corrupt copper. All I do know and believe is that we should investigate all the evidence and that's what Nick is not doing. And, while he's not doing that and I've been barred from doing that, I'm happy to give you what help I can so that you can reach your own conclusions about what happened in this case."

"Thank you," said Rivers. As he ushered her to the door, he said: "I'll contact you with anything I get but – for the next couple of days – I could be in Scotland."

• • ● • •

"You did what?" Nick shrieked.

"I went to see Roy Faulkner in prison," stuttered Charlotte.

"For what precise purpose?"

"I know Roy is not a murderer. We grew up together, Nick."

"Yes, I do know that and he fucked you when you were eighteen. I do know that, too."

"Nick," said Charlotte, tears welling in her eyes. "You've always said that you accepted my explanation that he didn't."

"Well, he wanted to. That's bad enough."

Charlotte wanted to argue that the two were not the same thing – but could see that arguing the toss with Nick in this mood was probably not a good idea. Instead, she pursued another line. "Nick, he's innocent," she said.

"Charlotte," he replied, moving menacingly towards her, "don't meddle in affairs you know nothing about. Any man who can twice try and stab a friend in the back by stealing his girlfriends and go on to have him beaten up is not to be trusted – and there's an end to it."

"So you're basing this case on the fact that he started going out with Gillian Bird when it was obvious to all concerned that you and she had nothing in common. You must be – because he had an alibi for the night of the beating and there's no truth in the suggestion he stole me from you. We're still together thirty years later."

"More's the pity," he said.

"Do you mean that? Because if you do."

Nick relented. "No, I don't. I'm sorry. Of course, I want you around." The subtext here could well have been because it won't look good if my wife storms out on me on the eve of a murder trial where an old friend of hers is the accused, thought Charlotte, rather than a suggestion that there was still any love left between them. Nick began pacing up and down the room.

"Charlotte, which one of the two of us is a detective?" he asked.

"Don't be silly, Nick. You are, of course," she replied.

He moved menacingly close to her again. "Don't tell me not to be silly," he said. All right, she thought, be silly. She restrained herself from voicing these thoughts, though.

"Good, we're making some progress," he said. "Then leave the detective work to me – and get on with your knitting."

"I don't knit," she said.

"Don't be pedantic. You know what I mean."

"I would – except you've got it wrong."

"Did you not hear what I said?" He was back in her face menacingly. "I said leave...." he raised his hand and slapped her hard on the left cheek. ".... the detective work....." he brought his hand back to give her a backhander on the right cheek ".... to me." A further right-hand slap on the left cheek followed.

Charlotte rubbed her cheek. Tears welled in her eyes – but she knew she had been cowed by Nick. She would not raise the issue again while Nick was in this mood.

"I think I shall go upstairs," she said.

"Good place for you." He was not looking at her. He was holding his right hand and rubbing it where it had had contact with her cheek.

It was at that moment that the front door opened and a cheery voice called out from the hallway.

"Hi Mum, Dad. I'm back from Uni," it said.

"Sarah?" said Nick. "We weren't expecting you." He turned to the snivelling Charlotte and whispered: "Go upstairs and clean up – you don't want Sarah seeing you like that," he said.

"No," she said turning on her toes. "You don't want Sarah seeing me like this."

It was too late. Sarah was in the kitchen before Charlotte could move out of it.

"How are you both?" She looked at Charlotte with the red weals on her face. "Oh, my God, Mum, Dad, what's happened?"

Charlotte moved towards her daughter. "It's all right, nothing for you to worry about," she said. "Mum and Dad have had a little disagreement but it's all sorted now." She kissed her daughter.

Sarah stared at her father. "You hit her," she said.

"Your mother was getting hysterical. I had to calm her down," he said.

"I'll just go upstairs and freshen up," said Charlotte, wiping away the tears from her eyes. "Then we must see about getting you some supper."

As she left the room, Nick turned to his daughter. "I shouldn't have done it," he said. "I've got a big murder trial coming up tomorrow and your mother was shouting at me, telling me I'd got the wrong man. I've put a lot of work into this case and I had to stop her."

"You shouldn't be trying to excuse yourself to me, Dad," said Sarah. "You should be doing it to Mum."

"Of course," said Nick "Let's go into the living room." Once there, he walked over to the drinks cabinet and poured himself a scotch. "Would you like anything, Sarah?"

"A glass of white wine, please," she said. He poured it for her. "I'll just go upstairs and see if Mum's all right," she said.

"Of course," he said. "Take her a drink, too." He poured another glass of white wine. As Sarah left the room, he sat back in an armchair and took a sip from his scotch. He reflected. Inwardly, he was glad Sarah had come home. Charlotte would be doing her best to paper over the cracks and make sure everything was all right for her. She would don a stiff upper lip. That, he reflected, would help him get through to the end of the trial.

• • ● • •

Loch Rannoch was a village about seventy miles north-east of Edinburgh from where Rivers had picked up a hire car. As he drove towards his destination, he could not help reflect on the beautiful scenery and wonder how Les Craven – who by all accounts was not the most aesthetic of men – had managed or even bothered to acquire a cottage in such an attractive part of the country. He began to wish he had invited Nikki up with him to take part in reconnoitre of Craven's cottage – and then realised it would have been impossible. She had a full-time job and he had a pressing timetable- the case against Roy Faulkner was due to get underway in court the following morning.

He reflected for a moment. Had it been wise to undertake the journey all on his own? If Les Craven was already a murderer, would he baulk at taking out a second person? If he was not and had taken Kate Williams prisoner, he could be equally dangerous. It was the type of occasion where he and Jo would have gone in mob-handed in the old days. After about a two-hour drive, he alighted on the address he had been given for Les Craven's country home. The word cottage seemed a trifle inadequate to convey the nature of the building. Built in granite stone, it sat back from the road and – he reckoned – was more like a mansion than a cottage. It had three windows at the front and on the top floor.

He parked his car in the cobbled driveway and made his way to the front door and rang the bell. It took a couple of minutes for any signs of life to emerge from the building and – when they did – he was confronted with a man who must have been well into his seventies. It obviously was not Craven.

"I'm sorry to trouble you," said Rivers, feeling a sense of relief surprisingly come over him as he realised he was not facing a confrontational encounter with a possible killer. "I'm looking for a Les Craven."

"He's no longer here," said the man who spoke with a thick Scottish accent.

"No longer? He was here then?"

"I bought the house off of him," said the man. "About a month ago."

Ah, thought Rivers. Before Kate's disappearance. "Do you know where he is?" Rivers continued.

"No, he's moved to another address. He hasn't given me any details as to where. Is that all?" The man seemed anxious to shut the door and get back to whatever he had been doing.

"I wonder if I might prey on your time a little bit longer," he said. "You see, I'm a private detective and I want to talk to Mr Craven about a possible crime down south in England."

"Oh," he said.

Rivers detected no note of surprise from the man. Maybe he had worked out what everybody else seemed to have done in their dealings with Craven. He was, without doubt, a man with no positive charisma. "Did you meet him?"

"He showed me round the house, yes." The man was still hanging on to the door as if he was desperate to shut it as soon as possible.

"Did he live on his own here?"

"I never saw anybody else."

"I wonder, would you mind telling me how you found out that this house had come on the market?"

The man looked irritated now. "Look," he said, "if Mr Craven is guilty of a crime down south, it's got nothing to do with me. I came to Loch Rannoch for a bit of peace and quiet for me and my wife after I retired. It seems I'm not getting it today."

At that a voice piped up from inside the house. "Who is it, Gerald?" said a woman.

"I promise you that's the last question," Rivers said.

"It was from an estate agent in Leuchars – Stirling's."

"Thank you," he said. With that, he turned on his heels and made his way back to the car. As he opened the door to get in and drive away, he noticed a curtain twitching in one of the downstairs rooms. Perhaps the woman of the house was trying to get a look at him. Maybe she was more interested in chatting to unannounced company than her husband had been. He resolved to try and come back at some time when the man of the house was out to see if he could bend her ear for more information about Les Craven. He sat in the driveway looking at his route map before resolving to drive back to Leuchars. It was about half an hour away, he guessed, back towards Edinburgh. Once there, he soon found Stirling's the estate agent. The man who greeted him seemed full of bonhomie and more inclined to chat than his previous encounter. Rivers shoved a note in front of him with the address of the cottage/mansion on it. "I wanted to ask you about that," he said.

"Ah, I'm afraid it's been sold, Mr….?"

"Rivers."

"Mr Rivers. It's no longer on the market."

"I know I've just been there," said the private detective, "but I was interested in trying to contact the previous occupant – a Mr Craven. Did you find him somewhere else to live locally – or did he give you a forwarding address?"

"Why do you want to find him?"

"I'm a private detective. I'm investigating a crime he might have been involved in."

"Ah." The estate agent nodded. Again there seemed to be a sense that it was not exactly surprising someone should be linking Craven to a crime. "No, we didn't find him anywhere else to live," he said. "He didn't want us to. He did give us a forwarding address, though."

"May I have it?"

"I'm usually reluctant to hand over details of our clients," said the other man. He opened a drawer at the desk where he was sitting, indicating he was minded to make an exception in Rivers' case. He rummaged around for a few moments. "I've still got it here because he hasn't settled up his final bill," he said. He handed a card to Rivers. It had on it the address of the house he shared with Sian in Newhaven.

So Les Craven really had disappeared and all Rivers' attempts to trace him seemed to have come to nothing.

CHAPTER NINE

Roy sighed. It was a deep sigh. He was waiting in a cell at the Crown Court at Lewes – waiting to be taken up in the dock and to be formally charged with the murder of Kate Williams. He ran his fingers through his hair. There seemed to be less of it now than there had been since this whole ordeal had started. His hairline was definitely receding. He wondered whether it was as a result of the stress he had suffered during the past few weeks. How could it have come to this he pondered? One answer came to him: Nick Barton.

At that stage the door opened and the prison officer who had escorted him to the court that morning came in.

"Someone to see you," he said. "Come with me."

Patrick Saunders and a fairly rotund man with longish curly hair who also had a receding hairline awaited him in a room set aside for accused meeting their legal representatives. It was Spartan; it reminded him of a police interview room.

"How are you?" Patrick asked.

"Oh, great," said Roy. He stared fixedly at the table that separated him from his two legal representatives.

"Chin up," said the rotund man. "You're soon going to be on parade."

The man's accent reminded him of some of the boys he had been at school with. His school had been perhaps a cut above being a minor public school – the sort parents sent their children to for the benefit of its name. This man would have fitted in well there. Or Sandhurst. There was definitely a touch of the self-confidence of the military in that accent, too.

"This is Sir Joshua Partridge," said Patrick. "He's going to defend you."

Roy nodded. He remained quiet. Quite frankly, he couldn't think of anything to say to the man who possibly held his freedom in his hands.

"Well, say something, old chap," said Sir Joshua, trying to maintain an air of joviality. "Look, things are not as bad as they seem. There's no body. The thing they're relying on is the DNA evidence."

"Planted," said Roy firmly. "By Detective Chief Inspector Barton."

Sir Joshua mused for a moment. "Juries are sometimes loathe to believe that the police would stoop to such levels," he said, "and you've got no proof that he did."

"Other than the fact Kate Williams was never in my room, never in my car – let alone lying dead in a suitcase in the boot. And Detective Chief Inspector Barton – Nick – has harboured a grudge against me since his teenage years."

"That's not proof," said Sir Joshua. "That's just your statement. We might be on a sticky wicket there."

And you're the one telling me to keep my chin up, thought Roy. He sighed again. The idea of relying on a cricket loving military public schoolboy to sway the minds of twelve honest men and women representative of a rather larger swathe of society did not appeal to him.

"Why?" he asked.

"Well, they might not buy this grudge thing. It is a long time to harbour a grudge."

"He probably hasn't harboured it all the time," said Roy. "It was probably reawakened by just seeing me again."

"We'll try it on," said Sir Joshua, "But you're going to have to sound convincing. None of this 'oh, poor me' whiney stuff'."

Patrick Saunders butted in at this stage. "I'm sure Roy will do himself justice once he gets into the witness box," he said. "Besides we've got those testimonials on his behalf to read out – two respected leaders of headteachers' organisations, a former Secretary of State for Education. Pity we couldn't get the current one to deliver but it's still quite an impressive list." He took a piece of paper from his pocket and glanced at it. "Some respected academics, too," he added.

A wry smile came over Roy's face. "Yes, I wish now I'd been kinder to the government in some of the things I wrote. I could have got that endorsement from the current Secretary of State, then."

"At least it's not only endorsements from the Left. There's one here from a minister in the last government who says he respects your integrity and looks forward to you holding the education world to account now he's retired from office."

Sir Joshua held his hand out so that he could see the list. "Michael Renshaw." He sounded impressed. "Represented a constituency around here. Some of the jurors might even have voted for him."

"Trouble is," said Roy. "None of these people know what I might do in a moment of madness. The prosecution is bound to lay that on with a trowel."

"Better to have the testimonials than not have the testimonials," said Sir Joshua. "Look, I'd better go upstairs and get dressed for the occasion." He touched Roy's arm as he made for the door. "Remember, chin up."

Patrick stayed behind as Sir Joshua left the room. "Don't worry, Roy," he said. "We've got a sporting chance."

"Not you as well," said Roy.

"What do you mean?"

"All this, 'chin up', 'sporting chance'," he said. "I half expected Sir Joshua to say something like 'may the best man win'. Perhaps he'd like to toss a coin to determine the result of the trial."

"Look, you've got a good man batting for you in Sir Joshua," said Patrick. He groaned when he realised the impact his latest metaphor had on Roy. "I'll have to go now," he said. The prison officer who had been hovering around outside the door came in to take him back to his cell.

"It won't be long now," said Patrick as he disappeared up the stairs to the court house. "Ten minutes, I should think."

Roy managed a smile but his mind went back to the person who had put him in this predicament – Nick Barton. He recalled that night at the youth club thirty years ago when they had decided to call time on Roy and the Rivettes.

• • • • •

Nick had set up his drum kit at the youth club that evening and was using the empty church hall for rehearsal time. He was not often the first member of the band to arrive, Roy reflected as he and Johnnie Simons joined him that evening. He had already had a heart to heart with Johnnie. His application for a place on a journalism training course had been accepted, he had been informed by letter earlier on that day. It meant he would be moving to Harlow and that he would have to find digs there. He might get back at weekends but might not. The digs would be there at the weekends if he wanted to make use of them. He did not really know what he would be doing. It depended on how well he got on with his new colleagues on the course. What it did mean, though, was he would not be able to devote as much time to the band as he would have liked.

"I'm sorry, Johnnie," he had told the organist. "I feel I've led you on by saying there's a place in the band – and then pulling out myself."

"One thing's for sure, the Rivettes won't continue without Roy," said Johnnie. "No singer, no songs." He mimicked the Jamaican accent of Bob Marley as he spoke these words. Johnnie touched Roy's arm. "Don't worry, man," he said. "We're all growing up. We've got to decide what we want to do in life. You're not going to be the next Mick Jagger. I'm not going to be the next Alan Price."

"Thanks," said Roy, smiling.

"You might have disagreed with me," said Johnnie with a chortle. "Shall we do this last gig at the youth club, then?"

"Let's go out in style," said Roy as they approached the door of the parish hall and found Nick practising on his own. He had planned to tell Nick of his decision after the gig but when he saw him there on his own he thought it was the right time to let him know. Besides, he thought, all the members of the band had the right to know it was their last performance. "Charlotte not with you tonight?" he asked Nick as he approached him.

Instantly he realised it was the wrong question to ask. "Why do you want to know?" asked Nick frostily. Roy realised the drummer's jealousy and suspicion had not abated.

"No reason," said Roy. "I was just making conversation." He paused. "Nick," he began tentatively.

"That sounds as if you're going to say something I don't want to hear," said Nick. He was not looking at Roy as he spoke but instead busiest himself with altering the height of his cymbals. Roy thought he was deliberately avoiding eye contact.

"I don't know whether you'll want to hear it or not," said Roy. "But I'll be going away to college in September. I don't think I can keep going with the band. I think this could be our last gig."

Nick showed no emotion. "Oh," was all he said.

"So I thought I ought to tell all the band."

"Tell all the band what?" It was Graeme McAndrew who had just arrived in the company of Barrie Read. Barrie was furiously puffing away on a cigarette. Roy was not the only one to look at him quizzically. As far as they could all recall, Barrie did not smoke.

"Tell all the band I'll be leaving to go to college in September."

"So this is it?" asked Graeme.

"This is it. I wanted us to give one more rousing performance."

"One more rousing performance?" asked Barrie. "Why, when did we do the last one?"

"Come off it, Barrie," said Roy. "We've had some good times together."

"We may have had some good times. I'm not sure about anybody who was listening to us, though. I mean, what a band. A Boy Scout with big ears on the drums, the poor man's Mick Jagger blurting out lyrics, little surfer boy here," (he pointed at Graeme) wanting to play different songs all the time. Not realising our voices couldn't cope with two part harmonies – let alone four."

"And you, a horrible pot-smoking little shit," said Nick.

That was it, thought Roy. Barrie was smoking a marijuana joint. He should have detected it by the smell. Roy turned to Johnnie.

"Don't know how you've managed to escape in all the cross-fire," he said to him.

"Familiarity breeds contempt."

"If that's the way you feel, fucker, why not come and sort it out outside?" said Barrie to Nick.

"Little surfer boy doesn't think that's a good idea," Graeme intervened. "On the other hand it would be interesting to see who would win. You're a bit weedy," he said to Nick. "And you," he added turning to Barrie, "you're stoned."

The hall had now filled up. Barrie looked as if he was getting ready to throw a punch at someone – only he could not work out whether it should be Graeme or Nick. It was Johnnie who tried to calm the situation down. "Look, you four guys have played together for months – even a couple of years," he said. "Is it too much to ask of you to put your differences aside for one more evening? After all, everybody has come here expecting to hear you and enjoy themselves."

Graeme and Roy were quick to agree to Johnnie's suggestion. Barrie might have done but he appeared to have a dazed expression on his face. At least he was no longer in a hostile mood. Nick looked at his four colleagues. "Okay," he said. "Just give me a minute." He left the parish hall walking in the direction of the toilets. When he came back, his mood seemed lighter than it had done before. "Okay," he said. "Let's give it some wellie." With that, he sat at his drum-kit and crashed the cymbals.

Roy took the microphone and surveyed the scene. There was no Gillian Bird, he noticed. Then he remembered: she had told him her parents were taking her away for a week's holiday in the Isle of Wight. There were quite a few girls, though. Time to impress, he thought. They started off with a rollicking version of 'Good Golly, Miss Molly', then slowed down for 'Like I Did' and had just embarked upon 'You'd Better Move On' when the dancing was brought to a shuddering halt by the arrival of the police.

"All right," said a police sergeant. "Everybody stay still. We have reason to believe there are illicit drugs on the premises. Everybody will be searched."

Roy immediately looked at Barrie – realising the bass guitarist could be in trouble. He seemed deep in conversation with Graeme. The police began by searching the audience and dismissed them from the room one by one. They saved the band until last. Johnnie was soon eliminated from their enquiries. Then they moved on to Graeme. To the guitarist's surprise, the policeman who was searching him brought a packet out of his pocket.

"What's this, sir?" he asked aggressively.

Graeme took one look at it. "Jesus Christ," he said. Without waiting to draw breath, Graeme turned round and aimed a punch in Barrie's direction. It caught him a glancing blow on the cheek and he fell backwards. Two police officers immediately moved in on Graeme and pinioned his arms behind his back. "You're under arrest for assault and the suspicion of being in possession of an illegal substance," said one of the officers as he handcuffed Graeme's arms behind his back.

"But he wasn't," stuttered Roy as the two police officers took Graeme from the room.

"Excuse me sir," said a third PC as he put a restraining arm on Roy's shoulder. "We'll come to you in a minute."

Another police officer had made his way over to where Barrie was propping himself up on Johnnie's organ after reeling backwards from Graeme's punch. "Are you all right, sir?" he asked. Barrie nodded his head. "I'll have to search you as well," he said. The police officer found some cigarette papers in Barrie's pocket. He also could not escape the smell of marijuana that was emanating from Barrie's mouth despite the bass guitarist trying to keep it firmly shut. "I think, sir, you had better accompany us to the station as well," the police officer said. "I have reason to believe that you may have been in possession of illegal substances, too."

Barrie was not handcuffed but led away from the youth club by two officers. Roy overheard one saying to the other: "Looks like we've got a case of the other bloke supplying drugs and this one possessing." Their decision to handcuff Graeme and just walk away with Barrie seemed to indicate they did not believe Barrie represented a violent threat but thought Graeme did. The first two officers were back in the hall by now and quickly searched Roy and Nick. Nothing was found on either of them.

"Right," said one. "We're closing this event down now. You would all be wise to go home." The remaining members of the band waited until the crowd of teenagers had dispersed. "Wow," said Roy to Johnnie. "I didn't expect that for my last gig."

"Are you all right?" asked Johnnie.

"Fine," said Roy, "but I'm a bit worried about Graeme."

"Not Barrie?"

"I could have sworn Graeme didn't have any drugs on him. I think I'd better go down to the police station and see what happens."

"I'll come with you," said Johnnie quickly. It took him about twenty minutes to pack his organ up and drive the two of them down to the police station.

Once inside, they asked at the front desk what had happened to Graeme. The sergeant behind the desk went away and told them he was being questioned.

"You'd be better off going home," he said. "It could be a long time."

It was. Two hours, in fact, but Roy was not moved to go home. Johnnie appeared happy to wait with him.

At about midnight Graeme emerged from the inner recesses of the police station. He took one step backwards as he saw Roy and Johnnie. "Hey, what are you two doing here?" he asked.

"We couldn't think of anything better to do on a Sunday evening," said Roy. He hugged the guitarist as he went to sign himself out. "What happened?"

"Arrested on a charge of possessing an illegal substance," he said. "Bailed to appear back here again in a month's time."

"And the assault charge?"

"Dropped. Barrie said he would refuse to testify. He also denied that I had supplied him with the drug – so that charge was dropped in the end."

"So he came up trumps in the end?"

"Came up trumps? How do you think the drugs got into my pocket in the first place?" said an irritated Graeme.

"Let's get you home," said Johnnie. "Both of you," he added.

• • ● • •

Nick Barton arrived in court that morning early for a chat with his prosecution counsel before the trial got under way. Alan Dale was a sharp-suited fresh-faced young man from the Crown Prosecution Service. Efficiency was his by-word. He had been swotting up on the case for the last three days.

"Trouble is," said Dale. "This man is a well-respected journalist. You can expect a string of character witnesses saying he would never ever do anything like this – and you cannot contradict that."

"He was an amoral womaniser in his teens," said Nick, "but I suppose that doesn't amount to a can of beans in this case."

"Not unless you can suggest he attacked another of his women friends at some stage in his life, no."

"We have the DNA evidence," said Nick

"Yes, and they're going to suggest you planted that. Are you up to defending yourself on that charge?"

"Of course I am," said Nick aggressively. "It's the last resort of every guilty man to say that the police planted the evidence. You should know that."

"Come across a bit hurt that it should be suggested you tampered with evidence when you take the witness stand. Don't go all arrogant on me. You have a fine record of never having been up on a charge of contaminating evidence – or ever having been up on a disciplinary charge, Nick. Remember that."

Others were gathering as the two continued to talk to each other. Nick was aware that, as a witness, he would not be allowed into the court before he was called to give evidence.

"I have a good feeling about this one," said Nick. "I'm confident we'll get a conviction."

"Oh, are you?" said a female voice piping up behind Nick. It was Angela. She was accompanied by Jane McAndrew. "As confident as you are of escaping a murder charge for killing Graeme McAndrew? This is his sister. Care to tell her what part you played in her brother's death?"

Jane looked a little embarrassed at Angela's confrontational approach to Nick. The detective looked at her intently. "Jane?" he asked tentatively. "What are you doing here?"

"Is it true what Angela just said?" she asked.

"Of course not."

Alan Dale stepped in. "I should be careful what you say, Mrs....?"

"Hopkins, Ms Hopkins," replied Angela. "I have been very careful. I've accused Detective Chief Inspector Barton of murdering Graeme McAndrew. You work for the Crown Prosecution Service. You should investigate my claim."

"I don't have to listen to this," said Nick. He turned on his heels to leave the room.

"That's right. Run away, your sins will find you out, Detective Chief Inspector," said Angela.

"I'm going to have the court attendant throw you out of the building, Ms Hopkins," said Alan Dale, "if you don't desist from making these inflammatory remarks."

"That's all right. I've made my point." She and Jane began to move as if to join Patrick Saunders at the other end of the corridor. She turned, though, before, leaving. "I don't believe I caught your name," she said.

"That's because you never asked for it and I didn't give it to you," said Dale.

"Perhaps you would now. Jane," she said turning to Graeme's sister, "will be coming to see you at the end of this trial to lay a complaint against Detective Chief Inspector Barton and produce evidence of his involvement in the death of Graeme McAndrew."

Dale sighed. "Well, if you hang around for long enough you'll find out my name anyway when I'm introduced to the court," he said. He reached into his breast pocket and brought out a card. "I'm Alan Dale. I won't say I shall look forward to hearing from you."

Nick turned back to Alan Dale when Angela had moved out of earshot. "She's talking nonsense," he said.

"I hope so, Nick."

Angela, meanwhile, was bending Patrick Saunders' ear. "Can you not raise the issue of Graeme McAndrew's death?" she asked him.

"Who would we call to give evidence?"

"Me," said Angela defiantly.

"You know nothing about it."

"Well, Jane, then. She could say how he ignored her pleas for help. And what about Charlotte then?"

"Charlotte is Nick's wife. You won't find her giving evidence against him."

"You've got to stir up a hornet's nest. It's my Roy's whole future that's on the line."

• • • • •

Nick thought carefully about the case as he left the court that morning. He was told it was unlikely that he would be called as a witness until the following day. He went back to the police station to bury himself in some paperwork as he continued to contemplate giving evidence at Roy Faulkner's trial. He was within a hair's breadth of sending his old adversary away for life.

His mind, too, went back to that night at the youth club when Roy had told him the band would be folding for good. He could not remember feeling much emotion at the news. He enjoyed playing the drums but he would not miss any camaraderie as a result of the band packing up. As far as he was concerned there was none.

He remembered his attention being drawn by the entrance of Barrie Read, furiously puffing away on what later proved to have been marijuana joint. He had never liked Barrie. Indeed, he reflected, it would not have been unfair to suggest that nobody really liked Barrie. The bass guitarist only seemed to have one interest in life – himself – and if anybody got in the way of him furthering his interests he was a dab hand at stitching them up.

Nick reflected on this as he saw Barrie smoking his joint. The memory of the altercation between the two of them as the five of them contemplated the break-up of Roy and the Rivettes was still fresh in his mind. That was when he first thought of trying to cook Barrie's goose once and for all. A quick call to the local police station could bring that about. He thought about the power he had in his hands: the power to ensure that Barrie Read was possibly even put away in prison for a while. Actually, he reflected, that probably would not happen. A first offence, with no suspicion of dealing in the drug, would probably just merit a caution but it could be the start of something nasty spoiling Barrie's life. With hindsight, it could also have been the moment when he first persuaded himself that a career in the police service beckoned. The opportunity to put away people who were the dregs of society – the power that could be at his disposal as a policeman was quite alluring. Okay, Barrie Read might not have been the dregs of society but – to Nick at that moment – society would be best served by Barrie facing criminal charges and an upset to his way of life rather than a blind eye being turned to his criminal habit.

Nick was also ruminating on the fact that that evening was to be the band's last gig. He shrugged his shoulders. So what? However, he took a different line in conversation with Roy. He needed a moment to reflect on it, he said. He got up from his drums and ostensibly made to go to the toilet. Instead, though, he went to the telephone kiosk on the road from the church hall to the church itself and dialled the local police station telling the desk sergeant who answered that drugs were being dispensed openly at the youth club. Having done that, he returned to his drum-kit without a word and then told the band he was ready to play their last gig.

He was the only member of the youth club not to be surprised when the police arrived mob-handed about fifteen minutes later. He feigned surprise at their entry, though. As they started searching the audience at the youth club, his gaze wandered to where Barrie was standing. He could see that he was deep in conversation with Graeme. He could see him taking something out of his pocket and slipping it into Graeme's without the little surfer boy – as Barrie had accurately described him – noticing.

Barrie was planting the drugs on Graeme. In that split second, Nick realised he could have told a police officer what he had witnessed. However, he decided not to. For one thing, it could alert suspicions that he had been the one to have tipped the police off in the first place if it was realised he had been keeping his eye on Barrie. For another, he did not really care if Graeme got charged, too. He did not really like the guy. He was a bit of a waster. No job, no discipline in his life. Just a little surfer boy, he thought.

He watched as Graeme tried to deck Barrie and the two of them were escorted from the premises by the police. He heard the police call time on the youth club event and started dismantling his drum-kit by himself. He could see Roy engaged in earnest conversation with Johnnie. He never said good-bye to Roy that evening and indeed only saw him again for one or two fleeting moments before he went off to college. He did, however, briefly chat with Johnnie who moved over to him with an outstretched hand.

"I guess it's the parting of the ways," said the organist. "We never really got to talk but I thought you played the drums really well."

Nick accepted the handshake. "Thank you," he said. It was the first time he could remember anybody connected with the band giving him an iota of praise. "It won't sound sincere now," said Nick, "but I thought that some of the pieces you played on your organ showed real promise."

It was Johnnie's turn to smile now. "You've had a rough deal from this band," he said. "A lot of disrespect."

Thank you, thought Nick. At least someone had noticed it. "I can stand up for myself," he said, "and I will be doing so in future. These guys had better take note."

Johnnie smiled and left. Had that been a threat he was to ask himself later? Nick was left on his own to contemplate his part in the beginning of the downfall of Graeme and Barrie. Both of them were given suspended sentences when their cases came to trial. In Graeme's case, it served just to make him feel it was even more difficult to get a job and led him to taking the job as potman at the local pub – and an acquaintanceship with alcohol that never dimmed in his last few years. In Barrie's case, he lost his job as a result of the court case. The next few years found him facing a series of charges as he sought to replace his lost income with a series of burglaries – the proceeds from which he used to buy more drugs. He eventually died of an overdose.

In the present, Nick reflected, what had happened to Graeme and Barrie showed he had the power to shape and destroy lives.

The night's events, though, were not without their consequences for him either, though. It must have been about three weeks later that he was making his way home after band practice with the Scouts that three people approached him as he got out of his car outside his home. He did not recognise them. They were wearing masks. The one in front was wielding a baseball bat and swiftly hit him on the side of the head. He collapsed to the ground with the force of the blow. Whoever it was moved to strike him on the head with a second blow as he lay on the ground. The second person laid a restraining hand on his shoulder. "Hey, go easy, man," he said. "We just wanted to teach him a lesson."

"That's what I'm doing, little surfer boy," said the first person who then whacked him on the side of the head again. As Nick slipped out of consciousness on the ground, he caught a brief glimpse of the first attacker's striped bell-bottom trousers. Barrie, he thought. At this juncture, the one named as "little surfer boy" made it clear he was walking away from what was happening – as did the third person who never spoke a word. When Nick came round, he reflected on what had happened. They must have realised he was the person who had tipped the police off about drugs at the youth club. It had been Barrie and Graeme, he thought, but who was the third person? Only one name came to mind. If it was action by the band, it could only have been Roy.

He then felt his ribs. Whoever had attacked him must have hit him again while he lay unconscious on the ground. They felt sore and swollen. Once he had got back inside his house, he telephoned the police and – to their credit – they came round immediately. However, after he had given them all the information he had he could tell they were pessimistic about their chances of bringing a prosecution. They did interview Roy, though, and found he had an alibi – in a bitter irony, he had taken Gillian Bird out to the pictures that night. He had kept the tickets and also correctly answered a probing sergeant's questions about the plot of the film they had seen. Graeme had also taken a girlfriend out that night – and had been seen in a pub by a couple of friends. Barrie's alibi was that he had been with his father mending his bike. In the end, no charges were brought.

Nick accepted the police's decision but thought to himself that the assault demanded far more serious punishment than the police and the courts would hand down. I'll get my own back, in my own time, in my own way, he pledged to himself.

• • • • •

Rivers began reading the *Scotsman* again as he sat in his car about a hundred yards away from Craven's former cottage. He was waiting for the man whom he knew as Gerald to leave so that he could see if his wife would be more accommodating and allow him into the house.

As luck would have, Gerald appeared to be staying put. He had been there for three hours before he saw the man leave the house, get into a car and drive away, He needed no second bidding to try his luck with the woman whom he assumed to be the wife.

"Is that you, Gerald?" came a voice from inside the cottage. "Have you left something behind?" The woman opened the door and upon seeing Rivers merely said: "Oh."

"Philip Rivers," he said flashing a card in front of her eyes. "Private detective. Nothing to worry about but I'm investigating the man who had this cottage before you. I thought you might be able to help me."

"Oh," said the woman. She took the card from him and reached into her apron pocket to bring out a pair of spectacles. "Seems all right," she said. "Connie Latham." She offered him a hand to shake.

By his estimation, she must have been in her mid-sixties. She had a bit of a limp, he noticed, but she was quick to invite him in and sit him down.

"Would you like a cup of tea?" she asked.

"Thank you," he said. It was wise to respond in the affirmative. It would make her feel at ease – as if there was no rush to get down to business, "Tragic case," he said. "We believe he may have been responsible for the kidnapping of a young woman."

"My goodness," she said. "I didn't actually meet him but Gerald did. Said he was a bit of a rough diamond. I'm not sure what I can do to help."

"Have you done any work on the place since you moved in?" asked Rivers.

"No."

"In that case would you let me look around?"

"Surely. Do you think?" She paused. "Do you think his kidnap victim may have been held here?"

"It's possible," said Rivers.

"Well, Gerald didn't notice anything – but he's not that good at that type of thing. If he did hold her here, there's an ideal place. In the cellar."

Rivers had an image of Gerald alighting on a woman bound and gagged in the cellar and deciding it was not his business to do anything about it. He put the thought to the back of his mind and allowed Connie to lead him down to the cellar. It was quite cavernous. There was a recess at the back which looked as if it had been used previously for the storage of perhaps vintage wine bottles.

"Have you been down here before?" he asked.

"Just to look around. We haven't really disturbed anything."

Rivers continued with his search and went into the recess area. Under what would have once been a wine rack, he found something. It was dirty but it looked as though it was a comb. "Do you mind if I take this with me?" he asked.

"No. Oh my goodness. You think it may have belonged to her."

"Difficult to say. Could have been dropped by anyone. Even Mr Craven himself. So it might not mean anything." He resolved to go. "Thank you, you've been most helpful." He thought he ought to take his leave as soon as possible. He was sure Gerald would not have been happy about his wife fraternising with him.

Once he was back at his car, he took his mobile out of his pocket and dialled the number of Brighton police station. "Francesca Manners, please," he said when the station answered.

"Hallo," said a woman's voice on the other end of the telephone.

"Francesca?" She replied in the affirmative. "It's Philip Rivers. I've just come from Les Craven's old cottage. I've found something very interesting. A comb in the cellar. It could have been dropped by anybody but it could have been dropped by Kate Williams. It's a perfect place to hold someone hostage. I'll send it off to you immediately to get it DNA tested. How are things going?"

"The trial started today," she said. "It's expected to last about a week."

"So I'd better get my skates on."

"Yes."

He needed no second bidding and went straight to the Post Office to send the comb to Francesca Manners. Then he thought for a moment. He was in a race against time to try and prove Roy Faulkner innocent. He could do with some help, he reckoned. He telephoned Nikki. "Any chance you could come up here for a few days? I think I'm on to something but it's needle in a haystack time again. I think Craven held Kate Williams hostage here. I've been to his old cottage but he's moved on from there. I need to find him."

"Okay," said Nikki. It was a Friday. She had no conferences on until the middle of next week – and her employers were quite happy to give her a couple of days leave to sort out what she said was "a sudden emotional problem". They knew that her close friend had just been recovering from some kind of a nervous breakdown and assumed something had gone wrong with his recovery programme. She rang back to tell Rivers she could join him.

"Good," he said. "Could you also go down the hallway from my flat- and see if Mark Elliott could come up here with you as well?"

A couple of hours later both of them had booked themselves on a train to Edinburgh with the thought of renting a hire car when they arrived at the station.

• • ● • •

Alan Dale adjusted his spectacles as he got up from his chair to address the court.

"My Lord, members of the jury – the prosecution's case is this. That, in the early morning of Saturday, May 3, the accused Roy Faulkner." He took time out to point at him and hold him in his stare for a moment "did murder Kate Williams," he began.

"The two were journalists assigned to cover the National Association of Headteachers' annual conference in Brighton which began that Saturday morning. They both arrived the previous evening and ended up having a meal on their own together at an Italian restaurant in the Lanes. These facts are not disputed.

"They then went on to a night club – the Lucky Star – where the accused admits he stayed until 2.30 in the morning when he says he left Miss Williams, whom he also admits at that stage to be tipsy from the drink they had both consumed – as he realised he had to get up for work the following morning.

"No witnesses have come forward to say they saw them leaving separately. No witnesses, hotel staff or anyone, saw Mr Faulkner arriving back at the hotel on his own."

Roy tried to catch Sir Joshua Partridge's eye at this point. He wanted to impress upon the barrister that no witnesses had seen them arriving back together, either. He saw Patrick Saunders leaning forward to speak to Sir Joshua and hoped he was making the same point. Sir Joshua nodded.

"It is the prosecution's case that Mr Faulkner – who has a reputation as something of a womaniser – invited Miss Williams back to his room where something went wrong. They had a row. Maybe she changed her mind and didn't want to sleep with him."

Sir Joshua managed to persuade his portly frame to rise from the bench. "Objection," he barked. "Pure conjecture."

"I apologise," said Alan Dale. The judge, whom Roy felt had given a passable imitation of being asleep, nodded. "The jury will disregard that remark," he said.

Easier said than done, thought Roy. Dale had managed to implant the idea in their subconscious even though the judge had told them to dismiss it from their conscious minds.

"Something happened," continued Dale. "DNA confirms that Kate Williams had been in Mr Faulkner's room. DNA next confirms that she was in a suitcase found in Mr Faulkner's room. It then goes on to show she had been in the boot of his car. I think the jury will see that these are not places that an alive Miss Williams would visit so the prosecution maintains Mr Faulkner killed her – it may well have not been a premeditated killing but a spur of the moment accident. He then sought to cover up what he had had done by placing her body in a suitcase and transporting it to the boot of the car.

"Sadly, CCTV cameras in the car park were not working at the time so we have no sighting of Mr Faulkner putting the suitcase in the boot but – fast forward to mid-morning – and we do have evidence that Mr Faulkner drove out of the car park and returned a couple of hours later. When initially questioned by the police, Mr Faulkner made no mention of this trip. It was only when it was brought to his attention by the police that he admitted he had driven up to Beachy Head for a couple of hours – a place that holds memories for him. We maintain that it will hold memories for him in future – bad ones – because that was when he dumped Miss Williams' body." At this juncture Dale paused for a sip of water.

"Is that it?" asked the judge. Roy warmed to him. He appeared to be quite sharp and maybe suggesting the prosecution had not done enough to persuade him of their case. Patrick Saunders had looked him up on the internet the previous evening and told Roy that Lord Justice Anderson had a fine legal brain and was considered by most of the barristers who had come before him to be scrupulously fair. He was also in tune with the world around him. If the history of Roy and the Rivettes came before the court, it was quite likely he would have heard of numbers like 'You'd Better Move On'.

Mr Dale shook his head. "I'm sorry, my Lord, I was merely pausing," he said.

"Fine. Carry on."

"We have evidence of Mr Faulkner's state of mind that evening. The journalists who were covering the headteachers' conference were all invited to a reception by the headteachers that Saturday evening. Kate Williams, obviously, did not turn up – whereupon the accused became agitated. So much so that one of his colleague, Mark Elliott, was moved to phone her and ask her to phone either him of the accused immediately because he "thinks he might have killed you". We have a copy of that voicemail which we can play for the jury." Dale pointed to a court official who was tending a tape recording and nodded. The voicemail was played.

What he's not saying, thought Roy, is that Mark must have thought she was still alive after talking to me. Otherwise, he would not have made the phone call.

"So there you have it," said Mr Dale. "Mr Faulkner and Miss Williams go out to a night club. She returns to his room. Her body is placed in his suitcase which is then placed in the boot of his car. He then drives it to Beachy Head where he disposes of the body. Later that night he feels agitated about what he has done – agitated enough for a friend and trusted colleague to try and find out if she is still alive. That is the nub of the prosecution's case."

"Admirably succinct, Mr Dale," said the judge.

"I should like therefore to call my first witness."

The judge looked at his watch. "You can do that, Mr Dale, after we have broken for a spot of lunch," he said.

"Court rise," said an usher as Mr Justice Anderson left the room leaving the participants to ruminate on how the first morning of the trial had gone.

"At least they haven't sprung any surprises on us," Sir Joshua said to Patrick Saunders as he collected his papers and made for the exit. "Be a huge moment this afternoon, though. I'm assuming Detective Chief Inspector Barton will be their first witness. I had been thinking Dale would spend a lot longer on his opening submission. Maybe Nick Barton thought the same and we can catch him off guard."

• • • • •

"I call Detective Chief Inspector Nicholas Barton," said Alan Dale at the start of the afternoon's proceedings in the court room.

His voice was echoed by an usher and Nick stepped through the door and made his way to the witness box. He looked straight ahead of him, never glancing from side to side, and was sworn in.

"You are Detective Chief Inspector Nicholas Barton and you were put in charge of investigating Kate Williams' disappearance and subsequent murder," said Dale.

"That is right, sir," said Nick stiffly. "We were apprised of her disappearance by her sister, Barbara, who lives in Brighton. Despite being assigned to cover the National Association of Headteachers' conference in Brighton she had made no contact with her national newspaper – something which was completely out of character.

"And foolish if she wanted to keep her job," interjected Dale.

"Precisely." Nick cleared his throat. Roy was trying to fix him with a stare but the detective was looking fixedly at the prosecutor. A sweat bead formed on his forehead – unusually for him.

"By process of inquiry, we ascertained she and the accused had been at the Lucky Star night club until the early hours of Saturday morning. That was the last time she had been seen."

"What led you to upgrade this inquiry into a murder inquiry, inspector?" asked Dale.

"What you said," replied Nick. "It would have been career suicide for her just to have stopped contacting her paper – and those that knew her best, her sister and her journalist colleagues could not believe that she would risk that. Then there was the accused, Roy Faulkner. I just had a hunch he was not telling the truth when he said he had abandoned a tipsy woman at a night club at 2.30 in the morning. It's not the sort of thing a decent man would do."

Oh yes, and he murdered her instead, thought Roy. Obviously, the sort of thing a decent man would do. Nice one, Nick.

"I began to investigate him and subsequently found evidence of her DNA in his bedroom, in his suitcase and in the boot of the car – leading me to only one conclusion."

"And that was?"

"That he had killed her. You don't ask someone to get into a suitcase in the boot of your car if you're just taking them out for a drink. Also, he failed to mention that he had driven to Beachy Head at midday on Saturday – a time when you might have thought he would have been doing his duty and reporting on the conference. He only admitted it after we confronted him with evidence that his car had left the car park."

"Detective Chief Inspector, you're satisfied with the DNA samples you obtained? I ask this because I believe the defence will challenge their authenticity."

"DNA is DNA and – as to any suggestion that I or one of my officers planted the evidence – well, I have full faith in all of my team."

"And yourself?"

"No-one has ever suggested that I have ever acted in a way other than scrupulously fairly in the investigation of cases that have come my way. I maintained that high standard in this case." He allowed himself a stare at Roy at this moment as if to say: Come on, have the guts to challenge me. You'll lose.

"It is, therefore, in your opinion, a straightforward case."

"Yes, sir."

Dale nodded and turned on his heels. "Your witness." he said to Sir Joshua Partridge.

Sir Joshua struggled to his feet and manoeuvred his paunch around his desk so he could approach Nick in the witness box.

"You know Roy Faulkner, don't you, Detective Chief Inspector?" he said.

"We grew up together."

"Do you like him?"

"We performed in a rock band together when we were teenagers." Nick almost managed a blush as he admitted this. It was not the sort of thing you expected to be on the CV of a policeman.

"Not really an answer, is it? Evokes a cosy image of rebellious teenagers all together having a lark when the fact is, you hated him."

Dale rose to his feet. "I'm not sure where we're going with this line of questioning but it seems irrelevant to me, my Lord," he said.

"And to me," said Lord Justice Anderson. "What are you trying to say, Sir Joshua? Spit it out."

"I'm trying to establish a motive for the Detective Chief Inspector to want to frame my client for this killing, your Lordship."

"Which I didn't," said Nick.

"Detective Chief Inspector, you're there to answer questions. Kindly wait for them to be put to you," said the judge. "Go on, Sir Joshua. But don't go round too many houses."

"Very good, your Lordship. You've harboured a grudge against my client for years over a girlfriend you once had – and you couldn't believe your luck when he turned up as the main suspect in a woman's disappearance."

"I hadn't seen him for thirty years. It's a long time to harbour a grudge."

"Precisely."

"I meant I didn't have one."

"You could have easily obtained access to his room, to his suitcase and possibly even his car to plant the evidence."

"But I didn't. It was uncovered as a result of routine police work."

"I don't believe you."

"The jury must be the arbiter on that," interjected Lord Justice Anderson. "Kindly disregard defence counsel's last remark," he said to the jurors.

"There were two other members of the band you didn't like, weren't there, Detective Chief Inspector, and they're both dead."

Nick looked shocked. Dale rose to his feet.

"My Lord," he said, "the Detective Chief Inspector is not on trial here."

"I'll move on," said Sir Joshua.

"No," said Nick. "You won't. It's true Graeme McAndrew and Barrie Read are both dead – one in a car accident and the other as a result of an overdose of drugs. Sad accidents, both of them but of no relevance to this case."

Lord Justice Anderson rose to his feet. "Counsel, my chambers," he said firmly. He turned to the jury. "I am going to have to debate a matter with counsel for the prosecution and the defence. Court is adjourned for the time being."

The court rose as Lord Justice Anderson was followed out of the room by Dale and Sir Joshua

"What is going on out there?" he asked Sir Joshua once all three were seated in his chambers. "Are you accusing Detective Chief Inspector Barton of murder?"

"I thought the jury deserved to know a little bit more about the Detective Chief Inspector's history."

"Do you consider he should be charged with murder?"

"I was merely going to suggest that fate sometimes seems to take a hand when it comes to people who have crossed the detective chief inspector."

"Weasel words. Not good enough. Either you put the record straight when we return to the court room or I order a retrial."

Sir Joshua thought for a moment. He had used the oldest trick in the book to plant a seed in the jury's mind. It was planted and – if there was to be a retrial – there was a strong possibility he would not be allowed to allude to the matter again. "I'm happy to say there is no evidence of his involvement in their deaths," he said.

"Are you happy with that?" the Lord Justice asked Dale.

"I'm not happy, no."

"But you'll accept my ruling." It was not a question and the three of them then trouped back into court.

Sir Joshua then addressed the court. "Before the adjournment I alluded to the death of two former band members who had played with Detective Chief Inspector Barton in a band some years ago. I was not going on to suggest the detective played any part in their deaths."

In the public gallery, Angela frowned. "There was evidence given to my client, though, that he gloated over their deaths when he heard of them. I was attempting to show you what kind of man he was – the kind that could have stooped to tampering with evidence to get back at someone he disliked. The kind who harboured a grudge for years – and let it fester."

"If I may intervene," said Nick looking at the judge.

"Wait until Mr Dale has his chance to put further points to you," came the reply.

"A couple of other points," said Sir Joshua. "We are told that Mark Elliott's voicemail in which he said that Faulkner 'thinks he may have killed you' to Kate was evidence of my client's state of mind. Do you know Mark Elliott?"

"No."

"So you don't know that he's the kind of chap who would make light of such a remark – and think it was a joke?"

"A joke in poor taste, I would think," said Nick.

"A joke nonetheless and not evidence of agitation on the part of my client. That was not a question, by the way." Nick sat glumly in the box waiting for the next question.

"You do know there was a witness to the fact that someone coerced Kate Williams into a car outside the Lucky Stars night club on the night of her disappearance – long after my client had departed the scene to go to bed?"

"There was a woman who claimed a friend who is now dead had seen that."

"You chose not to believe her?"

"I interviewed her. Her evidence at best was hearsay and – when it came to the crunch she refused to give evidence. I came to the conclusion this court would not miss out on any evidence by not hearing what she had to say."

"You didn't try to dissuade her from giving evidence."

"That's not my job," retorted Nick. He was feigning anger well, Roy thought.

"I know it's not your job – but I put it to you that you only went to see this woman to persuade her not to give evidence so you could pursue your persecution of my client."

"No," said Nick. He decided not to elaborate on his reply.

"Where's the body?"

"I'm sorry?"

"In a case of murder, it's usual for there to be a body – that of the victim."

"Oh," said Nick. "Well, I assume it's buried somewhere up on Beachy Head. That's where your client drove to with it in the boot of his car after he had killed her."

"It's not possible then that Kate Williams is still a prisoner of the man who abducted her from the night club. The white van man that my client and Miss Williams were talking to earlier in the evening of her disappearance."

"No-one abducted her. Her DNA is in the boot of your client's car."

"Not possible that she may have had some kind of a breakdown – and disappeared of her own accord. She had a stressful job working for one of our tabloid newspapers."

"I can't think why she would voluntarily get into a suitcase in the back of your client's car before staging her disappearing act – which she would have had to do if that were to be the case."

"Unless you, the man who gloated over Graeme McAndrew and Barrie Read's deaths, had planted the evidence in the boot of my client's car out of malice."

"Which I didn't."

Sir Joshua lowered his glasses down his nose and fixed Nick with a stare. "That is all, Detective Chief Inspector." he said. He smiled as he passed Alan Dale on the way back to his seat.

"Redirect?" Dale asked the judge, getting swiftly to his feet.

"Of course."

"Detective Chief Inspector, did you gloat over the deaths of these two band members?" Dale, having not been pre-warned that their deaths would crop up in the trial, could not remember their names.

"No sir."

"And will you gloat if Roy Faulkner is given a life sentence for the murder of Kate Williams?"

"I will take satisfaction in a job well done by the police," said Nick. "But gloat? No." He looked hard ay Roy as he spoke.

"And, just to put the record straight, did you tamper with any of the DNA evidence in this case?"

"No, sir, I did not."

"I have no further questions."

"Step down, Detective Chief Inspector Barton," said the judge. Nick buttoned his jacket and left the witness stand. The beads of sweat were now not only on his forehead but under his armpits, too. He was glad his ordeal was over.

CHAPTER TEN

Angela made a bee-line for Sir Joshua Partridge as he left the court that day. "Why didn't you pursue the deaths of Graeme McAndrew and Barrie Read?" she demanded to know.

He was about to reply just as Jane McAndrew caught up with Angela and stood next to her waiting expectantly for the answer.

"Who's this?" asked the barrister, irritated.

"Jane McAndrew," she said proffering her hand.

"I'm Graeme McAndrew's sister."

Sir Joshua accepted her handshake and then mopped his brow. "I'm sorry for your loss," he said, suddenly adopting a more sympathetic tone. He then turned to Angela. "Because it wouldn't have helped us," he said. "We have no proof that Detective Chief Inspector Barton had anything to do with their deaths. Indeed, in the case of Barrie Read, he appears not to have known about the death until a while after it happened. What we do have is evidence that he gloated over their deaths – and would be likely to do the same thing if a similar fate befell Roy Faulkner. Now, obviously he can't kill Roy that easily – so what better than to take advantage of the opportunity to put him away for twenty years by finding him guilty of murder? We have left that impression with the jury."

"Not strongly enough," ventured Angela. Jane nodded.

"I'm sorry you think that. I think we left a few seeds of doubt about Detective Chief Inspector Barton's evidence in the jury's mind. However, if you think you can do my job better than me." His voice tailed off. "Besides," he added. "The judge wasn't about to let me pursue that line of enquiry. Now, if you don't mind, it's been a long day and I have to go back to my chambers to sort one or two things out before I go home." Actually, to the wine bar across the road from chambers, he thought to himself.

Angela seemed oblivious to what he had just said. "About the defence you're presenting."

"Yes?" he said. His voice betrayed just that little sense of irritation again.

"Are you going to mention the man in the white van?"

"No, I think I'll give the jury a lecture on the life-span of a rhinoceros instead," he said sarcastically. "Of course, I'm going to mention white van man."

"Good – and what about Philip Rivers?"

"What about Philip Rivers?"

"Well, are you going to call him as a witness so he can tell the jury about his enquiries?"

"What? So he can tell the jury he has been scouring the land to find this man – and hasn't had any success? I don't think so. He could be taken apart in cross examination. Best, again, just to sow the seeds of doubt in the jury's mind and leave them to come to their own conclusion." The thought of a glass of red wine was now looming too large in his mind's eye to concentrate on anything else. "Now, you really must excuse me."

Angela decided not to pursue Sir Joshua any further. As he walked away, though, she muttered to Jane: "That man is going to lose the case for us – I'm convinced of it."

• • ● • •

Nick went straight back to the police station after finishing giving his evidence and marched up to Francesca's door. He did not observe the usual courtesy of knocking on it before entering. Instead, he flung it open. "What the hell have you done?" he asked her.

"Good afternoon, Francesca, how's your day been?" she said – annoyed at his method of entry.

Nick approached her desk and stared directly at her from across the table. "I repeat – what the hell have you done?"

"What do you mean?"

"I mean, how did Roy Faulkner's defence know about Marie Coombs? How did they come to suggest that I might have frightened her off from testifying?"

"I....I don't know."

"Oh, yes, you do," he said banging his fist on the table. "The only way they could have found out about her is through you. Are you deliberately trying to undermine my case?"

"Nick, you know I have issues with the way you have conducted the case. I think you've taken a blinkered attitude towards it. If the evidence hasn't supported your theory that Roy Faulkner is guilty, then you're just not interested in it."

"The evidence does support my theory that Roy Faulkner is guilty. Just look at the DNA evidence."

"Yes, well...." began Francesca. Then her voice tailed off.

"Come on," said Nick. "Come on, don't be shy. What are you trying to say?"

"I think you know what I'm trying to say."

"Remember, Detective Sergeant Manners," he said – adopting a menacing tone, "I have friends in high places in this police force."

"Yes, I know that." said Francesca. Then she bit her tongue for intervening.

"Oh, you do, do you? Then you'll realise that when this case is proved and Roy Faulkner is put where he belongs there will be consequences for you. I don't think we'll ever be able to work together again as a result of your insubordination. You'll be transferred from here." He turned as if to leave the room but stopped just before reaching the door. "Or worse," he added before finally departing.

Francesca breathed a sigh of relief at his departure. She ignored his threats. She had rather expected them. She picked up one or two papers from her desk and started to read them. She found it difficult to concentrate, though. Her thoughts were interrupted as the telephone rang.

"Detective Sergeant Manners," she said.

"Forensics here," came the reply. "The comb you sent me for DNA testing."

"Yes?"

"It's not Kate Williams'."

"Are you sure?" It was a silly question. They would not have rung her up to tell her a lie but the truth was she was beginning to wonder just how much control Nick was having over events. She pulled herself together. That really was a thought too far. Nick had not even known she had sent the comb for DNA testing. He could not have intervened in the process.

"Do you want me to carry out any other tests on it?"

"No, thanks, just leave it for now. I'll get back to you later."

• • ● • •

Nick sped away from the police station that evening. As he stopped at the traffic lights at the end of the road, he drummed with his fingers on the dashboard. Francesca had not been the only person to betray him. Charlotte must have done so, too. Probably when she went to visit Roy Faulkner in prison. He completed the drive home in fifteen minutes rather than his usual twenty. As he entered the front door, Charlotte came to greet him.

"How did it go?" she asked him.

"You probably know just as well as me," he said.

"What?"

"Well, the defence seemed to know all about my reaction to the deaths of Graeme McAndrew and Barrie Read. I wonder how they found that out."

"Oh."

"You might well say 'oh'. From you, obviously. Honestly, I don't know – it's bad enough having my Detective Sergeant going behind my back to try and undermine the case I have built up but you – you're supposed to be my wife." He walked past her and into the living room where he wrenched his tie off and sat down on the settee.

"Get me a drink," he ordered. "Scotch. Neat. No ice. Double."

Charlotte thought she had better do as she had been bidden. She poured the drink from the cabinet in the far corner of the room and took it over to her husband. He snatched it from her and gulped it down. "Another," he said, holding the glass out to her.

"Darling, don't you think?"

"Another," he repeated, "and don't call me Darling. You don't mean it." She refreshed his glass and brought it over to him. "Honestly," he said, snatching it from her, "I've a good mind to give you a darn good beating again. You deserve it."

"I wouldn't do that," said a voice from the doorway. It was Sarah, his daughter. She had been upstairs reading and had heard the sound of what seemed like raised voices and decided to come downstairs and investigate.

Nick decided against swigging the second glass straight down his throat. "I'm sorry," he said. "I didn't realise you were in."

"Obviously."

"I'm sorry, love, I've just had a bad day."

"And that's justification for threatening to hit my mother? I don't think so."

"Well," began Nick. He stopped. He could not think what to say so sipped his drink instead.

"Maybe," said Charlotte, plucking up the courage to speak, "maybe you deserved a bad day."

"What do you mean by that?" he snapped.

"Maybe Roy Faulkner is not the murderer you think he is."

"That's got nothing to do with you," he snapped.

"Yes, it has," she continued. "Roy was a good friend to me in my teenage years."

"I'm well aware of that," he snapped again. "I was outside in the car, remember. That night you decided to invite him in for a drink – and he fucked you."

"I remember that night very well. And it wasn't him that fucked me." A look of astonishment came over Sarah's face. "Sorry, darling," Charlotte added.

Nick remained silent. He did not want to go down that road any more. Not while Sarah was in the room, anyway. He sighed.

"Okay," he said. "I'm sorry, too. Maybe we should all keep our cool and let the trial take its course."

"I'm not aware of anyone else in the room losing their cool, Dad," said Sarah.

Nick nodded. "Point taken," he said. He realised he had nothing to gain from pursuing his aggressive line towards Charlotte – at least not while Sarah was staying in the house. He sipped his drink slowly now as a thought struck him. "You're not going to spring any more surprises on me, are you?" he asked.

A frown came over Charlotte's face. "What do you mean?" she asked.

"Like testifying for Roy Faulkner?"

"I haven't been asked to."

There was something in her tone that suggested to him that she would be quite happy to do so.

"Don't," he said. "Look," he added, "I think I'll go down to the pub for a couple of pints." It was quite out of character for him to do so but neither of the two women in the room moved as if to stop him. It seemed to him as if neither of them really wanted him there. "Don't worry," he said, "I'm not going to get hammered. It's just that – after today – I'd like to sit just quietly on my own for a while and I don't think I can do that here." He picked his glass up with the remnants of the whisky in it and went into the kitchen to pour the contents into the sink – as if to prove to Charlotte and Kate that he meant what he said about not getting hammered.

Charlotte decided to offer him an olive branch. "Do you want some dinner when you get back?" she asked.

Nick smiled. "No," he said. "I'll get something at the pub – but thanks for the offer." He left telling himself to get a grip on things. After all, the case was still strong. Roy Faulkner might still be convicted on the DNA evidence. These displays of petulance would only serve to undermine his confidence. Those that witnessed them would believe he had little faith in his case.

Meanwhile, Charlotte poured herself a drink after he had gone and offered one to Sarah who accepted. They both sat down.

"You shouldn't let him threaten you," said Sarah.

"He didn't really," said Charlotte who seemed always to have an ability to see the best side of people.

"He said he wanted to give you a beating."

"But he didn't."

"Only because I came into the room – and he has hit you before. We both know that."

"Only the once," said Charlotte.

"Once is enough, Mum," protested Sarah. "I would never stay with a man who hit me."

"Darling, I've been with him for thirty years."

"I notice you didn't say thirty happy years."

"No." It sounded like she was agreeing with her daughter.

"Then what are you going to do?" asked Sarah.

"It's not as simple as all that," began Charlotte, "but I do think that once this trial is over …" She paused.

"Yes?"

"Once this trial is over, I should move out. If Roy is found guilty, I don't think I could live with your father. I'm sure he's innocent and therefore that must mean your father planted the evidence against him."

"If you're sure of that, why don't you tell someone?"

"What proof do I have?" Then she answered her own question. "Just the fact that Roy Faulkner is a decent human being."

"Maybe you should volunteer to tell the trial that?"

"No," said Charlotte, "that would be a step too far. But I shall be leaving you father once it's all over."

"I'll stay around for the summer," said Sarah. "Make sure you're all right." Charlotte smiled and squeezed her daughter's hand.

• • ● • •

"So it's not Kate Williams comb?" said Rivers as he received the information from Francesca Manners. "That's odd." He thought for a moment about the implications of the discovery.

"What do you think that means?" asked the Detective Sergeant.

"Well, logically it means someone else was in that cellar."

"You mean?" Francesca's voice tailed off as she caught up on the implications of what they had just been told.

"Either he was holding two people in that cellar – or he never held Kate Williams a prisoner there. That could mean she's now dead. And that doesn't really help Roy Faulkner. It means we've got nothing to link Craven to Kate Williams." He paused for thought. "Unless, of course, we find her DNA in a search of the cottage. Could you organise that?"

"I'm not exactly flavour of the month here," said Francesca. "I don't think I could get permission to organise a trawl of the cottage – just on the off chance it might have Kate Williams' DNA in it. You could say that of a lot of places."

"So what do we do?" It was a rhetorical question. Rivers was thinking out loud. He answered it himself. "We find out who's DNA it is."

"Chances are whoever it is will not be on our files," said Francesca.

"I know but if we had an idea who that person was we could check it out against that person's DNA."

"But we don't."

"Natalie Craven," said Rivers. "Craven's wife. She's gone missing. She was filing for divorce until a few weeks ago and then her solicitor heard nothing further from her."

"But why would Craven want to kidnap his wife and another woman?"

"I'm not a psychologist," said Rivers. "I can't even look into Craven's mind and decide why he decided to kidnap Kate Williams. Let's find out who the DNA belongs to and then try and piece the whole thing together." He paused for a moment. "Perhaps he wanted to degrade her, forcing her to watch while he sexually assaulted another woman."

"Yuk," said Francesca.

"Come on, you must have come across worse things in your life as a copper. Anyhow, let's find out if it is her, first of all. Go down and see her solicitor, Stephen Aymes. He can show you to her house. You can do this, can you? They'll give you time to investigate this?"

Francesca gave a wry chuckle. "They don't seem to mind what I do – so long as I keep out of their way. Nick made it clear there would be serious repercussions for me if Roy Faulkner was found guilty. The very least would be transfer to another station."

"I would have thought getting away from him would be a bonus."

"You may not understand this but he's been a good policeman. It's just that he seems obsessed with proving Roy Faulkner guilty." She stopped what she was saying. There was no point in trying to persuade Rivers that Nick Barton had his good points. "I'll go down to Natalie Craven's tomorrow morning and bring back something so we can test her DNA. I won't be able to get a team to go down there with me."

"Good luck," said Rivers as he switched his mobile off and

turned to the two other people in the room – Nikki Hofmeyr and Mark Elliott.

"Did you hear that?" he asked. They both nodded. "So what do we do now?" There was a silence – only broken by the sound of Rivers' mobile ringing again.

"Philip Rivers," he said as he picked up the call.

"Patrick Saunders," said the voice at the other end. "We're trying to put our defence strategy together. Angela's here with me. How are you?"

"I'm fine but you don't really want to know about my welfare. I'm making progress slowly."

He heard another voice from the other end of the line.

"That's not good enough," it snapped.

"Good evening, Angela," said Rivers politely.

"What do you mean by that?" asked Saunders. "Only, I'm trying to work out whether it would be worth our while calling you as a witness tomorrow."

"I wouldn't have thought so," said Rivers. "I'd better go."

"You mean you've got nothing to report? What a waste!" came the loud retort from Angela.

"No, I mean what I said. I'm making progress slowly. Les Craven did hold someone prisoner in his cellar in the cottage he lived in in Scotland. Trouble is he's moved on and it wasn't Kate Williams."

"So he's got no connection with Kate Williams and you've just been wasting all that bloody money we've been lavishing on you."

"What a bitch," exclaimed Nikki out of earshot of the mobile. Rivers motioned her to silence.

"No," he said. "It doesn't mean he hasn't also been holding Kate Williams captive. It's just that we can't prove that yet."

"Do you know where he is now?" asked Saunders.

"Not yet," said Rivers.

"Oh God. Words fail me," said Angela.

Rivers smiled. That, he thought, would make the rest of the telephone conversation more palatable.

"So what are you going to do now?" asked Saunders.

"Trawl all the estate agents around the area and ask them if they've rented out a cottage or dwelling with a cellar – and then go and visit them all. If we start at the crack of dawn we could have the operation completed by nightfall."

"We'd best leave you to it," said Saunders.

"Give me the phone," said Angela. Oh God, thought Rivers, she's rediscovered her voice. "You'd better bloody come up with something," she said. "I heard that you were washed up, hadn't worked for months. Now it looks as though that's true. Trouble is my Roy's whole future is dependent upon you. Get your act together."

"It is together," he said slowly but – as he shut down the mobile phone rather abruptly – he reflected. "I can see where she's coming from," he said. "She's about to lose her partner because I can't find Les Craven."

"I would say you've done a darn good job getting as far as you have," said Mark. "Les Craven's gone missing. He doesn't want to be found. Yet we're on the verge of doing precisely that."

Nikki simply moved towards him and squeezed his hand. "Don't lose faith in yourself, Philip," she said. "We haven't."

He smiled. "Well, at least we've got one thing to be thankful to Angela for," he said.

"What's that?" asked Mark.

"Her anger at least prompted me to come up with a strategy while I was on the phone. We'll have to trawl through all the estate agents tomorrow morning. Face to face visits, I think. I can pull rank on them as a private detective."

"Investigative journalist mould for me," said Mark. "You know when I came into this job I was shown an article by a famous journalist saying what the three qualities of a successful journalist should be – a plausible manner, rat-like cunning and a little literary ability. Time for me to show the first two. Sod the third."

Rivers looked at Nikki. He sensed she was nervous. "I'll be all right," she said.

"Some ground rules," continued Rivers. "If you find someone has rented a cottage with a cellar, don't go and check it out on your own. If Craven has kidnapped two women, he'll be dangerous. We all go together to anywhere we find. Secondly, he may not have rented the cottage in his own name. If he has kidnapped two women, it would hardly be surprising if he had an accomplice and – if he doesn't want to be found – it'll have been booked in their name." He paused. "Until tomorrow, then," he said.

"Until tomorrow," they chorused.

• • ● • •

Angela woke like a bear with a sore head the following morning. She looked at her watch and noticed it was approaching 10am – the time she should have been in court to support Roy. Truth was, though, she had felt so angry the previous evening. Nobody seemed to care about defending Roy. Sir Joshua Partridge didn't seem too concerned about her partner's future. Philip Rivers seemed to be making little or no progress and was just enjoying a holiday in Scotland with his floosie and a journalistic chum at Roy's expense. She had returned home from Patrick Saunders' flat needing a drink – and another drink – and another drink. Hence the sore head. She was not used to it.

She prised herself out of bed and dressed as quickly as she could and drove to the court. She may well have been still over the limit, she reflected as she noticed a police car behind her. Luckily she was doing no wrong and it did not stop her. Much to her amazement, she managed to make it to the court by 11am and signalled to Patrick Saunders to step outside for a moment.

"What's happened?" she asked.

"We've had two witnesses," he said. "Kate Williams' sister who said she would have valued her career too much to have done a bunk and her news editor who said much the same thing. The prosecution has wrapped its case up and Sir Joshua is about to start our defence." Angela nodded, which hurt her head, and the two of them made their way back into the court room. Sir Joshua was just getting to his feet, a manoeuvre which took more time than Alan Dale would have done.

"My client is innocent," he began. "He has no history of violence, no history of aggression towards women. On the night in question, he accompanied Kate Williams – a journalist he neither knew well nor would have had much in common with – to a meal in a restaurant. He hadn't meant to dine with her alone. The table was booked for six – but the other four just didn't turn up. After the meal, they decided to go on to a night club near the hotel – the Lucky Star. They resumed drinking and my client will admit that Miss Williams did look a little the worse for wear when he looked at his watch and saw it was 2.30am and decided he had better go back to the hotel to bed if he was to cover the conference adequately for his paper that morning. End of story. With hindsight, the only thing he regrets is leaving her at the night club and not insisting he escort her back to the hotel." Sir Joshua paused and mopped his brow.

"The story doesn't end there, though," he said. "While my client never saw Miss Williams again, she disappeared off the face of the earth and he became the main suspect in a police murder investigation. The prosecution's case is that her DNA was found in my client's room, the boot of his car and his suitcase. Ergo he must have killed her. He also drove to Beachy Head the following morning. Ergo he must have dumped the body. There is, though, an alternative explanation. While the two of them were at the night club, they got chatting to a man who went on and on about his divorce and what a difficult time he was having. White van man on account of the van he was driving and which he left parked outside the night club. Now, my client is a modest man and realised that white van man wasn't really interested in him. He was interested in Kate Williams – and why wouldn't he be?"At this juncture Sir Joshua removed a photograph of Kate Williams from his pocket and showed it to the court room.

"White van man's name is Les Craven and he has something in common with Kate Williams. He went missing from the face of the earth on the same night that she disappeared.Yet the police seem not to have investigated this – largely because of Detective Chief Inspector Nick Barton's obsession with the theory that my client killed Miss Williams, an obsession which was borne out of their teenage years when there was friction between the two of them over girlfriends. If only the police had been more awake to Detective Chief Inspector Barton's obsession, they would never have let him lead on the investigation into the case. If another police officer had conducted the case, it is quite possible – nay, even probable – that we would not be here today. Quite simply, Detective Chief Inspector Nick Barton planted the DNA evidence condemning my client."

Alan Dale rose to his feet."Objection, there is no evidence ...."

"I withdraw the last sentence," said Sir Joshua, a smug smile forming on his face.

"Jury will ignore counsel's last remark," said the judge.

Sir Joshua then reworded his remarks more cautiously. "Quite simply, it is the defence's contention that Detective Chief Inspector Barton planted the DNA evidence condemning my client," he said, "but let's move away from Detective Chief Inspector Barton's motives," said Sir Joshua. He paused for a moment – possibly in an attempt to allow the jury to reflect on them for a moment longer. Alan Dale was about to rise to his feet again when Sir Joshua resumed.

"So what do we know about Les Craven?" he asked. "Well, the answer is we don't know that much," he said. "We couldn't find him – so my client hired a private detective to try and find him. This man, Philip Rivers, is still searching for him – but so far to no avail. He left the house in Newhaven he was sharing with a woman at the same time as Kate Williams went missing. He had a cottage in Scotland. He left there, too, leaving no forwarding address other than the house he had already vacated in Newhaven. Members of the jury, you might think that is suspicious. Mr Rivers is still searching for him. When he finds him, we might have a better idea of what really happened to Kate Williams on that night."

At this juncture, Sir Joshua paused to pick up a sheath of papers from his desk. "My Lord, ladies and gentlemen of the jury," he began, "I have here a sheath of testaments as to the accused's good character. They come from former education ministers, teachers' organisations, people of different political persuasions and none. I will not take up the court's time by reading them all to you but I would ask that they be distributed to the jury. They will show that my client is a journalist of considerable expertise, writing about a serious subject – education – for a serious publication." Sir Joshua smiled to himself. "He's not a saint. You might think that no journalist is but you will see that he is a man of impeccable character who has never been prone to fits of violence. There is no reason why he should want to murder Kate Williams and I suggest to you he did not. That concludes the opening submission for the defence," said Sir Joshua as he sat down.

● ● ● ● ●

Angela, who had been holding her head in her hand at the beginning of Sir Joshua's address, now perked up. "Well done," she muttered under her breath.

Rivers took the mobile out of his pocket. It was Francesca. "I've been down to Natalie Craven's house and brought some things back which might have her DNA on them," she said.

"Have you had a result back yet?" asked Rivers.

"No," she replied. "I should have by tomorrow."

"This isn't causing you trouble in the force?" asked Rivers, concerned.

"No, thankfully I still have a few friends left who will help me."

Rivers smiled. "Good," he said. "So you should."

"How's it going?" Francesca asked after she had soaked up the compliment.

"I've visited four estate agents already," he said. "I've got one that rented out a house with a cellar. To an Angus Roughhead. It could be Les' accomplice – if he had one."

"You haven't gone to see it then?"

"No," he said. "I've told the troops we shouldn't make an approach on our own. Les Craven could be dangerous. He's obviously unhinged."

"Wait just a minute," said Francesca. "I've got a call on my landline. It's forensics." Rivers could hear her taking the call. "It's a match then? Good. Thanks for being so quick." She turned her attention to Rivers on the mobile. "Did you hear that?" she asked. "It is Natalie Craven."

"Wow," said Rivers reflecting on the implications of the finding. "That puts a different complexion on things." He remained silent for a moment. "Potentially, it means, we could be looking for a killer." Mark and Nikki froze and began listening more intently to Rivers' conversation. "I'd better get on with things down here."

• • ● • •

"I call Roy Faulkner to the stand," said Sir Joshua Partridge. Roy made his way to the witness box and affirmed that he would tell the truth. After the niceties of giving his name to those assembled in court, Sir Joshua began to question him.

"What was your relationship with Kate Williams?" he asked. "I won't call her the deceased because as far as I can see there is no evidence that she is dead."

"There was no relationship. She was just a fellow journalist covering the same conference as me."

"You were with her in the Lucky Star night club at two-thirty in the morning?"

"Yes, and then I left her to go to bed."

"What state was she in?"

Roy smiled – an uneasy smile. "She was a little bit the worse for wear from drink," he said.

"And you didn't think you should have escorted her back to the hotel to make sure she got there safely?"

"With hindsight, I obviously should have done. If I had, I wouldn't have been here charged with her murder and she wouldn't be wherever she is now."

"I see." Sir Joshua fidgeted with his spectacles. "She never came to your room, then?"

"No."

"Or was in your car?"

"No."

"Or was stuffed into a suitcase in your car?"

"Certainly not."

"So why is her DNA in all three places?"

"I don't know."

"Perhaps Detective Chief Inspector Barton put it there?"

Alan Dale rose indignantly to his feet. "Objection. The witness can't possibly know the answer to that question."

"Withdrawn," said Sir Joshua. He turned to Roy. "You don't need to answer that."

Roy shrugged his shoulders, "He might have done, I suppose."

A red-faced Alan Dale returned to his feet. Lord Justice Anderson waved him aside."Jury will disregard that last remark,"he said.

"Do you know Detective Chief Inspector Barton?"

"Yes, we grew up together."

"Were you friends?"

"I like to think we were at one stage but we had a disagreement about girlfriends."

"Is it fair to say you stole his girlfriend from him?"

"Not so much stole. I ended up going out with a girl he had been going out with previously."

"And that caused him some angst?"

"She said he tried to run her over on a zebra crossing after she had started going out with me."

Alan Dale rose slowly to his feet this time."My Lord, this is all childish stuff which happened three decades ago," he said. "What relevance does it have today?"

"Goes to the relationship my client had with Detective Chief Inspector Barton,"said Sir Joshua.

"Then why do we not have this girl – or woman – here to confirm or deny this story?"asked the judge.

"She is dead, my Lord,"said Sir Joshua.

"I see. How convenient. So we can make up any story we like about what she might or might not have said thirty years ago,"said Dale. Then added:"Presumably, she did not die from injuries received on that zebra crossing,"he added sarcastically. "Or is this another murder Detective Chief Inspector Barton has committed?"

"Obviously she wasn't dead as a result of what happened or she wouldn't have been able to tell my client the story,"said Sir Joshua."She died of cancer three years ago."

"This is getting us nowhere,"said the judge."I think you've established the fact that your client believes there was no love lost between him and Detective Chief Inspector Barton. Can we move on?"

"Yes, my lord,"said Sir Joshua. He turned to Roy in the witness box. "Let's go back to the night Kate Williams disappeared," he began. "Was there anybody else that you met in the night club?"

"Yes," he said, "a man I now know to be called Les Craven. He began talking to us about his divorce. My counsel is right. I don't think he wanted to get to know me. I'm sure he wanted to get to know Kate. She was quite a stunning looker." Alan Dale was furiously writing notes as a result of this answer.

"And was he still there when you chose to leave the night club at two thirty in the morning?"

"I don't know. He may have been."

Sir Joshua changed tack again. "Why did you drive to Beachy Head the following morning?"

Roy shifted from foot to foot. "My grandparents used to live in Eastbourne. We often used to go to Beachy Head for lunch when I came to visit them," he said. "I just wanted to connect with my memories."

"And you didn't have a body in the back of the car that you wanted to dump somewhere up there?"

"No, certainly not."

"Thank you," said Sir Joshua, "that will be all." He walked back to his seat. "Your witness," he said to Alan Dale as he passed him.

Dale rose. "Mr Faulkner, are you the kind of man who leaves a drunken woman whom you've been dating alone in a night club at two-thirty in the morning?" he asked.

"No, sir."

"Oh, so you didn't? What did you do then? Take her back to your hotel room?"

"No, sir," replied Roy. "I hadn't been dating her."

"So then it's all right to leave her on her own at two-thirty in the morning," said Dale.

"Never mind about that. No need to answer." He paused for a moment. "You fancied her, didn't you?"

"No, I have a girlfriend."

"I didn't ask you that, You fancied her, didn't you? Can I

repeat your words from your earlier testimony? She was, you said, a stunning looker."

"I don't fancy everyone I think is a stunning looker," Roy replied.

"Perhaps not everyone, Mr Faulkner," Dale continued. He donned a perplexed look. "Mr Faulkner, isn't it a bit incredible to suggest that Detective Chief Inspector Barton is so eaten up with jealousy thirty years after you started going out with the girl he had been dating that he's decided to frame you for this murder?"

"I wouldn't have expected it," admitted Roy.

"So it is incredible? Let's lay that story to rest then," said Dale. He paused again.

"You did think you might have killed her, didn't you?"

"No."

"That's what Mark Elliott seemed to suggest in his voicemail to Kate Williams the following day, isn't it?"

"Mark was joking."

"In which case, he's got an appalling sense of humour."

"No," said Roy. "With hindsight, in view of what has happened, he would wish he hadn't said it but – at the time – he was fully confident that what he said would be followed by a call from Kate saying she was all right."

"But it wasn't and you knew it wouldn't be, didn't you, because you had killed her? Isn't that so?"

"No."

"I beg to differ from you, Mr Faulkner," said Dale. "No more questions."

Roy was released from the witness box – the judge saying he would reserve until the following morning counsels' and his own summing up. In the dock, Roy tried to steal a glance at Angela but she had her head in her hands. He took it from her posture that she did not think he had given that good an account of himself in the witness box.

CHAPTER ELEVEN

Angela sat through the morning session in the court house as Alan Dale and Sir Joshua Partridge gave their closing arguments. It was as expected. Alan Dale concentrated on the DNA evidence suggesting that Kate Williams' body had been placed in the boot of Roy Faulkner's car. Whatever had been said about Roy's impeccable past by various dignitaries from the world of education was irrelevant. The question was whether he was capable of committing this crime in the present. It could have been an accident. He could have attacked Kate Williams on the spur of the moment as a result of anger fuelled by drink. It would have been better for him if he had confessed to this immediately and then he might have earned some sympathy but constructing a smokescreen by blaming the investigating police officer of conducting a vendetta against him and falsifying evidence was the recipe of a desperate man.

Sir Joshua, for his part, laid emphasis on the fact that there was no body, no proof of murder, no motive for murder. He argued that you could tell something about a man's character if an army of well-respected citizens said how upright, honest and non-violent he was. Oh, and then there was white van man. He, argued Sir Joshua, held the key to this mystery rather than Roy Faulkner. If only he could have been found, this trial may never have happened.

In truth, thought Angela, the speeches were competently delivered but they were unlikely to have swayed any of the jurors one way or the other. She began to pay more serious attention as Lord Justice Anderson began his summing up of the case.

Nick, for his part, was calmer than he had been during the past few days. No longer confronted by what he saw as Francesca Manners' betrayal of trust, no longer dealing with similar behaviour from his wife, Charlotte, he was able to devote his attention to the matter in hand. He thought Roy Faulkner had not given that good an account of himself in the witness box the previous day. He, like Angela, thought that both barristers had been no more than competent. He was beginning to believe he would be vindicated. There was no longer any evidence of sweat underneath his armpits or on his brow.

As for Roy, no-one – not even Angela – could tell what he was thinking. He seemed to be listening inscrutably as the events unfolded in the court room. To Angela, it looked almost as though he felt the case was not about him, that he had eavesdropped in on another hearing about somebody else and was listening intently – keen to find out what the result was but not believing the deliberations could have a dramatic effect on his own future. He was, quite simply, like a journalist listening to events unfold and preparing to write up his own impartial account of them at the end of the day. However, she could tell that even he was summoning up a new level of intensity as Lord Justice Anderson began his summation of the proceedings.

"Ladies and gentlemen of the jury," the judge began, "you have listened intently to the ebb and flow of evidence in the past few days and now it is you turn to decide what happened to Kate Williams on the night of May 2, morning of May 3.

"According to the prosecution, the facts are simple. Her DNA was found in the defendants' bedroom, the boot of his car and inside his suitcase. That, they argue, means he must have killed her and driven her body away from the scene of the crime to protect himself from prosecution. It goes no further than that. They do not feel they have to establish motive. Oh, they have a stab at it by suggesting it is a love tryst gone wrong. Presumably

Kate Williams withdrew her consent from sex at a time when it provoked maximum anger from the accused. That is not proven, though, but does not need to be in the light of all the other evidence. As to the fact they have been unable to produce a body, that again is an irrelevance, they argue. You have heard that Kate was an enthusiastic reporter – unlikely to have put her job in jeopardy or indeed ruin her career by suddenly disappearing and therefore not carrying out her duties to her employer. If you believe the DNA evidence, you should convict the accused. That is the kernel of their case.

"On the other hand, for you to believe that the accused is innocent, you have to accept that the police planted the DNA evidence to incriminate the accused. You have to accept that the police – actually not the police in general but Detective Chief Inspector Barton in particular was so upset by an incident that happened thirty years ago that he could brook no answer to the crime in hand other than believe the accused was guilty of it. We have not had any evidence put before us here as to whether the force backed the way Detective Chief Inspector Barton pursued this case but equally we have no evidence that they did not.

"We have heard a lot of talk from the defence about a white van man who tried to befriend Miss Williams at the Lucky Star night club but – despite an extensive investigation by a private detective hired by the accused – no evidence about him has been forthcoming. All that we have is that he talked to Miss Williams – and, incidentally, the accused – in the night club. That, we are told to infer, is evidence that he may be responsible for Miss Williams' disappearance or murder."

At that moment Angela felt as if she could not hold herself back. "Shame," she shouted. "Disgraceful."

Lord Justice Anderson screwed up his eyes to stare at Angela intently. "Remove that woman from the court room," he said. Two ushers immediately went over to where Angela was sitting.

One took her firmly by the hand and led her out of the court room. "My Roy is innocent," she shouted as she reached the door. "Innocent."

Patrick Saunders excused himself from the court room and found Angela sobbing outside – an usher still restraining her by placing a hand on her shoulder. Presumably he felt she might be preparing to rush back into the court room and usher a new volley of expletives against the judge if he did not maintain a hold on her.

"It's all right," said Patrick. "I'll take care of this." The usher looked doubtful but let go his grip. He remained around by the door as if to protect the court room from whatever Angela and/ or Patrick could cook up.

"I'm sorry, Patrick," Angela blurted out through sobs. "That was so unfair. He was telling the jury to find Roy guilty – and he's not."

"I know, I know, Angela," said Patrick soothingly, "but remember who you are and where you are and think how you can offer the best possible support to Roy." He paused. "It's not by shouting at the judge."

"No," she sniffed, wiping away the tears. "I don't suppose I can go back into the court room?" she asked within the usher's earshot. He shook his head.

"She's the accused's partner," explained Patrick.

"Look," said the usher bending a little. "Write a note to the judge apologising for your outburst and I'll see that he gets it at the break. Promise not to do it again and maybe we'll get you back in for the afternoon session."

"Thank you," said Patrick. He looked at Angela. She did not respond for a moment. It was unlike her to apologise for anything but Patrick could sense that she was weighing up the pros and cons.

"I'll do it," she said eventually.

"Good," said Patrick. "Now if you don't mind, Angela, I'll go back inside and tell you what happens afterwards. Will you be all right now?"

Angela nodded. She sniffed once more and removed the last evidence of sobbing from her eyelids. Once Patrick had disappeared inside, she sat down and began to compose her note to the judge.

Patrick realised that the judge had come to the end of his summing up.

"It only remains for me to say," said Lord Justice Anderson, "that the time has come for you to leave this court room and go and do your duty." They filed out one by one and slowly made their way under the supervision of an usher to the jury room.

Nick was smiling now. The judge's summing up had bolstered his confidence. He even allowed himself a smug look in Roy Faulkner's direction which seemed to say "Got you, you bastard". Revenge is a dish best served cold, he thought to himself again.

"Just a thought," said Rivers as he rang Francesca Manners on her mobile again. "We're building up a list of people who have hired cottages with cellars –where Kate could have been held. It's possible Craven booked it in a false name and used someone's stolen identity to confirm the agreement. It's a long shot but could you check out the names of some of his associates. Your best bet would be to visit Sian – the woman who rented a room in his home." He gave her the address.

"Okay," said Francesca. She seemed less than enthusiastic, he thought.

"Will that cause you problems?" he asked.

She thought for a moment and then smiled inwardly. "No," she said. "I'm like the proverbial spare prick at a wedding now the trial is going on. Nick doesn't want me anywhere near the court room and – to be honest – I don't want to be there either." She paused for a moment before saying emphatically: "I'll do it."

"Good," said Rivers. "We'll speak soon."

"Yes," said Francesca, "but you three be careful. You could be on the track of someone who has no compunction about killing."

"I know," said Rivers.

• • ● • •

Angela had given up pacing up and down as she awaited the jury's verdict. "It's been three hours now," she said. "Surely that's a good sign? If they were going to accept the judge's direction, they'd have been back by now."

"Maybe," said Patrick Saunders, "but three hours is not a long time for a jury to deliberate."

"What do you think Roy is thinking?"

"I don't know," said Patrick. "He was keeping a remarkably level head in court, I thought."

"And I wasn't."

"I didn't say that," said Patrick.

"You didn't have to."

As they spoke, a smallish young man approached them. He had wizened features and was not dressed in one of the sober grey or brown suits that most of the male participants in the court room were wearing. His clothes were reminiscent of an earlier age – a flowered shirt, a mohair jacket, a red tie.

"I couldn't help but hear you mention Roy's name," he said. "I used to be a friend of his. Johnnie Simons."

"Johnnie Simons? The organist with the band?"

"I don't think many people would know me by that epithet now," he said, smiling, "but yes. The same."

"What are you doing here?" asked Angela.

"I read about the case in the papers," he said. "I was curious."

"So you must have known both Roy and Detective Chief Inspector Barton in their younger days?"

"Yes," he replied, "although nothing surprised me more

than to find out that Nick had become a senior police officer. I wouldn't have said he was cut out for it."

"There are a lot of people in support of Roy who would agree with you," said Patrick Saunders.

"No, not for that reason," said Simons. "He was a bit – well, nerdy when he was young. A good drummer but definitely nerdy."

"Would that he had stayed a nerd," sighed Angela. "You must have known Graeme McAndrew and Barrie Read, too?"

"Yes. Barrie Read was not a nice man," said Simons. "I think the splitting up of the band spared me from having to have anything more to do with him. But Graeme? Well, he was a real sweetie."

"A real sweetie?" echoed Angela. An interesting picture of the band was emerging – a nerd, a sweetie, a bad influence and, of course, Roy and Simons himself.

"What do you think of the idea that Nick nursed a grudge for years and was just dying to see Roy put away for this murder?"

"I think he was badly treated by the band – because he was a nerd. There was also no doubt that he and his girlfriend weren't suited to each other. She was far more Roy's type."

"So are you sympathetic to Nick?" asked Angela, a certain frostiness sounding in her voice.

"No. He forfeited that with his treatment of Graeme. I spoke to Nick the night after he met Graeme in the pub – just before his death. I remember him almost gloating over the fact that Graeme seemed to have hit upon hard times and become an alcoholic. It turned me off him. I didn't speak to him after that. I tried to seek out Graeme to see if I could help him – but he died just a few days later."

"So you kept in touch with Nick after the band broke up – but not Roy?"

"I liked Roy – but he didn't need any help with his future. I thought Nick did. Nick was also badly beaten up around that time. He thought it was members of the gang trying to get even with him over shopping them to the police."

"I don't think Roy ever heard that," said Angela,

"He thought Roy was one of those involved – although nothing was ever proved. In the end, though, I lost sympathy for Nick. Also, he didn't seem to have needed any help in getting himself into a senior position in the police force. Amazing."

"So what are you expecting will happen?"

"What I expect to happen and what I want to happen are two different things," he said. "I expect Roy will be found guilty of murder. There's too much respect for the police in our society. The jury won't believe that Nick is capable of framing Roy is such a cold and calculating way. What I hope will happen is that Roy is found innocent and Nick's tactics during the investigation come under scrutiny from his superiors."

"Sadly, I have to agree with you," said Angela. "So if Nick's a nerd, Graeme is a sweetie, Barrie an evil influence, what is Roy?"

"He was the epitome of cool. A pouting, sexy front man for the band. He seems quite cool today, too, remarkably."

"And you?"

"I'm the kind of Svengali of the band. I see all, I register all but I'm only on the periphery. I don't intervene."

Patrick smiled. "You could have had the ingredients for a successful band. Maybe you shouldn't have split up and then we might not have been in the situation that we face today – with two band members dead and another facing life imprisonment.

"Wouldn't have worked," said Johnnie Simons. "We weren't that good." With that, he smiled and took his leave of them.

"What an odd bloke," said Patrick.

"Odd – but interesting," replied Angela. "We could have done with his evidence yesterday – evidence of Nick gloating about what he perceived to be Graeme's downfall. We should have tried to find him. Also, the beating."

"That wouldn't have portrayed Roy in a good light – although I'm not saying he had anything to do with it."

"It would have given weight to the theory that Nick was conducting a vendetta against Roy.

"Maybe we should be taking a note of these things. For the retrial."

They were interrupted at that moment by a series of movements behind them. The ushers seemed to be in a hurry to take up their positions in the court room.

"I think the jury's returning," said Patrick.

"I'm not sure I can go through with this," said Angela.

"You've got to," said Patrick. "This is not about you and what you can go through. It's about Roy and being in court so that he can see you're there and in support of him. He may be Mr Cool in Johnnie Simons' eyes but he's not that cool today. Believe me."

The tone of Patrick Saunders' voice struck a chord with Angela and she followed him back into the court room. She sat down just in time to see Roy being brought up from the cells to take his place in the dock. She smiled at him and showed him that her fingers were crossed. He smiled at her. He still looked like a journalist who was reporting on these affairs rather than the man whose whole future was in the hands of those twelve men and women who were returning to the court room to deliver their verdict.

• • • • •

"Right," said Rivers, "what have we got? I've got Angus Roughhead with a cellar. You," he said turning to Nikki, "have got Kevin Summers with two cellars. And you, Mark, have got Jim McLaughlin with a cellar and Frances Brady with two cellars."

"The jackpot," said Mark smiling.

"Now, I think we can eliminate Frances Brady. A woman is hardly likely to have been involved in Kate's disappearance."

"Stranger things have happened," said Mark.

"All right," said the private detective. "Maybe we put her at the bottom of the list, then. Would that make you happy?"

"Suits me."

"I think we ought to try and cover them all tomorrow. They're within a thirty mile radius of here so there won't be any difficulty fitting them all in – except we'll have to go a bit carefully. We can't just barge in and say 'excuse me, but we believe you've got a woman held prisoner in your cellars'."

"Or two women," said Mark.

"Right. Now which order shall we go in?" He was interrupted at that stage by a call on his mobile. "Hallo," he said. "Philip Rivers speaking."

"Rivers, it's Francesca Manners," said the voice at the other end of the phone. "I've been to see Sian and looked through Les Craven's papers. It seems he was employing two people at his repairs business – a Douglas Halliday and a Kevin Summers."

"Kevin Summers?" queried Rivers.

"Yes."

"That's interesting. He's one of four people who have recently rented cottages with cellars in them where Kate Williams could be held." Rivers smiled and gave a knowing wink to his two companions. "I think we've got our man – or men," he said.

"How's the court case going?" asked Rivers, changing tack.

"I haven't heard anything," she said, "but I think it's reaching the end. The feeling was that the jury would be sent out today. So no time to waste?"

"No." With their conversation at an end, Rivers turned to his compatriots. Nikki put an arm around his shoulder.

"Well done, Philip," she said. The progress made in the case was final proof, she thought, that he had recovered from his depression.

"I must confess I'm quite excited by all this," said the private detective. He drew a deep breath. "It shows I can still cut it," he said and – with that – he gave Nikki a cuddle. "It's been quite a journey," he said. "A few weeks ago I was all washed up. I didn't know if I'd ever be able to tackle another case. My detective agency, my life was in ruins – but...." He stopped for a moment and sighed.

"I can do it," he said. "I can do it." Nikki gave him a peck on the cheek. "I don't even have to convince myself of that anymore," he added.

"So what do we do now?"

"There's no time to lose," said Rivers. "I think we should go in to this Kevin Summers' address first thing tomorrow morning. Our aim will be to free the woman or women- we can leave any arrests up to the police. What we've basically got to do is make sure we get Kate Williams out of there and present her to the court in Lewes as soon as possible. After all, you can't have a murder trial if the victim is sitting large as life in front of you."

"I agree," said Mark.

"Remember, though, she may be traumatised by her time in captivity," said Nikki. "Just the mere fact that we can prove that we've found her should be enough to stop the trial."

"Yes, you're probably right," said Rivers.

The trio spent the rest of the evening eating dinner and watching some television.

"Right then," said Rivers to his colleagues as they prepared for bed. "We're going in tomorrow morning."

• • • • •

"Ready?" said Patrick to Angela as they prepared for the members of the jury to file back into the court room.

"As ever," she responded. She had written a note to the judge during the lunch interval and he had conveyed a message through Sir Joshua Partridge that she would be welcome back in court as long as she behaved herself.

"Now, behave yourself," said Patrick, emphasizing the judge's message and giving her a little squeeze on the arm. They watched as the jury filed back to their seats. Angela tried to scrutinise their faces for clues as to what their verdict might be. They seemed inscrutable, though. She glanced over at Roy. For the first time now, she could see signs of nervousness in his mannerisms. He was clinging to the side of the dock with his hands. No more the uninvolved outsider – the journalist reporting on the case. Realisation appeared to have dawned upon him as to the seriousness of his situation.

The clerk to the court went through the formalities. Roy was asked to stand while the jury delivered their verdict. There was a hush in the court room as the clerk asked them whether they had reached a verdict. They had.

"On the charge of murdering Kate Williams, how do you find the defendant?" he asked.

The foreman of the jury, a bespectacled man with grey hair and beard who must have been in his sixties, cleared his throat. "Guilty," he said.

"No," screamed Angela. "You're wrong." Roy closed his eyes for a second in the dock before managing to regain composure.

Lord Justice Anderson rapped on his desk with his gavel and fixed Angela with a stare. "Quiet please," he shouted. "Madam, if you continue to misbehave yourself, I shall have no alternative but to bar you from this court room permanently."

Angela took matters into her own hands and stormed from the court room – whereupon Lord Justice Anderson turned his gaze to Roy.

"Roy Faulkner, you have been found guilty of the murder of Kate Williams," he said. "You will be remanded in custody overnight and brought back to this court for sentencing tomorrow morning. Take him down." One of the security staff took Roy by the arm and led him from the dock down to the cells below – whereupon Lord Justice Anderson got up from his seat to leave the room. "Court will rise," said an usher as he made his way from the scene.

Nick Barton sat back in his seat and allowed himself a broad smile before getting up and making his way over to Alan Dale.

"Congratulations," he said. "I thought it was touch and go."

"Don't thank me," said Dale. "Thank the judge. I think his summing up was crucial."

"Yes," said Nick. He could not quite make out whether Dale was trying to intimate that he felt he was going to lose the case until then. Stuff it, he thought on reflection. It doesn't matter now.

Meanwhile, across the court room, Sir Joshua Partridge was collecting up his papers and showing no emotion.

"I'd better go and see if Angela is all right," said Patrick.

"Oh, yes," said Sir Joshua with heavy emphasis. "We must all find out whether Angela is all right."

Patrick excused himself. He had been sitting behind Sir Joshua and now fidgeted with his jacket buttons – in a sign of nervousness – as he made his way from the court room.

He caught up with Angela outside who – by now – was crying.

"Don't worry," he said. "We'll lodge an appeal."

"How?"

"We'll get Rivers to have a closer look at Barton to see if he can dig up some dirt.

"Fuck Rivers," said Angela. "Where is he now? He's done nothing to help my Roy."

"That's not the case," said Patrick. "I'm sure...." His voice tailed off as he saw Nick Barton coming out of the court room in the company of Alan Dale. "Oh, no," he said as he saw Angela moving towards him.

"I hope you're proud of yourself," she said as the detective walked past her.

"Very," said Nick smugly. "I've just brought a murderer to justice." He stopped and looked at her in the eyes. "I'm prouder of myself than your boyfriend has any right to be of himself."

He was just about to move on when Angela grabbed him by the arm.

"You ought to be ashamed of yourself," she said. "You're a crook, a...."

At this moment she felt a restraining hand being laid on her by one of the security staff. Patrick moved towards them but was at a loss what to do. "I think we ought to go and have a word with Roy before he's taken away," said Patrick in an effort to persuade Angela to move away from the situation.

"Oh, yes," said Angela, wiping away another tear from her eye and seemingly coming to her senses by releasing her grip on the detective's arm.

"She's not going anywhere," said the security official. "You may go downstairs and see if you can get access to your client but she is leaving the building."

He tightened his grip on Angela's arm and started frogmarching her towards the door.

"There's no need for that," said Patrick, panting as he tried to keep up with them.

"I shall decide what there's a need for and what there's not a need for," said the security official. Angela by this time had relaxed and become a meeker version of her former self. She allowed herself to be escorted from the building. Patrick turned back and resolved to go and meet his client. As he returned to the building, he was just in earshot of a comment Nick Barton was making to Alan Dale.

"I should imagine Roy Faulkner must be thanking his lucky stars if the alternative to the evening he's going to have was an evening with that," he said, jerking his head to where Angela had just disappeared from the court house.

Patrick thought of intervening but then decided it was best not to bother. From the silence that greeted the comment, he thought that Alan Dale had not appreciated it either. Instead, he went down the stairs to the cells and asked one of the officials if he could have access to Roy. He was ushered into a cell.

"Roy, I'm so sorry," he said.

Roy managed a smile. "Not as sorry as I am," he said.

"No," said Patrick. He paused. "Words are a bit pointless at a time like this," he said.

"Yes," said Roy. For a man who relied on words to earn him a living he, too, found himself incredibly short of them at the moment.

"Rivers is still trying to find out what happened to Kate. I'm sure he'll come up with something."

"Yes," said Roy again.

Patrick was at a loss for words himself. "Look, I'll see you here tomorrow for the sentencing," he said. "Don't give up hope."

"No." Patrick made as if to leave but Roy stopped him as he made his way to the door.

"Patrick, just a moment," he said. "Thank you."

"Thank me? What for?"

"For believing in me. The way you said 'Rivers is still trying to find out what happened to Kate'. You don't think I murdered her."

"No."

"Well, thanks. And thanks, too, for being so calm."

Patrick looked at him and grinned. He wondered if that had been a veiled reference to Angela. "Angela would have been here now – but she had to be escorted from the court house," he said.

"Why does that not surprise me?" said Roy, managing to conjure up the faintest evidence of a smile.

• • • • •

Francesca Manners was still in her office when Nick Barton returned to the police station following the end of the trial. She just happened to be going to get a cup of coffee when he walked by on the way to his office.

"I can see I'm not going to get any congratulations from you," he said curtly.

"There's no point in us having a row," she said.

"None at all," he said, "since you won't be with us for very much longer."

At that moment their contretemps was interrupted by the arrival of Chief Superintendent Rimmer. He had a large smile on his face. His neck gave one the impression of bobbing up and down feverishly inside his collar again. He held out a hand to Nick.

"Nick," he said beaming. "I knew you'd do it. Well done."

"Thank you, sir," replied the detective. He was almost blushing as he sought to take maximum pleasure from Francesca witnessing this scene.

"This is a high profile case," said Rimmer. "The murder of a tabloid journalist by another journalist. They'll want you to give a press conference tomorrow."

"They?" queried Nick.

"The media," said Rimmer firmly. "Oh, and the powers that be." He looked around himself mysteriously. "It'll be good for the police's image – managing to solve this one."

Nick nodded. "By the way, can I have a word with you tomorrow?"

"Yes. What about?"

Nick looked at squarely into Francesca's eyes. "The future of Detective Sergeant Manners," he said. "As you know, she has been less than helpful on this case."

"I'm sure we can arrange something," said Rimmer. Francesca turned on her heels and walked back to her office. Nick smiled – and relaxed. As he did so, he was aware of suddenly becoming very tired. He uttered a sigh.

"Are you all right, Nick?" asked Rimmer.

"Yes, I think I've suddenly begun to realise how much of a strain this has all been. My integrity being under question, you know. Would you mind if I went off home now? I feel quite tired."

"No, not at all. You deserve some rest."

• • • • •

"What the hell have you been doing all this time?" It was the kind of call Rivers could have done without late that evening. "You know Roy's been found guilty?"

Rivers remained silent for a moment. Angela's call was the first indication he had been given of the result of the trial. "He's being sentenced in the morning," said Angela.

"Look," said Rivers. "Don't give up hope. We think we may have found where they're holding Kate Williams."

"Think? Don't you know?"

"We're going there tomorrow morning."

"But that's too late."

Rivers swallowed. "No, it won't be," he said. "They'll release Roy the moment Kate Williams turns up alive."

"Yes, but can't you see it would be better if you could do that before Roy was sentenced to life imprisonment rather than after? And why are you going there tomorrow morning and not the police?"

"You know why," said Rivers. "The police aren't interested in Les Craven."

"Well, I hope you know what you're doing," said Angela – the tone of her voice suggesting she did not believe he did. Rivers reflected for a moment. He had to admit he did not. He did not know what would confront them when they turned up at the house rented in the name of Kevin Summers the following morning. He turned to Mark as he put the telephone down on Angela. She had seemed to want to prolong the conversation but he saw no useful purpose in doing that.

"Are you ready for tomorrow?" he asked Mark.

"Think so," said Mark tentatively.

"You know – your presence is crucial," said Rivers. "You're the only one of the three of us that Kate Williams knows. That could be very reassuring for her." He walked over to Nikki and held her hand. "We'll start reasonably early tomorrow," he said. "Set off about 8am?"

He and Nikki made for the bedroom while Mark poured himself a large whisky before he, too, retired for the night.

"You've come a long way," said Nikki as they lay in bed together.

"You mean from the gibbering wreck who could hardly get out of bed in the morning?" said Rivers. "Yes, but there's a part of me that doesn't want to get out of bed tomorrow morning, either."

"That's understandable," said Nikki. "Nerves. You wouldn't be on your toes as much without them."

"I guess not," he said, holding Nikki close to him and giving her a kiss on the lips. He thought for a moment before kissing her again. "I know this is an insane moment," he said, "but – will you marry me?"

"What?" Nikki sat bolt upright in bed.

"What is it?" asked Rivers

"Well, I wasn't expecting that. We've only...."

".... known each other on and off for nearly thirty years."

"Yes, more off than on. We've only got together again very recently."

"And we wouldn't have done that if I hadn't expected it to last. I'm not about to walk out on you again, Nikki. Honest."

"I didn't think you believed in marriage."

"Nor did I but suddenly it seems like an attractive proposition. You've always been there for me, I know that. Now it's my turn to prove that I'll always be there for you – and this is the best way I can think of doing that."

"Think about it, Philip. You're emotional now. If you still feel the same way about it in the cold light of day, my answer's yes."

"Good."

"Hey but not now. I want you to ask me again in the cold light of day and I want to see that you're still as intense about it."

"In other words, sleep on it?"

"Sleep is a very good idea considering what we've got to do tomorrow morning."

Only it wasn't so easy for the two of them to get to sleep that night. Nikki couldn't believe that – after all those years – Rivers had finally come to the conclusion that he wanted to marry her and that it was not just a spur of the moment decision that he might come to regret. Rivers, for his part, felt relaxed, fully confident he would be able to summon up just as much emotion to ask Nikki again the following morning. And she had already told him that her answer would be yes. So the hard part was over. Gradually they drifted off to sleep.

• • • • •

Nick turned into his driveway that evening – glad to be away from the police station. He had some fences to mend with Charlotte, he knew, but he felt confident he would be able to do that. More confident, in fact, than he had been of winning the case against Roy Faulkner.

"Hello, Charlotte, I'm home," he said as he unlocked the door. It was, in truth, the most loquacious greeting he had given his wife in years.

He could not, though, have been prepared for what he saw in the hallway. There was Charlotte, with an overcoat on and a suitcase by her side, ready to make an exit from the house.

"Charlotte?" asked Nick, "what are you doing?"

"I'm leaving you, Nick."

"Wait!" He paused for a moment. "It's all over now."

"It is between us."

"No," said Nick. "I won't let you leave." He grabbed her arm but she shook herself free. "The case is over. I've been exonerated – if I needed exonerating. The jury accepted my version of events. Why can't you?"

"Because I know you were lying." She paused for a moment – "and I can't live with a man who hits me. I won't forget that, Nick. Ever."

"Please," said Nick, grabbing hold of her arm again.

It was at that moment Sarah stepped from the kitchen. "I think Mother's made it quite plain what she wants to do, Dad," she said. "Don't stand in her way." Sarah was also accompanied by a suitcase. "I'm leaving with Mum," she explained.

"But where are you going?"

"My sister's," said Charlotte. "Nick, it's no use. Our marriage has been dead for years. It's only after you hit me that I had the courage to realise it and act upon it."

"So we're leaving," said Sarah firmly as she walked to the front door and held it open for her mother.

"Don't try and stop us."

Nick sighed and moved away from the doorway. "Do I get to see you again, Sarah?" he asked.

"I'll be there for Mum while she tries to put her life back together," his daughter said, "but, no, I'm not going to cut you off without as much as a penny. You've made mistakes. Mistakes which can't be undone but you are still my Dad."

"You know I was proved right today."

"Those weren't the mistakes I meant, Dad. The mistakes were in your relationship with Mum."

"OK," he said as he watched them both leave. "I'll see you soon, Sarah," he said as if to reassure himself. "Charlotte?"

"Goodbye, Nick." With that, they got into Sarah's car which was parked on the road just outside the house.

He watched them go and then turned back to go inside. A fine victory, he thought. Roy Faulkner might be behind bars but here he was in a prison of his own – on his own in his own home with no-one to talk to. Revenge didn't seem like a dish served cold at that point, he reflected. He would almost be prepared to forgo it to get back his private life. Then he smiled or rather sneered. No, at least that upstart Faulkner was behind bars. That was something to take from the way the day had turned out.

CHAPTER TWELVE

The woman woke up early that morning. She rubbed her eyes with her left hand to remove some of the sleep from them. Her right arm was still chained to the bed that she lay on – as it had been for most of the time she had been incarcerated in that cellar. Around her was shelving where, in any normal cellar, bottles of wine would be stored. The shelves were empty – and bleak. Like her whole existence.

Kate could just about see into the car park through a slit in the wall on the far side of the room. As she looked out on to the drive way of what she presumed must be quite a swish mansion, she could see the white van in which Les had brought her there was not there. She assumed he must have gone out to buy food or get some newspapers. He would be back soon and then her torment or torture even would start all over again. She had lost track of time but it seemed to her that she had been incarcerated in this place for weeks now. She had been beaten, repeatedly raped – almost to the point where she accepted what Les was going to do to her and no longer tried to resist him. She sighed.

Suddenly, she became aware of a noise – the sound of a car coming up the driveway. She looked through the slit. She could not see it clearly but she was aware it was an ordinary car and not the white van that Les Craven drove. As she watched she could barely make out three figures getting out of the car. One of them, a man, turned to his two companions and obviously said something to them but she could not make out what it was. They then disappeared from view and the next thing she heard was a knock on the door. There was a gap of a few seconds then a further knock. It confirmed to her that Les was not at home.

Emboldened by that knowledge, she then shouted as loudly as she could. "Help, I'm in here," she screamed at the top of her voice. "In the cellars. Please help me. Help."

She did not know how far her voice could carry but all she heard was a third knock on the door and then nothing. A few moments later she could see through the slit in the window that the three people – it looked like two men and a woman – had walked back to the car. She thought one of them looked familiar but she could not see that well. Then it dawned on her.

"Mark," she cried. "Mark Elliott." It was obvious her voice did not carry. There was no recognition of her call from the man she could identify as the tabloid journalist she knew. The three got inside and – a few moments later – they drove off. "Hell," said Kate out loud. "They've gone."

Surely they would be back, though. If it was Mark Elliott, he had come a long way to find her. Within minutes, there was the sound of another vehicle on the gravel driveway. Through the slit she could see it was the white van that Les drove. She reflected. It had only been a few moments since the other car had driven away. If the occupants had wanted to do business with Les – as she was sure they did, was there a chance that they might have seen the other car approaching and they would come back? She fervently hoped so. In the meantime, though, she braced herself for another attack by Les.

A few moments later, she heard a key in the front door lock and then Les appeared at the top of the stairs leading down to the cellar. He had a grin on his face – a malevolent grin that Kate had come to recognise by now. He had a newspaper in his hand which he flung over to Kate,

"Go on, have a look," he sneered. "You've been murdered. "That guy you were with in the night club has been found guilty of your murder."

Kate grabbed the paper and there – prominently displayed on the front page -was a picture of Kate looking beautiful as she had done in the days before her incarceration. Next to it was a less than flattering photograph of the "award winning reporter", as Roy was described, who had been found guilty of killing her. "Shit," she said.

"Yes, shit," said Les, a beam in his eye. "Amazing. Read it. They found your DNA in the boot of his car, in his bedroom, all over the place. What were you up to before I got my hands on you?" He laughed.

"I don't understand," said Kate.

"It's perfectly simple," said Les. He crouched down next to her and held her chin in his hand. "There are crooks all over the place. In the police force, too, I shouldn't wonder." He had a mug of tea in his hand and held it up.

"Let's drink a toast," he said. "To Detective Chief Inspector Nick Barton," He drank from the mug. "Nick, you have just made my life so much easier," he said. "No-one's looking for you now, Kate. I could even kill you and get off scot free. They've found the person that killed you, Kate. Roy Faulkner," He kissed her firmly on the mouth and then withdrew his face from her and slapped her on the cheek.

"Come on, you can manage a bit of a warmer response that that." He then put his hand on her knee and moved it slowly upwards, lifting the skimpy mini skirt she was wearing. It eventually came to rest at the top of her leg when he appeared to admonish himself. "Time for that later," he said. "I've work to do first. And don't you go heaving a sigh of relief. We'll get round to that later. Who knows? You might even enjoy it sometime."

He moved to climb the stairs but turned to Kate as he reached the top.

"Where's my manners?" he said. "I'll get you a cup of tea as well." He held her chin in his hand again. "Say, thank you to uncle Les."

"Thank you," mumbled Kate.

"Again – so I can hear you."

"Thank you," she almost shouted.

He hit her across the face again. "Naughty, naughty," he said. "Show due respect to your seniors. Otherwise, you know what we do to naughty girls. Give them the kind of spanking they deserve." He smiled. "There, doesn't her little face light up at that? It's really what she wants. Gagging for it."

Kate restrained herself from spitting at him. "Thank you," she said again – this time the tone of her voice having moderated to somewhere between the mumble and the screech. It seemed to satisfy Les Craven. He moved away from her. "I've got work to do. Chopping wood for the fire. Preparing a proper breakfast and then I'll turn my mind to what fun we can have."

● ● ● ● ●

It was, of course, Rivers, Mark Elliott and Nikki who had approached the mansion earlier in the day. "We could wait," suggested Mark.

"No," said Rivers, "if he saw us in the driveway, he might panic. I'd far rather have him answering a knock on the door."

Mark still did not seem happy with the situation. "Suppose the girls are inside," he said. "Couldn't we just break in and rescue them?"

"How? It looks like quite a fortress. I don't fancy breaking down the door. What equipment have we got?"

"I suppose you're right," sighed Mark. "It just seems – well, so near and yet so far."

"I know. Remember, though, he could be a killer. We have to tread carefully.""

The trio traipsed back to their car and turned round in the driveway to make their exit from the mansion. Indeed, it did look like a fortress. It probably dated back to the 18th century at least, thought Rivers, with a solid wooden front door and steel girders imposing a lock that would have made it impenetrable from the outside to any interloper. They turned right to go back to the local village. There had been a coffee shop there where they could wait until they tried to make contact again. However, as they drove away Rivers could see behind him in his mirror a white van turning into the mansion's driveway.

"Someone's come back'" he said as he watched the car turn. "Shall we give it another go?" The other two nodded. It was a delicate manoeuvre to turn round on the winding lane – giving Les time to disembark and get inside the mansion.

"Mmm, fits the description of Les Craven," said Mark. The three of them then got out of the car. Rivers felt a cold shudder go down his spine as he approached the front door. Nikki hung back a little. Mark stood foursquare by Rivers' side. Rivers knocked on the door.

"Who is it?" came a voice from inside.

"We're lost," said Rivers. "We wondered if you could help us get back on track."

Les Craven sighed. "All right," he said, – reluctantly opening the door. He stood in the doorway facing Rivers.

"Actually, we've come here to see one of your guests – Kate Williams," said Rivers, moving into Les Craven's space and attempting to get past him into the room.

"I don't know what you're talking about," said Craven. "There's no-one of that name here."

A muffled cry could be heard. Rivers deduced it was coming from the cellar. "What's that then?" he asked.

Les shoved Rivers in the chest and slammed the door shut. Rivers steadied himself and banged on the door again. "Come on, it's three against one, It's all over," he said.

"I do have an advantage over you," said Les as he opened the door slowly. Rivers could see he now had a shotgun in his hand.

"Come on, Craven, you're not a killer," said the private detective. He fervently hoped he was right. He moved a step towards him.

"I will use it," said Craven menacingly, "and the woman gets it first. So back off and drive away."

Rivers thought quickly. Craven was obviously banking on them protecting Nikki. He reckoned the white van driver would never be able to shoot the three of them before being overpowered.

"Okay, Nikki," he said, "let's get back into the car." As Nikki moved towards the car, Rivers could see Craven's eyes were on her and were not watching him all that closely. He hurled himself at Craven with as much force as he could muster. The gun went off hitting Nikki in the side near her breast as she got into the car. Within seconds, though, Rivers had overpowered Craven and was pummelling him with his fists.

"You bastard," he cried. "That one's for Nikki," he said. He raised his fist again and added: "And this one, too."

Mark moved over to calm him down. "Come on," he said. "That's enough. Let's see to Nikki." Mark took possession of the gun. "I'll keep my eyes on him while you look after her," he said.

Rivers went over to where Nikki was lying on the gravel pathway. She was unconscious. There was blood spurting from her side and breast. He felt her pulse. She was still alive. He took a mobile phone from his pocket and rang the emergency services.

"Police and an ambulance," he said. "There's been a shooting. A woman is seriously injured." He then read off the address from a piece of paper he had pocketed earlier to guide him to the mansion. He went back to the car and took out Nikki's handbag. As luck would have it, there were a number of tissues there which he used to staunch the flow of blood from her breast. He could see she was still breathing.

"What about the prisoners?" asked Mark.

"We've got enough on our plates trying to hold on to Craven until the police arrive," said Rivers.

"I'll keep the gun trained on him," said Mark. "You have a look."

"Okay, I'll go inside and see what's happened," He took a look at Nikki and held her hand. "Hang on in there love," he said. "I am sorry. I thought I could knock Craven off balance before he had time to fire the gun. Help will be here soon." He caressed her hair tenderly. "Oh, and I still want to marry you."

Tears welled in his eyes as he said this. Mark looked at him quizzically, "Yes, I proposed to her last night," said the detective. "She said she'd say yes if I repeated the proposal in the cold light of day. Didn't want me carried away just by emotion." He couldn't stop himself from crying now as he looked at her unconscious body.

"I think you'd better propose to her again when you get her to hospital. One, she may not have heard you and two, this could qualify as a second emotional moment," said Mark dryly.

Rivers smiled. He thought he could feel Nikki lightly squeezing his hand as he held hers.

"I'll be back in a moment," he said. He went inside the mansion and saw that the door to the cellar was open. He stood at the top of the stairs.

"Kate Williams?" he called.

"Yes," came a reply,

He walked over to where she was chained to the bedpost. "Jesus Christ," he said on seeing the conditions in which she was held.

For the first time in weeks Kate managed a smile. "I'm sure you're not," she said, "but thanks for coming."

He looked at her again. "My name's Philip Rivers," he said. "That won't mean anything to you. I'm a private detective. I was hired by Roy Faulkner to prove his innocence on a charge of murdering you. Looks like I've just done that."

"Yes. I am still alive."

"I'll just go upstairs and get the key to unlock your chain. Don't go away."

She smiled "I'm not going anywhere," she said.

Rivers nodded and then paused for a moment before going upstairs. "By the way, is there another prisoner?" he asked.

A look of surprise came over Kate Williams' face. "No," she said. "Should there be?"

Rivers did not answer, wondering in his mind what had happened to Natalie Craven. He then walked upstairs and out on to the driveway again, He stopped to take a look at Nikki who was showing more signs of life now, noticeably breathing more easily but still unconscious. He kissed her on the forehead before making his way over to Craven. He held out his hand.

"The key," he said. "I want to release Kate Williams, There's no point in trying to hang on to your prisoner now."

Craven nodded. "It's in the top drawer of the sideboard in the kitchen," he said. He seemed to have accepted defeat.

"Thanks," said Rivers. Before he turned to go and fetch it, he spoke to Craven again. "Why did you do it?"

"It's a long story," said Craven. "I'd had a bad marriage."

"And that makes it all right? No, don't bother to answer that. I know the answer." With that, he went back into the mansion and collected the key from the kitchen. A few seconds later, he had freed Kate Williams. They made their way out into the open. Craven was still standing against the wall with Mark training the gun on him. Kate was rubbing her eyes to accustom them to the light.

"Mark," cried Kate as she realised she had been right about her second rescuer. She went up to him and flung her arms around him – almost causing him to lose control of the gun he was holding. "It's so good to see you."

Mark was a little taken aback by her warm welcome. They had known each other, yes, but only as acquaintances at conferences. And there had been a time when he had turned down her invitation to go to a night club in favour of re-joining the journalist pack for a late night drink at their hotel. He laughed inwardly. What a time to remember that! For her, he reflected, it was the first time she had come into contact with anyone she had known for several weeks. He put the gun down and embraced her.

Les Craven was in as quick as a flash. Before either Rivers or Mark realised what he was doing, he had grabbed the gun and was pointing it at Kate Williams.

"Either of you move and she dies," he said, "I could kill everybody here and escape," he said. "No-one would know what had happened."

"The police are on their way," said the private detective. "They know you're here. They know you've been holding Kate Williams hostage." Actually, reflected Rivers, the police who would arrive in a minute did not. It was only Francesca Manners that knew the truth. The other force soon would, though, he reflected. He looked at Craven. The man was obviously unsure as to whether to use his gun and he wondered if he had time to charge him again and knock him over before he could make any fateful decision to pull the trigger. His previous experience led to him treading the path of caution – although Craven in fact took the decision away from him.

"Okay," he said, "but I think I'll just be off, though." Training his gun on Kate Williams, he walked backwards over to his white van, got in and started up the engine. At that precise moment, though, the assembled party heard the sound of sirens and three police cars sped down the driveway – blocking Craven's exit.

"He's got a gun," Rivers shouted at a police officer who got out of the lead vehicle. The man nodded, turned round and shouted:

"Armed suspect in white van. Neutralise." Within seconds six police officers emerged from the two rear vehicles – all of them armed. Craven didn't have time to pick up the gun which he had discarded on to the passenger seat before six guns were trained on him. He put his hands up whereupon one police officer opened the passenger door and took the gun out of the car.

"Your message said someone had been shot," said the inspector from the first vehicle, "so we took the precaution of being armed. Now, would someone like to explain to me what's been going on?"

As Rivers began to offer an explanation, another siren sounded and an ambulance used the grass verge to pass the police vehicles and park itself in front of the mansion.

"First things first," said Rivers. "My girlfriend's been shot," he said. Within a few minutes, the ambulance-men had given Nikki an oxygen mask and were preparing to transport her to hospital. "I'd like to go with her," Rivers said to the police officer.

"Provided you don't mind being accompanied by two of my men," he replied.

"No," said Rivers. He boarded the ambulance with two police officers and they sped off.

"I suppose I'd better explain what's happened," said Mark, "It's this woman you need to worry about." He pointed at Kate. "She's been held prisoner in the most disgusting circumstances for the past few weeks. She is on your files as a murder victim. In fact, the so called killer of this lady, a friend of mine, was convicted of her murder only yesterday. The chap you've just seen departing in the ambulance is a private detective who my friend hired to find her. Detective Sergeant Manners at Brighton police has all the details of the case if you'd like to ring her. This," Mark was pointing to Craven, "is the one you need to arrest. Les Craven kidnapped her." He pointed at Kate again. "There's another missing woman he may have kidnapped, too. His wife, Natalie. I think now the best thing we could do, though, is take Kate somewhere where she can freshen up."

"We need to release Roy," said Kate anxiously. "He's going to be sentenced for my murder today."

"All in good time," said the inspector. "You don't need to worry about, Roy, is it? If he has been found guilty of your murder, the moment you show that you're still alive, steps will be taken to secure his release. Now, if you wouldn't mind all accompanying me to the police station we'll sort everything out." He turned to Mark. "That includes you, sir, just in case you haven't been telling me the truth."

• • ● • •

Rivers stood aside to let the nurse wheel the trolley with Nikki on it to the operating theatre. He touched her arm as it went past. "I'll be here when you get back," he said. The consultant had been optimistic about Nikki's chances but could not say when she was likely to regain consciousness. Left to his own devices sitting in the hospital, he told himself it was about time he informed his employer of the events of that morning. He got his mobile out of his pocket and telephoned Patrick Saunders.

"Hi, Patrick, where are you?" he asked.

"I'm just on my way to court for the sentencing."

"I've found Kate Williams."

"What?" Patrick sounded amazed and surprised at the other end of the telephone.

"Yes," he said. "She's alive. I wouldn't say she's well. She's been imprisoned, raped and tortured for the past few weeks but we've released her."

"That's wonderful news. Where is she now?"

"She's with the local police in Scotland."

"Do the police down here know about your find?"

"I'm not sure. The police here will want to hand Les Craven over to the Brighton police for questioning, I think. I thought I should ring you so at least the court could be informed of what has happened – even if the police wheels are moving slowly."

"Right. I'll let Sir Joshua know as soon as I get to court."

"Great. I'll tell Francesca Manners." With that, he rang off and dialled Francesca's number. As luck would have it, she answered the phone.

"Great news," he said. "We've found Kate Williams and she's alive. I don't know whether the Scottish police have informed you yet."

"Nor do I. I'm not exactly persona grata here at the moment. Nick Barton is having a word with the chief super sometime this morning – apparently about transferring me out of here."

"Well, Brighton is going to be short of detectives if he does that," said Rivers. "I can't imagine Nick Barton will survive the fall-out from this."

"No."

"Listen, I've got to go know. My girlfriend was shot during the rescue. I'm at the hospital waiting for the result of her operation."

"Oh, no, I'm so sorry to hear that. Good luck."

Rivers went back to check on Nikki's progress but was told she was still undergoing the operation. He nodded his thanks to the nurse who had explained the position to him and then went outside to use his mobile again – this time to telephone Mark.

"Kate's got cleaned up," said the journalist. "She seems to be making a good recovery. She wants to go down to Lewes to give evidence at the court case and get Roy freed."

"Have they tried to contact the police in Brighton about what's happened?"

Mark chuckled for a moment. "They rang through and were told they should speak to Detective Chief Inspector Nick Barton but he told them he was too busy to speak to them at the moment and that he had to make an urgent court appointment."

"He might have quite a few of those in the coming weeks," said Rivers dryly. "Did you tell them that it would perhaps be better to speak to somebody else?"

"I tried to – but they don't seem to think I'm the font of all wisdom here, which is a shame."

"Never mind." As he spoke he noticed a trolley with Nikki on it was being wheeled back to the ward. "Look, I've got to go now," he said. "Nikki's just come out of theatre."

"Okay." Rivers followed the trolley back to the ward – but was told Nikki was still under sedation and they could not guarantee when she would come round from the operation.

• • • • •

"I'm sorry but it's urgent," said Francesca. "I have to speak to Chief Superintendent Rimmer now."

"Yes, he did want to see you sometime today," said his personal assistant, "but I would have thought it was more of a question of him wanting to see you than you wanting to see him."

"Oh, he discusses confidential police matters with you, does he?" she said sharply and then she bit her tongue. If she wanted to get this woman on board as an ally to get her in to see Rimmer, it was perhaps not the brightest riposte she could have made.

"I'm sorry," she said, "it's just that there has been an important development in the Roy Faulkner case that I think he should be apprised of."

At that moment Rimmer himself came walking into the room. "Detective Sergeant Manners," he said. "I didn't think we had yet arranged an appointment for you."

"No, you haven't," she said, "but there's something I thought you ought to know. Kate Williams has been found alive in Scotland this morning. I think you will appreciate it's not the sort of information I could go to my superior with."

"And you have heard this through official police channels?"

"No, sir, I heard it from the man who found her. Philip Rivers, a private investigator hired by Mr Faulkner to protect his interests. He, too, felt he was unlikely to get a sympathetic response if he approached Nick Barton so he approached me."

"Where is she now?"

"As far as I know, she's still in Scotland. The local police are trying to unravel the situation. They have a suspect who is understood to have kept her in captivity since the night she disappeared from the Lucky Star night club."

"You would think they would contact us."

"They may have, sir, but maybe they would contact Detective Chief Inspector Barton first. He may have been difficult to find this morning as he's on his way to court."

Rimmer nodded. He asked Francesca where Kate had been found and then got his PA to contact the nearest police service to Loch Rannoch. Francesca relaxed. It looked as if he was taking her seriously. The PA handed the telephone to him. The voice on the other end of the line confirmed what Francesca had been saying.

"You said you had been called to a shooting?" he asked. He was informed that a woman – not Kate Williams – had been shot. Rimmer handed the telephone receiver back to his PA.

"It seems that I have an urgent message that I should convey to the court this morning," he said to Francesca, "and that I have an apology to make to you. Detective Chief Inspector Barton has some awkward questions to answer, too. If this girl is alive and living in Scotland, I fail to see how her DNA could have got into the boot of Roy Faulkner's car. Or at least, should I say I can only too easily see how it happened. Manners, you get over to the court-house – quickly as you can, I'd better find Barton and get this over with. Sorry business. He was one of our finest policemen."

Francesca focussed on the word "was". She thanked the Chief Superintendent and smartly left the office. Rimmer made his way to Nick Barton's office – only to find there was no-one there.

"Do you know where he is?" he asked the desk sergeant stationed just outside Nick's office.

"He said he had to get to court urgently," the sergeant replied. "He had a phone call just before he left. Seemed a bit put out by it."

"I'll bet he was." He thought to himself for a moment and came to the conclusion that he, too, had better go off to the court house to sort the situation out.

• • • • •

Patrick Saunders skipped up the steps to the court house. He saw Angela hanging around in the waiting area. She looked despondent.

"I've got some good news," he said. "Rivers has found Kate Williams. She's alive and well and in Scotland. He freed her from imprisonment this morning. Now tell me again he's a useless, spineless shit. Oh, and by the way, his girlfriend got shot in the rescue operation." Patrick had become tired of how Angela would routinely disparage the private detective – and so thought he would add the latter to evoke some sympathy for Rivers.

"Oh, well, that's wonderful news," Angela said, completely ignoring what she had been told about Nikki. Patrick sighed. Then Angela added impatiently: "So why hasn't my Roy been released?"

"Give them some time. Rivers has had a hard time convincing the police of his find, I think. Now, if you'll excuse me, I've got to find Sir Joshua Partridge."

At that moment Nick Barton walked into the waiting area. Angela immediately turned on him. "I'm surprised you're even showing your face here today," she said. "My Roy will soon be a free man."

"We shall see," said Nick stiffly. In truth, he did not know why he had come to court. It just seemed a lot better and more dignified than making a run for it – which would have been the other alternative. He would have to take whatever was coming to him, he reflected. A quick glance round the waiting room showed Patrick Saunders and Sir Joshua in earnest conversation.

There could not be any doubts as to what they were talking about. As he watched them, he became aware of a voice at his side. It was Alan Dale.

"Are you ready for this morning?" he asked him.

"As I'll ever be," muttered Nick.

Alan Dale looked at him in askance. It was quite obvious to Nick that he had not been told of the morning's developments. He did not feel it was in his interests to enlighten him, though. Dale glanced at his watch. "Time to get into court," he said.

Within a few minutes, they were all assembled in the court room. Roy was brought up from the cells to take his place in the dock. His face had a look of studied indifference on it. It was as if this was something he had to get through that day – like a visit to the dentist. Angela hit Patrick, who was sitting in front of her, in the back.

"Have you told Roy?" she asked.

"No," he confessed. "I didn't have time."

Angela sighed. "For goodness sake," she said. She tried to communicate with him with what looked like semaphore messages but was restrained by Patrick Saunders as Lord Justice Anderson came into the court room demanding a dignified silence. As he sat down, he motioned all those in front of him to do likewise. Sir Joshua Partridge was quick to his feet, though.

"My Lord, may I approach?"

Lord Justice Anderson seemed surprised at the request but granted it. "I should like to see you in your chambers," Sir Joshua said.

"This is most irregular. The trial is over. This is just the sentencing procedure."

"There is something you should know before you pass sentence. I would not ask were it not of the gravest importance."

"Very well," said the judge. He got up. "Court will reconvene in a few moments. I want to see both sides in my chamber." Alan Dale got up to join them, frowning and looking around himself as if in a vain attempt to get some inspiration and explanation as to what was happening.

"Well?" said Lord Justice Anderson as they arrived in his chambers.

Sir Joshua took the floor. "Kate Williams was found alive and well in Scotland this morning."

"Kate Williams?"

"Yes, the woman who was supposed to have been murdered," said Sir Joshua.

"I know very well who she is," said the Lord Justice. "I'm just a bit surprised. I wonder why the prosecution did not inform the court of this development."

"This is the first I've heard of it," said Dale.

"Ah, so it could be disputed information?"

"There's no dispute as far as I'm concerned," said Sir Joshua. "I gather she was found by a private detective hired by my client. There was a shoot-out and a man is in police custody who was allegedly harbouring her."

"I cannot throw any light on this situation, your lordship," said Dale.

"Well, go and find someone who can. We'll wait here."

Dale walked back into the court room and went over to Nick Barton. "I gather the murder victim has been found alive this morning," he said.

"So I understand."

"Well, why didn't you tell me?"

"I didn't know whether or not to believe what I was hearing."

"Oh, yes, you can believe it." The voice belonged to Chief Superintendent Rimmer who had just arrived in the court room. His Adam's apple was bobbing up and down nineteen to the dozen – possibly as a result of the anger he felt towards a detective who he previously found trustworthy.

"His lordship would like some explanation as to what's

happened from one of you," said an exasperated Alan Dale. "Chief Superintendent, I think it should be you. The Detective Chief Inspector doesn't seem very co-operative this morning."

"I'm not surprised," said Rimmer. He got up to join Alan Dale and the two of them made their way back into the judge's chambers. "I'll deal with you later," Rimmer said to Nick in a parting shot before he disappeared from the court room.

"Ah, Chief Superintendent, can you throw some light on events?" asked the judge.

"Yes, earlier this morning, Kate Williams – the subject of this murder inquiry – was found alive at an address in Scotland. A man who had been harbouring her is in police custody."

"An interesting dilemma," said Anderson. "This trial has concluded and the accused has been found guilty by a jury of his peers. My only function today is to carry out sentencing."

"You can't mean....," said Sir Joshua, almost springing to his feet.

"No, I have no intention of sentencing an obviously innocent man for a murder he has not committed." He turned to Alan Dale.

"You," he said, "must make a statement withdrawing the evidence in this case. I will set the defendant free. And you...." He turned to Chief Superintendent Rimmer.

"You should think seriously about arresting Detective Chief Inspector Barton for conspiracy to pervert the course of justice and perjury. We shall reconvene."

Sir Joshua and Alan Dale made their way into the court room. Sir Joshua made his way over to Patrick Saunders and explained what had happened. The conversation seemed to end with smiles on both sides and Roy leaned over from the dock to try and make out the course of events for himself. Patrick made his way over to him. "It's going to be all right," Saunders reassured him. "Rivers found Kate Williams this morning. The prosecution is going to withdraw its evidence and you will be released in a matter of moments."

Roy heaved a sigh of relief and sat back in the dock, feeling totally relaxed for the first time in weeks.

"Yes," he shouted. He stood up as the judge entered the court room. Lord Justice Anderson waived them all to sit down and Alan Dale got to his feet.

"I would like to make a submission on the part of the prosecution," he said. "New evidence has come to light this morning causing us to rethink our prosecution. Kate Williams, whom the accused is alleged to have murdered, has been found alive in Scotland and therefore it consequently follows that no-one can be charged with her murder. The prosecution withdraws its case."

"Thank you," said the judge. "Mr Faulkner.?" Roy rose again. "It appears there are no charges against you anymore. It therefore follows you are free to go."

Roy nodded. He tried to get out to join his supporters in the court room but realised the only way to exit the dock was from down the stairs to the cells. A wry smile formed on his lips. It seemed that – whoever had designed the court room – had not entertained the fact one day someone accused might be found not guilty and be free to join those who had supported them during their darkest hours.

"Members of the jury, you are dismissed from your task," the judge continued, "but before everybody leaves this court room I should like to make it clear that there are serious questions for the prosecution to answer. Someone tried to seriously mislead this court and I would like to make it clear that I expect that someone at the very least to face a charge of conspiracy to pervert the course of justice."

Roy looked over to where Nick Barton was sitting but could detect no emotion from the expression on his face. He just sat staring blankly ahead of him. Meanwhile, Faulkner's girlfriend was trying not to show too much emotion until the judge had left the court room. She muttered in a voice that she hoped was inaudible: "And you might apologise for so biased a summing up of the case, you old fart."

At that moment, the judge left the court and the assembled crowd did likewise. Angela, Patrick Saunders and Sir Joshua waited for Roy to come up from the cells. While they were waiting, Nick Barton made his way from the court room. He took no notice of anyone until he saw a familiar face standing at the back of the waiting area.

"Charlotte," he said sounding surprised. "I didn't think you'd be coming this morning."

"I'm not here for you, Nick," she said. "I came to see if I could do anything to help or support Roy. It now appears I don't have to." She paused for a moment and then said: "Goodbye, Nick, I expect it will be a very long time before I see you again."

Nick decided against replying. As he made as if to leave the court room, he felt a hand on his shoulder. It was Chief Superintendent Rimmer. "Nick, I think there are one or two questions that we have to answer back at the station," he said.

"Am I under arrest?"

"I'd rather do that back at the station instead of exposing the police's dirty linen in front of the public."

Dirty linen? Is that all I am to you after a period of thirty years successful service in the police force, he thought to himself. Okay I made one mistake. Alan Dale seemed to sense what he was thinking.

"You've only got yourself to blame for whatever happens now," he said. "We could do without police officers like you in the force." And I could do without police officers who present me with a case that is completely fabricated, he thought to himself.

Nick left the court room with Rimmer placing an arm on his shoulder – presumably to ward off any escape attempt. Once outside, he was ushered into the back seat of Rimmer's car. The Chief Superintendent sat beside him for the journey back to the police station.

Back in the court room Roy was not at pains to leave so quickly. Angela had made a bee-line towards him and flung her arms passionately around him almost knocking him over. Patrick Saunders shook his hand. Sir Joshua shifted nervously from one foot to the other.

"You seem a bit nervous, Sir Joshua," remarked Roy.

"If you want the honest truth," he said. "I'm a bit embarrassed that I couldn't get you freed through the evidence."

"If you're that embarrassed, you could always waive your fee," replied Roy.

Sir Joshua smiled. "I think not," he said, "but I tell you someone who is worth the fee you are paying him is that chap Rivers. What a masterstroke. Never heard of it happening before. A murder victim turning up just on the day her alleged murderer is due to be sentenced."

Patrick looked at Angela. "Did you hear that?" he said. She nodded respectfully.

Meanwhile, Roy was intrigued by the new addition to their gathering.

"Charlotte, what brings you here?" he asked.

"I wanted to support you, Roy. I knew Nick had been lying. I didn't think there was anything I could do about that but I just wanted the opportunity to let you know that I believed in your innocence."

He smiled. "Thank you," he said. "I'm sure there would have been something you could have done. Joined Angela's campaign to free me, for a start. I'm sure it would have included sit-ins at the police station, protest marches and that sort of thing. And what about you and Nick?" he asked.

Angela gasped for breath. "So this is Nick Barton's wife?" she said.

"Yes," admitted Charlotte.

"How could you?" Angela continued. "You must have known he was fitting Roy up."

"Knowing it and proving it are two different things," intervened Patrick Saunders. "The best possible proof was what turned up in Scotland this morning."

"Absolutely," said Roy.

"Nick and I are finished. I've left him. I should have done it years ago."

"Well," said Roy. "Thank you for coming today and thank you for coming to see me in prison." He touched her arm. "I'll be in touch," he said.

"No, you will not," said Angela firmly.

"I'll be in touch," Roy repeated very quietly. Charlotte smiled and turned away. Meanwhile, Roy turned to Angela. "I grew up with Charlotte," he said. "I've known her for years. Wives are not tainted with the sins of their partners. You will not attempt to dictate who I can and cannot see."

"Come on," said Patrick. "This is supposed to be a happy ending. Let's go for a drink. I think I could do with one."

"Agreed," said Roy. It was Angela's turned to have her arm touched by him. "Thank you for all your support, too," he said.

She smiled but – if truth be told – the word "too" rankled with her.

• • ● • •

"We thought we'd come round and see how Nikki was," said Mark as he arrived at the hospital with Kate Williams.

Rivers smiled. "It's just a question of waiting for her to come round from the operation," he said. "They don't know when that will be." He looked at Kate. She looked completely different from the bedraggled mess he had come across that morning. She and Mark had booked into a hotel that evening and had then gone shopping for some new clothes for her so she could discard the rags she had been wearing in Craven's prison cellar. Some lipstick and make-up also replaced the grime that had almost looked ingrained on her face.

"How are you, Kate? It must have been quite a bit of an ordeal," said Rivers.

"It was – and I don't think I want to go into all the details of it now. I spent most of the morning doing that at the police station and I gather I'll have to do that again when they transfer Les Craven to the investigating force in Brighton."

"Yes."

"They tried to be sympathetic but it was all a bit cold, a bit matter of fact."

"Yes," said Rivers again. He thought for a moment as if debating with himself as to whether it was an appropriate time to broach this next subject but then went ahead. "Do you know anything about what happened to Craven's wife?"

"Craven's wife?"

"Yes, she's gone missing, too."

"No," said Kate, a sudden chill going down her spine.

It was obvious to Rivers that she knew nothing. He felt it best to change the subject. "So what are your plans?" he asked her.,

"Get back to London and see if I've still got a job to go to. I… we've booked tickets for the first flight out from Inverness tomorrow morning."

"You're going with Kate?" Rivers asked Mark.

Kate intervened to answer. "I was a bit worried about making the journey by myself," she said. "I'm sure that feeling will go – but I don't feel up to it yet. Mark kindly agreed to accompany me."

"Are you going to be able to go back to work?"

"They've already been on to me to write the exclusive story of my ordeal. It's a bit tricky, though, with Craven already facing charges. I wrote them a shortened version of my nightmare for tomorrow's paper – you know, about how I was glad to be free again but I was a bit limited in what I could say. They said they want the full works for when Craven is convicted. It's a bit daunting – there are lots of things I don't really want to go into but I suppose many of them might come out in the trial. At least they still want me." She stopped talking for a moment. "They did say I could have a few days off to recover."

"Well, that's something, I suppose," said Rivers. "Look, I was going to phone Roy Faulkner and find out how he is. Do you feel up to talking to him?"

Kate smiled. "I think I can manage that," she said. They were sitting by Nikki's bed in the hospital. Rivers thought for a moment he could detect a low moan coming from Nikki in the hospital bed but – on closer inspection – there did not seem to be anything happening. He rang Roy's number.

"Hi," he said on his answering. "Philip Rivers. Just wanted to find out how you were."

"A free man."

Rivers could hear a background buzz on the other end of the telephone. "You're in a crowded room?" he asked.

"A bar. I haven't been in one of these for some weeks."

"Don't drink too much," the private detective continued. "I've got someone here who would like a word with you," he added. He handed the phone over to Kate.

"Hallo Roy," she said.

"God, am I relieved to hear that voice," Roy said. "It is you, isn't it, Kate?"

"Yes, it's me. Large as life."

"How are you?"

"OK, Roy. It's been a bit of an ordeal but the paper says I can have a couple of days off to recover."

"Don't rush back," he said.

"I don't intend to."

"What are you doing?"

270

"Celebrating my release." Someone at the other end asked him if he would like another drink. "I could murder another pint," he said. Then he smiled. "I suppose I shouldn't say that in case the police misconstrue it. After all, the pint won't be able to make an amazing dramatic re-appearance – unless I have far too many of them."

Somebody else started talking to him. "What? No, I haven't had too many. Not tonight."

"That must be Angela," said Mark quietly.

Roy turned his attention to Kate again. "Look, I'm sorry," he said. "I should have stayed with you at the night club that night. That – or insisted you come back to the hotel with me."

"Do you think I would have come?"

"No," he said bluntly.

"Also, I might have misconstrued your intention and slapped you round the face."

"That would have been preferable to what has happened to you over the last few weeks."

"Let's not get into that," said Kate.

"Okay."

"Well, I shall leave you to your celebrating, then."

"I'll see you on the road again soon, Kate," Roy replied,

Kate handed the mobile phone back to Rivers. As she did so, there were definite signs from behind them that Nikki was stirring again.

"I'll get a nurse," said Mark.

Rivers took Nikki's hand. "Hallo darling," he said as she rubbed her eyes. "You're in hospital. You were shot – but the doctors seem to think everything's going to be OK." He could see that she was smiling again.

"We'd better leave you two alone," said Mark sensing Rivers might want a private moment with Nikki. "Are you ready, Kate?"

Kate smiled. "Yes," she said and – extending her hand to Rivers – she added: "Thank you."

As the two of them made their way down the hospital corridor, she turned to Mark.

"Mark, I've got a big favour to ask of you," she said.

"Name it," he replied.

"I'm still a bit shell shocked, nervous about what's happened. I trust you. Mark, there are two beds in my room at the hotel. Would you stay in the other one for me? I'm just a little bit frightened of being on my own."

Crikey, thought Mark. What would Prunella think of this? Here was the most attractive reporter on the education beat asking him if he wanted to spend the night with her. Normally it was an invitation he would have given his eye teeth for – and then rejected. He did not take long to come up with an answer this time. "Of course," he said.

"I'll be all right after tonight," she added. "I'm going to stay with my sister down in Brighton tomorrow and she says I can stay there for as long as it takes for me to pluck up courage and go back to my flat in London."

"No problem," said Mark. He thought seriously for a moment, though. Perhaps Kate Williams was more psychologically scarred by her ordeal than she had let on.

Meanwhile, back at Nikki's bed, the nurse had taken her pulse and checked her blood pressure. "All seems in order," she said to Rivers as she departed.

"Hallo," said Nikki to Rivers when they were on their own. She squeezed his hand.

"How do you feel?" he asked.

"A bit woozy," she confessed.

"I'm not surprised. I was worried about you."

"I'd have been worried about me, too."

"What do you remember?"

"It's all a bit of a blur but someone inside the mansion started shooting and I just seemed to get in the way."

"Yes," said Rivers. "It was my fault. I thought I could knock

Les Craven off balance before he could shoot."

"You didn't fire the gun," said Nikki reassuringly.

Rivers paused for thought. Was this the right time, he wondered? Oh, hell, he thought. If it isn't I can always do it again – and again. "We had a little unfinished business from last night," he said tentatively.

"I remember," she said encouragingly.

"In the hope that this will be third time lucky."

"Third time?"

"I proposed to you on the gravel driveway outside the mansion just after you'd been shot. I thought it might buck your spirits up. You didn't hear me?"

"No, but it was a nice idea."

"So, Nikki Hofmeyr, at the risk of seeming boring and repetitive – I love you. Will you marry me?"

"Right question," said Nikki.

"Yes?"

"You didn't say the bit about loving me beforehand."

"And the answer?"

"Yes. Oh, yes." He leant forward and kissed her gently. "Then we shall get married," he said.

• • • • •

"So what did you do with your wife, Les?" It was the following morning and Francesca Manners had been given access to Les Craven for the first time.

"My wife? Nothing." Craven sounded surprised to be asked.

"We found her DNA in a cottage you rented in Scotland – before you moved to the one where you were arrested."

Craven looked shifty for a moment. "She came up for the weekend," he said. "It was before we split up."

"She's gone missing. Know anything about that?"

"No," he said emphatically. "I don't want to hear from her.

She's attempting to bleed me dry over the divorce."

"Have you killed her?"

"No," he said. "No way." He then permitted himself a smile. "I wouldn't have thought you'd want to bring anther murder prosecution without a body after the last one."

Francesca sighed. There was no evidence to charge him over his wife's disappearance. Still, he wasn't going anywhere. He was caught bang to rights over the kidnapping of Kate Williams. She resolved to stick to that charge but make further enquiries over the missing wife – further enquires which led her to organise a full scale search of Natalie Craven's house once she had finished questioning Les Craven. She went down to supervise the search herself.

"What are we looking for?" one detective constable asked her.

She had to admit she did not know. "Any evidence of a struggle which suggests she was abducted from here," she said.

They had been searching the house for about three hours when the front door was opened and a middle-aged woman stood in front of them. "Are you looking for me?" she asked.

"Natalie Craven?" asked Francesca.

"Yes. What are you doing?"

"Detective Sergeant Francesca Manners," she said offering her a hand to shake. "Am I glad to see you alive."

"You thought I was dead?" Craven's wife sounded surprised.

"We found your DNA in a house your husband had rented in Scotland. He is now in custody."

"I know," interrupted Natalie. "That's why I came back. I can feel safe now."

"Safe?"

"He did try to abduct me but I escaped."

"Why didn't you go to the police?"

"I just wanted to go away – to somewhere he wouldn't find me?"

Francesca's eyes narrowed. "You realise by doing that you put another woman through an awful ordeal?"

"No," said Natalie, "I refuse to take responsibility for any of my husband's actions."

Francesca frowned. "Sorry," she said. "Maybe I was a little bit hasty there. Did he abduct you, though?"

"He drugged me. Tied me up in the back of his van and in a cellar in the cottage in Scotland." Another question seemed to be forming on Francesca's lips. Natalie pre-empted the answer. "No, he didn't rape me," she said. "I escaped before he could do that – while he was sleeping."

"Nevertheless, it appears he could be facing some further charges as a result of what he did to you."

"I would hope so, Detective Sergeant. I would hope so."

POSTSCRIPT

"I was tired of women telling me what to do," said Les Craven. Francesca Manners listened patiently. "I wanted one to control. One that would always have to do what I said."

Francesca detected a coldness in his manner. His eyes started staring ahead of him. He then looked at Francesca in earnest.

"I want you to know I would never have killed Kate Williams. Never," he said.

"So you say."

"And I didn't mean to harm Natalie. Yes, I did abduct her but I was angry – over the way she was behaving over the divorce. When she escaped, I decided to move cottages – so she couldn't find me."

"Funnily enough, that's the last thing she would have wanted to do. Find you. That's why she didn't call the police. She wanted to get as far away as possible. But moving cottages was your first mistake. When you hired the new one in the name of Kevin Summers."

"I never thought anyone would make a connection between the two of us. I visited Kevin after Natalie escaped. I nicked a couple of utility bills from his place in case anyone wanted proof of identity from me."

Francesca thought for a moment. Charges against him for kidnapping his wife could wait, she reasoned. He would soon be sentenced for what he had done to Kate Williams, after all. Rivers had once told her he was surprised no-one could find a good word to say about Les Craven. After spending a few hours in his company interviewing him, she could understand why. When summing up his character, the word "weasel" seemed to form in her mind. He would be charged with abducting his wife – though the case might have to come to court separately.

• • ● • •

"What the fuck do you mean you're not going to write it?" said Grant Leftly rising from his chair in the newsroom and towering over the five foot four Kate Williams.

"I can't," she said. "I don't want to relive it again."

"Wrong answer. You did a great piece when you were freed about how dreadful your ordeal was in captivity. Now he's been convicted all you'll have to do is rewrite it."

"And you'd run my picture. And I'd have to walk the streets again with people pointing fingers at me and saying: 'There's that rape victim.' I don't want to go through it again."

"That's not the way this newspaper works. The newsdesk asks you to do something. You do it. End of."

Very calmly, Kate Williams looked him in the eye and said: "Then I guess we have to move to the next stage and consider what this newspaper does when one of its reporters won't write what they've been told to."

"That's easy," said Leftly. "Fuck off. You're fired. Don't come back."

"Okay," said Kate very quietly. She moved back to her desk and picked up her handbag and started putting her belongings in it – notebook, pen etcetera. She stopped what she was doing for a moment and sat down. Grief suddenly began to overwhelm her. She began to cry.

Leftly whispered to his deputy, who was sitting next to him. "Get a photographer up here. Fucking pronto." The deputy made the necessary phone call and – before Kate could even recover her composure – there was a photographer snapping away at her as she continued to cry.

"No," she said. "No. Get away." She made a futile gesture

aimed at trying to sweep the photographer out of the way but there was no power in it.

"Stop it," said Geoff Stevens who had been sitting on the other side of the newsdesk, shouting at Leftly.

"Sit down," said Leftly firmly. "This is nothing to do with you. Shagging rights don't give you any rights here."

Stevens was beside the photographer by now. "Can't you see you're upsetting Kate?" The photographer shrugged his shoulders.

"Got the photograph?" asked Leftly. The photographer nodded. "You can go," he said. "Great front page picture. The overwhelming grief of a kidnap victim as she relives her ordeal. Now all we need is the story," He stared at Kate in the eyes. "Write it," he said to her. She tried to wipe her eyes but ended up in a heap on the desk.

Leftly gave out a deep sigh. "All right, you write it, Geoff," he added. "You know the story like the back of your hand and some other parts of your anatomy, probably, too. Interview her or say she was too distressed to talk. I don't fucking care. Let's just get some emotional words to go with the picture. As for you, Kate, go home. You're no use to me here – a shivering wreck."

Defiantly Kate got to her feet. As she began to leave her desk, she turned to Leftly again. "Am I fired, then?" she asked.

"We'll talk about that tomorrow." He noticed out of the corner of his eye that Geoff Stevens was putting his coat on. "Where are you fucking going?" he asked.

"You told me to interview her – or have you forgotten?"

Leftly growled. "Get your copy in by 5.30pm." He was aware of a small man wearing the grey trousers of his suit with the sleeves of his white shirt rolled up standing by his side.

"A word, Grant," said the man. It was the editor, Paul Leaning, a man not known for using a hundred words when a few would do. They departed to his office.

"What have you done?"

"Oh, just some trouble with Kate Williams. She won't write a piece about her ordeal."

"And you fired her?"

"I've left her to stew on things overnight. We've got a tremendous picture of her sobbing her heart out."

"Do you think that was clever?" asked Leaning.

"Clever?" Leftly reacted as if he was flummoxed by the word. "I don't know what you mean, sir."

"Good headline for our opponents. Tabloid sacks kidnap ordeal victim for refusing to relive the trauma of her rape. You know she could have maintained anonymity after the first trial but she didn't because we asked her not to. Ring her and tell her that her job's safe. I don't want her going and talking to somebody else." He looked at his news editor closely. "You don't have to apologise to her. You can say it was my decision if you like."

"What if she steps out of line again?"

"The future's the future. The present's the thing."

Leftly nodded and went back to his desk and immediately rang Kate on her mobile. He got the ansafone. "Your job's safe, Kate, he said. "Just get Geoff to get a move on with the copy."

Kate had been travelling with Geoff by tube to her home when Leftly called. She picked up the ansafone call immediately she surfaced from the underground.

"Sounds like the nearest thing to an apology he's ever uttered," remarked Geoff. "Good news?"

"Yes," said Kate tentatively.

"What's the matter?" he asked her, sensing her indecision.

"I'm not sure I want to go back."

"That's understandable after the day you've had."

"After the weeks and months I've had," she replied.

"Think about it," he said clasping her by the shoulders. "You know they're not going to fire you. Stay there until you've worked out what you want to do." She nodded. "And in the meantime I'll stick by you," he said, kissing her on the lips after he had spoken. She did not recoil from him in the way she might have done immediately after her ordeal. It emboldened him.

"You know," he began tentatively, "if you're worried about money, you could always move in with me."

She smiled. "I've had more romantic propositions made to me in the past," she said. She squeezed his hand. "You're a sweet person," she said, "but I'm not ready for that yet." As she spoke, she wondered to herself: will I ever be?

• • ● • •

Nick Barton flicked a pellet of paper from one side of his prison cell to the other. He was into the third month of his three-year prison sentence for perverting the course of justice. He had been lucky. The judge had cited his previous good behaviour and commendations he had received for bravery earlier in his career. With any luck, with good behaviour, he could be out and back on the streets again within the year. Back on the streets, though, he thought. He would be. There would be no chance of pursuing his previous career with the police force. He smiled for a moment. Maybe he should try being a private detective. Perhaps take a few tips from Philip Rivers – the man who had largely been responsible for him being where he was. He shook his head. No, Rivers would not want anything to do with him.

He had hardly had a visitor since beginning his jail term. Only Sarah, his daughter, had turned up once. There had been an awkward silence between them as she could not forgive him for the treatment of her mother. She had, though, shown him a sense of loyalty by turning up and he had to thank her for that. As for Charlotte, there had been no sign of her. Sarah had let slip that she might be pursuing another relationship but had clammed up when he had tried to question her about it. In his mind's eye, he could not get rid of the thought that it could be Roy Faulkner. After all, she had taken the trouble to visit him

when he had been in prison. That, he thought, would be ironic –
an example of revenge being a dish best served cold better than
he could have conjured up, he reflected.

His musings were interrupted as a couple of warders entered
the room. "You've got a visitor," said one. "Actually, two," said the
other. "Come with us."

He glanced at his watch. It was not the normal visiting time
and he could not think who his two visitors could be. The
warders declined to enlighten him and took him to a sparse
office – not the normal visiting room – where two men in suits
were sitting at one side of a table. They were both detectives.
He was told he was going to be questioned about the death
of Graeme McAndrew. New evidence has come to light in the
shape of an eyewitness who had seen the whole episode.

• • • • •

"That was Rivers," said Roy Faulkner to Angela as he put the
telephone down. "Apparently, they've charged Nick Barton
with the murder of Graeme McAndrew. He heard about it from
Francesca Manners."

Angela smiled. "Couldn't have happened to a nicer person,"
she said.

The two of them were back together now. Angela had forgiven
him for his brief fling with Charlotte after she had split up with
Nick. It had not amounted to anything. More of a thank you for
believing in me than anything else. Or sympathy for her to have
had to put up with Nick Barton for thirty years.

Roy looked at Angela. She had been a staunch defender of
him during the days of the trial. She may occasionally go over
the top and be overbearing, he reflected, but she was better to
have onside than be against you.

"How come they got enough evidence to charge him?"
Angela asked.

"Rivers," replied Roy. He neglected to add: "You know, that shit detective you were always talking about." He had heard about her behaviour from Patrick Saunders. "He had a word with Jane McAndrew after the trial and then set off to interview people living off the green," Roy continued. "It's quite an exclusive area. He found out who had been living there thirty years ago. One of the residents was an employee of a foreign embassy and had seen what had happened and taken a number of the car but the following day he was called back by his embassy to the Yemen. Rivers tracked him down. He had meant to tell the police but in the rush forgot. Miraculously, he had still kept the number – although he didn't realise he had it when Rivers first questioned him. So he's not a rubbish detective," Roy could not resist himself from adding in the end.

"No," said Angela, getting her hands around a large gin and tonic. "Obviously not. So farewell Mr Barton for a number of years?"

"If this guy agrees to give evidence and there's every prospect that he will. He's back in the UK now."

"And you? What do you feel about this?"

"I can't believe it. I was stunned at the lengths Nick went to try and convict me. To find that he was also responsible for killing Graeme." His voice tailed off. "I can understand why he didn't like me. He thought I'd pinched his girlfriend – he thought I'd made a pass at Charlotte, too."

"Which you did thirty years later," said Angela tersely. "There was this beating, though," she added.

"Beating?"

"Nick was beaten up by three people," said Angela. "He thought it was you, Barrie and Graeme. Johnnie Simons told me." She paused. "You never mentioned it," she said reproachfully.

"Nothing ever came of it. I remember the police did come round and question me but I was with Gillian Bird at the pictures at the time it happened."

"Convenient."

"But true."

"He must have still believed it was you and Graeme."

"But Graeme was a nice guy. He'd never hurt anybody,"

"He was a waste of space in Nick's eyes. An alcoholic who was begging Nick for money. Nick's view – not mine. And he called Nick Big Ears."

"Nick must have planned it,"Roy continued."You can't tell me he just happened to be driving down the green when Graeme left the pub that night. He knew the route Graeme took home – and that road didn't lead anywhere."

"He planned his destruction of you, too. Only difference is he tried to use the law in your case not take the law into his own hands. Luckily it didn't work.""

• • • • •

"Why did you do it Philip?" said Mark Elliott as he helped the detective adjust his tie."I mean, it's not as if you were being paid for it."

"Jane McAndrew,"said Rivers."I felt so sorry for her. She was so forlorn thirty years after her brother died. I felt she needed some closure."

Mark smiled. "If you're going to be a successful detective again, you're going to have to stop doing freebies," he said. "Now, are we ready?" He glanced at his watch."We've got half an hour to get to the registry office."

"Ready,"said Rivers with a sigh,"Mark,"he said tentatively."I just have this horrible feeling. You know I walked out on Nikki thirty years ago. What happens if I let her down again?"

Mark put a reassuring arm on his shoulder."Just think about what it'll be like if you don't let her down,"he said."You'll be fine."

The private detective smiled."I'm ready,"he said.